UNINVITED

JOCELYN DEXTER

BLOODHOUND
— BOOKS —

www.bloodhoundbooks.com

Print ISBN 978-1-914614-97-2

ALSO BY JOCELYN DEXTER

Shh

Melanie
weird!

1

ME

My name is John. It isn't really, but I answer to it all the same. It's not my birth name, put it that way. It could just as easily be Paul, Steve or Dave. But I like John. It's a boring nondescript name. Unexciting. And I don't *look* exciting – you could pass me in the street and not give me a second glance; probably wouldn't even notice me at all. Except perhaps for my size. I'm big. Like a big old cuddly teddy bear. I look like a John. Someone you'd welcome into your home.

The name fits in with my immediate plans. Comfortable, unassuming, John. People never expect the unexpected with me. They only see my easy-going façade; the very John-ness of me.

I'd initially thought about simply breaking into the house, and surprising Rebecca. I had, after all, burgled many a property in my past. And indeed, had accessed this very house in particular. I could have used the spare key that was kept under the flowerpot. But this way was better.

I'd decided on the charm offensive. I could *do* charm: a lot of smiling, a lot of eye contact, a lot of meaningless compliments. And a lot of practice. I'd learnt quickly, absorbing all the information on how to finesse and delightfully engage others. Charm always took people by surprise. Common decency and politeness dictated that many people, especially women, were thrown by a show of gracious courtesy and they acted stupidly, without thought. By which time, of course, it was too late. Too late for them to see the error of their ways and I would be inside their house.

With them.

I stood in front of the large country house. Not your average chocolate-box cottage but a magnificent grey stone structure on three floors. I peeked through the open slatted venetian blinds, into a spotless modern kitchen. Nothing chintzy going on here.

Having already concealed my bigger and much heavier rucksack behind a large bush to the right of the front door, I hooked my two thumbs around the straps of my lighter rucksack, casually slung over my shoulders, and adopted a completely non-threatening stance. My legs were planted slightly apart, my black brogues so highly polished I could see my own reflection in them. My laces were, as always, tied with a double safety knot. I'd taught myself as a boy how to make my footwear more secure and enjoyed the added 'safety'. Proudly I'd shown my mother, but she'd had little time for praise: a busy lady. But I knew she was pleased. She'd patted me absently on the top of my head in a congratulatory way. Quiet, unspoken plaudits, but good enough for me.

The double safety knot had worked for me for all these years. I saw no reason to change a habit of a lifetime. Being prepared was a good motto, although I was no boy scout. Far from it. But I liked the principle of being ready for any eventuality.

Standing away from the threshold, not wanting to crowd, I plastered on my oh-my-good-gosh-boy-next-door smile, rang the bell and waited.

The woman who opened the door – Rebecca – was wearing her hair up and a flour-dusted apron which held her heaving bosom in place, and only partially covered her simple jogging pants and baggy jumper ensemble. Sunday lunch was already on the go. Flaring my nostrils I inhaled discreetly. Chicken. My favourite. At least I wouldn't go hungry on this particular venture.

Rebecca's eyes furrowed in slight confusion as she looked at me. I wasn't expected and she didn't recognise me, so it was a facial expression I'd anticipated. Sweeping my blond hair from my forehead in a boyish gesture, I beamed at her. A real, live full-wattage smile, showing off my perfect white dental work: boasting my little row of impeccably enamelled Tic-Tac-teeth. 'Rebecca, how lovely to see you again. You look marvellous.'

I opened my arms and gathered up her small frame, nearly lifting her off her feet. Planted a big wet one on her cheek and gave her a little squeeze. 'Roger told me how well you were, but he didn't tell me just how fan*tastic* you look. It really is lovely to see you again.'

Stepping past her, I watched her face drop as she realised I was suddenly and unaccountably on the wrong side of the door. I was *in*.

Her cheeks pinked, and she said, 'No, wait. Please stop. I don't know who you are.'

'It's me. You know *me*.'

I laughed softly and pretended a mock-hurt look that she had forgotten me so quickly. I held my hand to my heart, feigning distress. She visibly dithered; her innate good manners fighting with the fact that there was an uninvited man in her house.

I slithered my glance up and down her body. Taking the whole of her in. It had the desired effect. She blushed. I grinned

3

at her. 'I'm certainly all the better for seeing you, Becky. Is it through here...?'

Of course I knew where the kitchen was because I'd let myself in weeks before – just to familiarise myself with the lay of the land. I pointed quizzically as if unsure of the route but walked into the kitchen, and then like a divining rod, headed miraculously into the dining room as if by luck. Heard her hurried footsteps behind me. She laid her hand on my arm, her fingers gripping with a surprising strength.

'No, really, please wait. Look, I'm very sorry, but I'm still not sure who you are, and I wasn't expecting you.'

'Who *were* you expecting?' I smiled to take the bite from my words. 'Don't tell me Roger forgot to tell you I was coming for Sunday lunch? I've been looking forward to it so much. And of course I can't wait to see your daughter again – Lucy, and her new husband, Frank, as well. Do tell me they're still coming.'

My apparent intimate knowledge of her family and their plans for the day, threw her. Her cheeks still held an embarrassed tinge of pink but flared afresh again in an ugly crimson flush.

'Yes. I mean, no. Roger didn't tell me. Or I forgot. Probably my fault – it usually is. Brain like a sieve. And yes, Lucy and Frank *are* coming. As per. But I'm terribly sorry, I really can't quite place you. Who *are* you? How do we know each other?'

'*Rebec*ca, really. How can you not remember me? I can't believe it. I'm hurt.'

Her fingers interlocked with each other, creating a mass of reddened digits, her knuckles showing white. She was a veritable blaze of angst-ridden colour. 'Come on, Becky. Tell me you're only playing. You are, aren't you?'

She looked on the verge of weeping at her own social ineptitude. Rallying well, although laughably transparent in her attempts to redeem herself, she stretched her mouth into a smile

4

– so tight I thought her lips might split. 'Just give me a clue. I'm just dreadful with names and faces. Always walking past people who I've known forever.'

Collapsing down heavily on one of the wooden dining chairs, as if she were feeling faint from her utter uselessness and lack of etiquette, I almost felt sorry for her.

No, that's a lie. I didn't feel sorry for her. Not one little bit. I said, 'I haven't told you my name. My fault entirely. That'll help. It's John. Remember now? We last saw each other at Roger's Christmas party. Three months ago?' I spread my arms out in what could only be interpreted as charming. 'How could you forget, Becky? We all had such a laugh that night.'

She feigned a look of relief as she pretended to recall our non-meeting. Slapped her hands to her forehead. 'Oh, stupid, stupid me. Now I remember. John. How are you?'

'Certainly better now you know who I am. Sorry if I frightened you. You looked as if I were the bogeyman who'd come for Sunday lunch, instead of me, John. Don't worry, don't be upset. Easy mistake to make. We'd all had a bit too much of the old vino at the Christmas "do", so no hard feelings. I know I'm not exactly a stand-out type of man, am I?'

Again with the blushing. She jumped up. 'I'll get you a drink. Wine? Red or white?'

'Whatever you're having.' She hesitated because I'd given her a choice. Left it up to her. 'White would be lovely, thanks, Becky,' I said, coming to her aid.

I made myself comfortable at the solid oak dining table, my hands folded in front of me. I couldn't help but take the time to admire my beautifully and professionally manicured hands: the nails were buffed to a soft sheen, the cuticles were where they should be, and the tips of my nails were bright white, perfect crescents. Filed, smoothed. Delightful.

My rucksack sat on the chair next to me as I politely waited for my glass of wine. She brought it to me and sat opposite, looking pointedly at her watch. 'Roger will be home soon. Back from the pub. Two o'clock. He's never late.'

That much I knew. And estimated time of arrival for Lucy and Frank – they also ran like clockwork and would turn up at three.

We both sipped politely from our respective glasses and I leaned forward. Instantly, she recoiled. Tried to cover her rudeness by pretending a coughing fit. Getting up and walking around the table so that I stood over her, I rested the back of my legs against the adjacent chair to Becky. 'I'm a real townie – can't abide the country. Too much open space for me. However, I *do* concede, that on the face of it, *because* you have no other houses around you, you have your very own idyll of peace and tranquillity, with no one else close enough to spoil it. But do you know the worst thing about living in such a beautiful rural house like this? A secluded house like this? Do you know the one real pitfall of this set-up?'

She shook her head, her eyes suddenly rounder and eyebrows higher than they should be. I quickly bent in close, so that my mouth almost touched her face, and her hair tickled my cheek. I whispered in her ear. 'The worst thing about living here, Rebecca, is that no one can hear you scream.'

Then I headbutted her, right between the eyes.

2

ME

Tutting, I cleaned up the broken wine glass from the carpet. It had caught the edge of the table as it fell, as Becky fell, and I consequently had to mop up the spilt wine with wads of kitchen paper from a roll. Didn't want it to stain: it was a nice carpet.

More to the point, I wanted things to look normal; didn't want Roger glancing through the kitchen window and not seeing his wife slaving over a hot stove. He wouldn't be able to see her now at all, as she was hog-tied on the dining room floor, with an apple in her mouth to stop her shouting out. She looked uncannily and amusingly like a pig on a spit, adorned and decorated as if for a banquet. But at least she was quiet. And of course, breathing. I am not a complete beast.

The stuffing of the mouth with an apple was purely to stop her shouting out and warning Rog that all was not as it should be. That dinner might be a little delayed. But hopefully not spoilt. The masking tape which held the apple in place rather ruined the overall medieval look that I was going for, but it at least restrained her dribble that would otherwise have run free. A real plus.

I looked at my watch. Ten to two. Ten minutes. Frankly I was bored and couldn't wait for everyone to get here. Becky wasn't up for general chit-chat, so after a quick wander about, tidying as I went, I positioned myself on the hinge-side by the inside of the front door and simply waited.

Holding the carving knife with both hands, the tip of the blade pointed straight up.

Finally, I heard the sound of Roger's car pull into the lane and park outside the house. Bang on two o'clock. I had to hand it to the man, he adhered strictly to his own self-imposed timetable. It was an admirable quality – that of reliability, if a little nerdy for my tastes. He always looked a bit too much of an Anorak for me, showing a lack of spontaneity and a smidge too much of predictability and dullness. I'd like to say, 'Each to their own,' but I didn't really think like that.

And I actually *knew* that he was far from being Anorak-Man. Don't judge a book by its cover and all that. He had hidden depths. And he'd hope to keep those depths well and truly hidden. For his own sake.

Good luck with that.

I braced myself as I heard Roger shout out, 'Rebecca, I'm home.' And then he closed the door to find me standing there, staring at him. Instantly, at a glance, I recognised again, up close and personal, the weakness in him. Smelled the beer fumes coming from him. He reeked of it.

On impulse, I thrust my face to his. 'Boo!' Tiny flecks of my own spittle landed on his cheeks and his arms flew up in defence. He stepped back and in doing so, managed to stand on one of his own feet: he fell in an embarrassment of idiocy and cowardice, landing on his blubbery bottom.

You must forgive my theatrics, but I wasn't physically under threat from old Rog, so I had allowed myself the fun of simply frightening him.

He brought his hand to his mouth and I saw it tremble. 'Stand up,' I said. He did, his mouth slack. His face had undergone a weird sort of disintegration, almost disappearing, as if unsure of what expression to settle on.

'Hello, Rog, I'm John. Thanks for being on time. It's appreciated. Hang your coat up and we'll go and find your wife, okay? Suit you?'

He didn't move. Not a muscle. I had to step forward one pace, softly, softly so as not to frighten him to *death*, to check that he was still doing the old breathing in and out thing. And there it was; a raspy, whispery sound – his breath had taken on a whistle for the occasion. Odd.

I unlooped the corded twine that I had earlier placed on one of the coat pegs, lasso-style, and gently hung it around Roger's neck. Pulled it tight, but not too tight, and led him down the short hall to the dining room. Not really knowing why I bothered as he was very low maintenance, I manacled his hands together. Police issue handcuffs. Only the best. I knew a man who knew a man who knew a woman. It's good to have contacts in my world. Becky was already wearing a matching pair. I'd got four for the price of two. Bargain.

I didn't even have to wield my mighty blade at Roger. He was already completely cowed purely by my very existence in his house.

Bit pathetic I thought.

Leading him like a dog on a leash, I had to tug harder on the cord as his feet failed him. Like a horse refusing a jump, he planted himself at the entrance to the dining room. 'Come on, Roger, for pity's sake, don't you want to see your wife? Check she's okay? Christ, get a backbone, for God's sake. You're embarrassing me. And yourself.'

Roger was almost as nondescript looking as I. There was nothing that defined him physically, nothing that made him anything other than grey. Up close, he reminded me again of just how nothing-looking he really was. He wasn't, visually at least, a man to make you think, *Now there's someone I'd like to spend time with.* I sighed extravagantly. 'She's alive, Rog. Becky is alive and waiting for you. When I tug, you walk, right?'

He nodded. Barely. But it was something. I noticed a small drop of sweat trickle down the side of his cheek. And then it just hung there. Dangling in space, a droplet of fear, suspended from his chin. It quivered like a gelatinous blob and I had to stop myself gagging. I made a swiping movement on my own face, and then pointed at his jaw. He looked back at me blankly. 'Roger, pull yourself together and wipe your face. You're sweating.'

Disgusted, I had to look away. I wasn't overly keen on others' bodily excretions. Wasn't a fan of human fluids. I liked things clean. Very clean.

Blood was different. I didn't mind blood. Funny that, if you think about it.

Having got rid of the offending sweat, I allowed Roger to see Becky for the first time. His reaction was, as anticipated, a non-one. He remained immobile; his face seemed to have lost all ability of portraying any emotion. Becky, however, was, thankfully, a different proposition entirely. She reacted like a real person. Seeing Roger, she attempted to scream. She only managed grunts from behind the apple; *now* dribble escaped from the corners of her mouth.

I hastened my gaze over her drool, not wanting to linger on it. But at least she *tried* to communicate, whilst old Rog just looked down at her as if he'd never met her. Putting my hand on his shoulder I said, 'Roger, this is Becky. Becky, Roger.'

Appalled by his lack of *any*thing emotional, I pushed blank-man onto one of the dining room chairs and bound his feet, arms and torso to the chair with the cord. In an intricate but man-size version of a cat's cradle. Shoved an apple in his mouth just to keep a little symmetry going – piggy number two.

Gathering Becky in my arms like a child, I lifted her from the floor and gently deposited her in one of the other dining room chairs. Opposite her husband. Trussed her up in similar fashion to Roger. Their arms were able to bend at the elbows; other than that, their movement was severely restricted.

They made for an odd couple. Not an obvious pairing on the face of it. They seemed somehow mismatched. Uncomfortably so. I stood back to see what they'd do.

They eyeballed each other; Becky doing better with expressing her fear through her eyes, although they were both horribly swollen and blackened by the impact of my head. She used her eyes to convey to Roger that he needed to *do* something. *Any*thing. But Roger was proving to be a bit of a dud all round. I hoped he'd improve. With or without the apple. Stupid little piggy.

I settled in for the last two guests to arrive.

Then we could begin.

3

ME

Two people are harder to control than one, so I'd had to give this part of the plan a little more thought. Not a lot, because I wasn't expecting any difficulty. But it was, theoretically, double jeopardy. So, equally, double the fun.

Two more cords hung on the coat pegs; nooses-in-waiting, and the knife remained in my hands. Again, I was warned of their arrival by the sound of tyres on the lane outside, and the slamming of two car doors. Their laughter floated in through the closed windows and I knew it would be a very long time before either of them would be laughing again.

I assumed that Lucy would be the first through the door as she had the keys. When I'd watched them arrive over the previous weeks, for their free Sunday lunch provided by Mummy and Daddy, she'd always been the one to open the front door. I could only presume that today would be no different.

And I was right. I saw her swathe of long blonde hair first as it flew through the door, closely followed by Lucy herself. No faffing about here. Swift action was called for and before she was even fully over the threshold, I grabbed her from behind, the blade jutting into the bottom of her chin. Gasping, she struggled briefly, her hands instinctively grabbing my forearm. All it took was a teeny pressure on the knife from me, just a slight upward dig motion, and a drop of blood blossomed suddenly on her skin. She must have felt the droplet hot and wet as it swelled and dripped down her neck. She stopped fighting. Quick learner, our Lucy. Good girl.

Frank, much like Roger, had frozen. I backed away from the door, allowing him space to enter, saying, 'Take your coat off, hang it up and put that rope around your neck. Now.'

He looked at me. 'Go on, do it. Or I'll cut Lucy. Cut her deeper. Don't think I won't. Do you want me to prove my intent or will you take it as a given?'

Then he moved. Fumbled his coat off and stood there with the cord hanging from his neck like a forlorn rescue mutt. I threw him a pair of handcuffs. 'Put them on.' He did as instructed. 'Now, move slowly. Or I swear to God I'll slice your brand-new wife. Into strips. Imagine a paper shredder. Now imagine your wife. Understand?'

He nodded. Mute.

I smiled at him. He didn't smile back. Of course I was rather overplaying the bad man here. But it was a quick and effective method of making people do what you tell them. Fear was a useful tool in its place. I used what worked but it went against the grain. I preferred a little more finesse personally. Frightening people for the sake of it didn't fill me with any sense of accomplishment. It was unnecessary and uncalled for. But it was expeditious.

Still keeping the knife to Lucy's neck, I popped the fourth pair of handcuffs around her slender wrists. Pulling the noose tight around Frank's neck – all the better to lead him with, and still with a knife to Lucy's throat, I brought them both into the dining room.

Neither of them made any noise when they saw Becky and Roger sitting bound in their chairs, apples in mouths. Except for a little gasp from Lucy. A little inhalation that I might have missed were my ears not waiting for some sort of audible reaction.

Frank, without being told, silently went and sat in the third chair, his eyes continually flitting in my direction, following the knife, fixating on the knife. Frightened of the knife. He chose the chair diagonally opposite Roger. Waited like an obedient boy for his tying-up turn. Strange reaction but it made life simpler for me. I was already familiar with the way Frank operated so wasn't overly bothered. I dropped the end of his neck leash onto the floor and stood on it. I tied Lucy first, to chair number four and then roped in Frank.

All bound and remarkably unresistant, I took out the apples from Roger and Becky's mouths, using a napkin to avoid coming into contact with their spit, and then sat on the fifth chair. At the head of the table.

The constant moving of the knife stopped any one of them from even thinking of being difficult. But really, at this stage, their options were limited. We looked at each other. I beamed at them.

At last we were all here. But first things first.

'I'm hungry. I assume you'll join me if I make sandwiches?' I said.

'*What?* A sandwich. Christ. Who *are* you?' Lucy said.

'All in good time. Your mother can fill you in while I rustle up a little something to eat. Okay?'

Smiling to myself at Lucy's impatience, I pivoted on my feet and left them to it.

But Lucy had asked a good question.
Who was I?
I smiled.
They'd never guess.

4

REBECCA

R ebecca had a headache. Her whole face ached and she felt her eyes puffed up; her lids only able to open a crack. But a slits-view of her world was all she wanted now. It was enough.

She felt an embarrassment and humiliation that she'd been so stupid as to let the man in. Politeness had forced her to allow him entry, not knowing how to stop him without being rude. That politeness could be the death of her. Of her family. Stupid, stupid, stupid. She couldn't stretch to another adjective that quite summed up her idiotic behaviour. With the acknowledgement of that idiocy, inevitably she felt a deep sense of shame and guilt. Now her family was in danger – all because of her.

Fear ricocheted around inside her head. Taking a deep breath, she tried to calm herself. An odd, strained silence fell. Finally her daughter broke it, saying – her voice a childlike whisper, 'Mum – your face. What did he do? Are you all right?'

Rebecca nodded. Smiled. *Smiled – yes, really.* But honestly, in the grand scheme of things, she told herself, she just had two black eyes. Her tongue worried the corner of her lip where it felt like it had split. From having the apple in her mouth. A cold sore perhaps preparing to blossom at a later stage. Again, did that really rate as a major concern at this point?

Dear God, it could have been a lot worse. The man could have killed her, tortured her. Raped her. She should be grateful, although that particular emotion remained out of reach for the moment. Very out of reach. But she quieted her daughter with a firm but calm lie: 'I'm fine. Really, Lucy, I'm fine. Don't worry.'

Then she noticed the small drops of blood on her daughter's neck; some of it had dried on Lucy's top. Gesturing with her manacled hands to her own throat, Rebecca raised her eyebrows in question; dreading the answer. Lucy answered in much the same way; downplaying it. 'It's all right, Mum. He nicked me with his knife. Just the tip of it. Doesn't even hurt.' Lucy smiled and Rebecca smiled back. A rare union between them. A good time for it.

She crouched forward, straining her neck to get physically closer to her family. Didn't want John to hear them, although as Roger had picked this house for its very open-planned structure, picked every piece of uncomfortable and revolting furniture in it, she suspected that John would hear anything that was said: whispering or not. But what the hell? There was no other choice. An urgency threatened; she tried not to babble.

'What are we going to do?' she said, her voice at an emergency hissing pitch. 'We can't just sit here and do nothing.'

Frank shrugged, his face drawn and frightened. Suddenly he looked his age; twenty-two, the same as Lucy. Two children. And her husband sat, cowed and pale, detached. He stared at her. Helpless. She said, addressing all of them as they looked to her for help, 'Any ideas? Anyone?'

'What *can* we do?' Lucy's mouth twisted in frustration. 'We're tied up and he's got a knife. We don't have any options, do we?' A barely controlled panic, naked and raw, flowed from her.

'Roger? What do you think?' Rebecca said in desperation, unable to reassure Lucy.

He tried to sit up, puffed up his physical self that seemed to have shrunk since John's appearance. He tried for a derisive sneer at her question, but it fell well short. The bully had become the bullied. A small part of her was pleased. After all the years of mental torture that she'd endured since her misjudged decision to marry him, she didn't care if he was suffering. That he was at a loss. Strangely, it felt as if the tables were turned. With another man in the house, attacking them all, Roger had hugely diminished.

When push came to shove, it turned out, he was all bully and no bollocks, Rebecca realised. And quietly, and quite unexpectedly, she felt herself grow in strength at that realisation.

Her husband spoke, forcing some authority into his voice. 'Stop panicking. All of you. I have this under control. I know men like John. He's fundamentally weak.'

Rebecca gaped and saw that Lucy's facial expression aped her own. After twenty-three years of humiliation, verbal abuse, being ground down, feeling shame at her very own existence, Roger had systematically erased Rebecca's past life. Had effectively and very neatly obliterated her former self.

It had happened because she'd been caught unawares. And then, over the years, it had become a habit for her to be nothing.

But now, in this scene that was playing out for all of them, held hostage by a lunatic, wanting God only knew what from her and her family, she felt an unexpected calm wash over her. A forgotten residue of self-belief raised its head, unsure of its welcome. Self-belief was very out of practice, almost completely forgotten. But now it turned out to be most definitely willing to play. Rebecca welcomed it greedily.

She realised with a shock that it was she, and not Roger, who the family were depending on. At a time when the family should be unified, she finally, and with relief, released herself from her husband. Felt her resolve strengthen.

Anger overwhelmed her – much easier to give in to fury than to surrender to terror.

She said, 'What do you mean, you're in control, Roger? Of *course* you're not. *You have no control.* None. John has the power. He's got the knife and we're trussed up. What part of that makes you think you have *any* control at all?'

'Experience,' he said, faking it in John's absence: all bluster. 'I recognise men like John. All he wants is money. It's all they ever want. He'll go through the motions, trying to intimidate us, and then he'll just rob us of everything that isn't nailed down. You'll see. I'm right. I know I am. Trust me.'

Even Lucy couldn't hold her tongue: 'You're talking crap, Dad. Mum's right. We have to *do* something. He doesn't want money. If he did, he'd have burgled us already. He'd have been and gone. He wouldn't have interacted with us. He wouldn't still be here. We can identify him. Why would he go to these lengths just for money? You're wrong.'

'Maybe we should ask why John is here,' said Frank. 'Why *this* family?'

Lucy looked at her husband, seemingly surprised that he'd come up with a good question. Rebecca also thought it was an intelligent remark and one worth considering. Considering quickly. She smiled at him, and then her daughter. Even though she was terrified. Shaking. Desperate to know what to do.

All she could think to say were stupid and meaningless platitudes, but she said them anyway. 'Let's just see how it plays out. Frank's right. We need to know why John is here. What he really wants. To do that, let's listen carefully to everything he says, and for the moment, go along with him. Don't antagonise him. Just smile and nod at him.'

She did so as if to remind them all how to do it, but her fake smile felt so brittle she feared it might fall from her face, and that her lips would shatter into a thousand pieces as they landed unceremoniously on the table. Leaving a gaping chasm in her face, fit only for screaming. She swallowed; her mouth as dry as sandpaper. 'Come on, let's keep it together. Now, shh. He's coming.'

Lucy's words bounced around in her head. *We can identify him.* That wasn't good. Not good at all. It was a serious red flag and one which, for the moment, she would ignore.

There was one thing that she *could* do. The only thing that she could do. But was it enough? It was nothing really, but it was all she had.

She'd have to revert back to her former self – how she was before being wife-to-Roger and mother-to-Lucy. Go back to being Becky Bee, before she'd given up more than her name, and become Rebecca Twist. She'd do anything to protect her child. Anything at all.

With the advent of John, a complete stranger; a very probable *mad* stranger, a spark of her old self had put in an appearance: a hint of who she really was. Who she had been.

She needed to protect her young.

I can be the real me, again. she thought. *Finally.*

I can be the mother I should have been for all these years.

I can save my child.

This is my chance.

5

ROGER

R oger found himself inexplicably looking at his wife. Looking *to* his wife, as if she could rescue them all from this nightmare. Why was he doing that, he asked himself. He never... well, certainly not for many years, never in living memory if he was being honest, did rely on Rebecca. He'd married a feisty, independent, sexy woman. She'd turned into a middle-aged frump.

If he was being truthful, *he'd* turned her into a middle-aged frump. Not a difficult task. It had been soul-destroyingly easy – she was no match for him. She should have put up a better fight. But disappointingly, she'd failed at even that. Hadn't even tried. A too-easy conquest, which had taken away all-the-fun-of-the-fair. He preferred someone with a bit of resistance, but Rebecca had offered little. None, if he was being truthful.

And yet here he was, waiting for her to say something, or do something, that would save him. Save all of them. Maybe he hadn't killed off that magical spark within her that had so attracted him in the first place. If he had, he took partial responsibility for the death of that person. But really, it was her fault as well. She should have been stronger – a better contest for him. He'd expected, anticipated even, a good fight from her, but instead she'd given up alarmingly quickly. No fun to be had there. Now he was simply left with a boring and emotionally stunted wife.

She was embarrassingly weak and inconsequential. She made him sick.

Even so, perhaps she could still save him. Them. He hoped so. Because for the first time in his life, he didn't know what to do. And unexpectedly, Rebecca seemed to have risen to the occasion. Better than himself, he had to admit.

And this man, John. When he'd popped out from behind the front door, Roger had nearly had a coronary. His heart had thumped and lurched in his chest. His breathing had become tight. He'd felt physically sick.

He despised that John had made him feel so subservient. So frightened. So *vulnerable*.

Roger reminded himself that he was always the one in control. He ruled the roost, ruled his professional minions, ruled the world: an influencer, a person to whom others listened. Popular. Or perhaps feared would be a more truthful word. He liked that people feared him. That meant he was good at what he did best: controlling people and situations. Thus he remained a natural leader of men. And a most definite leader of women.

And yet, here he was. And as much as he despised his wife now, *here he was*, unsure of what to do next. Relying on *her*. Being at a loss as to his next course of action, seriously distressed him. An unfamiliar feeling. But all-pervasive.

More than distressed, he was so very frightened; for the first time in his life, he was truly frightened. And that didn't sit well with him.

He answered his wife's question. Explained that men like

John usually just wanted quick, easy money. But he didn't believe his own words. Knew he was only kidding himself.

At a loss, he turned to his daughter. Disgust filled him. Trying to ignore John's presence in the house, he decided to use an avoidance technique and concentrate on Lucy. Why did she insist on always dressing like a cheap tart? She looked as if she wouldn't do anything unless she was paid for it. And that wasn't far from the truth. Always cadging money from either him or her mother.

Lucy's false eyelashes fluttered as she blinked. Simply ridiculous. Like two dead spiders, they perched on her lids, both upper and lower, like dying arachnids – legs splayed in death on her cheeks. Long plastic nails were stuck on the ends of her fingers, covered with a red varnish and a dusting of glitter. The extra length made them more talon-like. Like sharp unattractive claws. And all that make-up slathered onto her face. With a fucking shovel. No finesse nor artistry. He failed to see how it was even possible that he had spawned such a slag. He hadn't brought her up like that. But that was bloody women for you. Bloody young women especially. He knew that for a fact.

It must be Rebecca's fault. It *was* Rebecca's fault.

But ironically, his wife seemed to have a better handle on the situation than he. Even Lucy recognised that they were seriously fucked. There was nothing they could do, physically restrained as they were. But how dare Lucy say he had been speaking crap. How *dare* she? Both his women, his wife and his daughter, had suddenly got ideas way, way above their station. Well, see how far their new-found courage got them. *Bitches.*

John had a knife. John had a very big knife.

Roger concentrated on keeping his bowels static. His innards felt like water which threatened to erupt from God fucking knew which orifice. He clenched everything and closed his eyes. Just for a second. He plastered on his I'm-in-total-control face and waited. He'd said his piece and had nothing more to offer.

Again, almost as if he couldn't help himself, Roger looked again to Rebecca. For help.

No, not for help. Definitely not that.

Just reassurance: that was all.

Or something less needy than that. Definitely less needy. Perhaps just a little show of camaraderie from her – a sense of being together in something that was too abhorrent to contemplate would be a nice gesture.

But bloody *some*thing. He'd accept anything at the moment.

It was time for Rebecca to find herself again. Stop being such a deadweight. Time for her to step up to the mark and fucking *do* something. Maybe her ineffectualness was his fault. Perhaps he'd done too good a job in destroying her.

Come on, Rebecca, he thought. *Please. Now is not the time for petty recriminations. If you can do something, then please, Rebecca, do it. Do it now.*

Help me.

6

LUCY

Lucy had very large breasts. All things were tit-centric for her and hers were things of pride in her big-bosom world. *And* hers were natural. Her buttocks were like buns of steel and her waist was almost slight enough that she could nearly, so nearly, clasp her fingers around her stomach so that they touched. Just above her belly button. Nearly. But not quite.

She was used to being stared at by men. Men were so easy. A quick flash of her tits, a quick flap of her eyelashes, a sudden turn and jiggle of her arse, and men were hers for the taking. Always had been. It was easy. Usually too easy – it was like a game that she always won.

Letting the conversation wash over her, and at least her mother was trying, she wondered at Frank's comment. *Why* was this happening? It was an astute thought from her gentle numpty husband. One of his better ones.

But this John though. He was different. Bland didn't cover it. More blah than anything. But dangerous blah. She doubted whether she could physically charm him. But you just never knew. She'd rarely found a man who responded negatively to her physical attributes.

It was something to think about anyway. A way of tricking him; getting him on side. Lulling him into a false sense of security and then... and then seducing him. And ultimately he would let her go. She needed to finesse her plan. Plan was too big a term for her rambling, skittering thoughts, but it was a seed of hope that she clung to. For the moment. Until she'd got something more concrete to work with.

Strangely, Lucy found herself looking at her mother. An automatic response to finding herself in danger. Tied and handcuffed, she'd turned without thinking, wanting her mother to help her. To save the day. Maybe it was what all children did when confronted with a life and death situation, but Lucy had never knowingly asked her mother for anything.

And expecting help from her father was a no-go. He was all about himself. Lucy and her mother didn't really figure in his life. They were just there. Like fashion accessories. Because it looked good for him. Marriage and a child was an expectation; had never been a real desire on his part. The presence of Lucy and her mother ticked all the relevant boxes. Her father, the conformer – a man who succeeded and did what was right.

On the surface.

But Lucy knew that she and her mother might as well have been white furniture scattered about the place. They might as well not have been there at all.

So she reminded herself that she was a grown woman – twenty-two. She realised now, sitting silently at the dining room table, that for all intents and purposes, she was on her own. She didn't even think of turning to her husband of six months, Frank. Knew it would be a waste of time. He was too wet to depend on. Despite his one intelligent question.

Right there and then she decided that she'd work this out for herself. Look after number one.

She'd never been a mummy's girl. She'd never been a daddy's girl. She supposed she was now Frank's girl. But she didn't believe that. Not really. So that made her nobody's girl.

And that meant she wouldn't be asking anyone for help. She'd rather die than ask.

7

FRANK

This wasn't how it was meant to go down at all. No fucking way. What was John playing at? He shouldn't be here. Not now. On a Sunday. Frank had told John the family's timetable: when they were in, when they were out. And Frank should know; he'd had to live here with Lucy for eleven long months before they'd been able to move into their new flat. Before they'd been able to escape and finally get married.

But now John had gone off-script. Seemed to have his own plan going on. It was all horribly wrong. Very wrong and far too real. Something beyond anything Frank could have imagined.

He questioned how well he actually knew John. Clearly not as well as he'd thought. As soon as he'd walked through the door and seen the knife at Lucy's neck, Frank had known that everything had gone tits up. He'd walked into total chaos and he knew he didn't want to be involved. Didn't want to be a part of it. If he was being honest, violence freaked him out a bit. It freaked him out a lot. And now here he was – *involved*.

He thought his best and only plan of attack was to follow John's orders. Pretend that all this was a surprise to him. Well, that part was true anyway. Instinctively he knew that for his own survival, he must keep up the pretence that he and John had never met. John was clearly playing the same game already and that suited Frank just fine.

John had told Frank that he'd break in when the house was empty. Frank, in turn, had told him where Rebecca kept all her nice pieces of jewellery, where the family silver was kept. An in-and-out job, John had said. 'I'll nick the stuff, and you, Frank, you can sell it on.' That's what John had said, and stupidly Frank had laughed and knocked back the second, or maybe the third pint John had bought him.

What the fuck had he been thinking? He liked Rebecca. Really liked her. Roger not so much – no surprise: he was an impossible man to like. If Frank was being honest, he'd just got carried away with his own apparent new criminal 'connection' and hadn't thought it would really happen. He hadn't thought it through. Couldn't believe John had taken him seriously.

Frank had been drunk. Messing about. Having a laugh. He hadn't meant it. *God.* He wouldn't even know who to sell the stuff to. He was just pretending. Thought he'd made that clear. It was just stupid showing off, a bloody joke. Of *course* he'd never condone the burglary of this house.

And now it was too late. But not too late to feel the shame.

He had *not* been expecting this. This was completely out of his league. He didn't even play in a league. No league would have him.

The more Frank considered their meeting in the pub, the conversations he and John had had – mostly drunken on his part – it occurred to him for the first time that perhaps he'd been used. That John had orchestrated the initial meeting, the following meet-ups, the backslapping pissed-up laughing. The whole friendship was a lie. John had manipulated Frank. And Frank had happily told John everything that he knew about the Twist family.

And now Frank was knee-deep in shite and didn't know how to get out of it. He'd do whatever John wanted.

He was so frightened that he had to clasp his handcuffed hands together to disguise their shaking.

Frank sat at the dining table, listening as the family tried to come up with a plan. He dug deep, clenched his toes in preparation, attempted to ignore his own fear and he'd spoken out. Asked what he saw as the obvious question. *Why?*

8

ME

I'd taken all of their mobiles and turned on the answerphone on the landline. Confiscated the very pedestrian contents of their pockets and put them in the kitchen. No weapons; no guns, knives nor other excitements found lurking about their persons. Nothing untoward nor surprising. Just the everyday, ordinary and extremely banal clutter that people accumulate as they go through their very average days.

Why are people so acquisitive? So hopelessly bound to useless possessions? It's not what you have, it's what you do with what you have that counts. Big difference.

Having left them all to it, I made a quick detour to the downstairs loo – made it risk-free for me. Removed everything available that could be hurled, tossed or stabbed into yours truly. Constant risk assessment and management had to be done, and consequently, having completed the task to my satisfaction, I was now safe.

I then allowed myself the luxury of remembering the first time I'd met Frank and paused as I thought it through. The first one of the family I'd actually spent real, quality time with.

I'd sauntered into Frank's regular watering hole. Buying a pint, I strolled over. 'Okay if I sit here?'

He looked up at me, assessed me, trying to see if I was worth sharing a table with. I'd observed him from the bar on previous nights, and knew he thought he was a bit of a lad. A chancer. Dabbled with a little bit of drug dealing. Only a few joints here and there, but enough to make him believe that he was on his way, and that he would eventually progress up the ladder and reach the dizzy heights of a super gangland boss.

Frank would never be a super anything. Nothing about him was super. He was an idiot who tried and failed to present the relatively easy persona of a tough bad boy. As it was our first real face-to-face meeting, I'd made an effort and had gone for the sharp but menacing look: all black from head to foot and wearing a perpetual scowl. I won him over with my winning wardrobe and fiendish attitude, and he said, 'Yeah, no worries, mate. Take a pew.'

Take a pew? Frank, as I was soon to confirm, was a sad walking cliché. After a brief pause, I poured a pint down my throat in one in order to prove just how manly I really was, although my stomach was offended by the onslaught of undesired lager. It would be my last pint that evening but my performance had won instant admiration from Frank. He laughed, in his laddish way. 'Good one, mate.'

'Yeah, thirsty. You want one?'

Delighted to have a pint bought for him, Frank accepted and sat with fresh pint in front of him. He gulped at it, and it went down the wrong way, and he coughed and spluttered. In general, Frank went down the wrong way. He recovered. 'Not having another yourself, then?'

I winked at him and bent closer to him as if sharing a secret. 'Can't. Got a job on tonight. Need a clear head. Do you get me?'

Frank nodded earnestly, his little middle-class head bobbing away in excitement and trying to contain the thought that he might actually be drinking with the real thing: an honest-to-God *real* criminal. 'Anything you need a hand with, mate? You know, like a driver or something?' He sat back and realised that he'd sounded a bit too eager and leaning forward again, said, 'Got a lot on myself at the moment. Just offering my services, if you get what I mean. No worries though. Don't sweat it.'

And all this fine English spoken in his clipped, reedy middle-class accent. Word choice alone does not a criminal make. Words in this case, were not dissimilar to the one swallow and the summer adage. But I didn't point that out. Instead I held out my hand, saying, 'Name's John. And you are?'

Frank rolled his shoulders, his weak and puny shoulder blades sticking out like two boomerangs through his tight T-shirt. 'I'm Frank. Nice to meet you. What brings you down this way?'

There wasn't any need for me to do any mental limbering up to be able to become Frank's friend. He was so obviously needy my physical presence alone was enough without trying too hard on witty banter. He took himself too seriously and any extra effort would be wasted. So I simply replied, 'Just passing through. Fancied a quick pint. In the area, you know. Dropped in to see my girlfriend. Well, one of them anyway.'

I laughed and he jumped straight in with his size nines. 'Would you like to see a photo of my girlfriend, Lucy? We're getting married soon. She's great.' He pulled out his mobile and then, realising that he was showing a soft side, too soft in his opinion, he said, 'She's a right looker. See? What do you think?'

Politely I sat and watched as he scrolled through countless, seemingly *endless*, photographs of Lucy Twist, striking poses, pouting her lips, sucking her index finger, running her hand through her golden hair, smouldering her eyes into the camera. 'Yeah, very nice. You've done well for yourself there.'

He beamed. Proud and puffed up. 'She's fucking great. The best. Look, here's another one, I love this one. See how she's looking at me?' He laughed, carried away with his own fatal attraction to women. 'Looks like she can't get enough of me, doesn't it? And she can't.'

'No, I'm sure she can't. Lucky her.' I did my best leer and added, 'Lucky you.'

My banal *banter* was drying up and clogging my throat with the tedium of it all. 'Same again?' I asked.

'Sure, why not. Thanks.'

I went to the bar, giving an added swagger to my walk for the benefit of the very puerile and very easily manipulated Frank.

The also very stingy, selfish boy who would apparently accept as many free pints as were offered.

Returning with a Coke, ice and a slice and a straw for myself, I sat down again.

'What's with the straw?' said Frank.

'Not manly enough for you?' I said. 'I like to look after my teeth. This way the sugar bypasses them and goes straight down my neck. Clever, don't you think? Appearance is what it's all about, Franky boy.'

There he went with the nodding again. So easily influenced I didn't even need to try. On any level. I moved it on a pace. 'So, tell me, any family come with that girl of yours? Minted, are they?'

The mere mention of Lucy made him smile. 'They're rich, yeah. Nice though. I like them. Lucky me, eh? In-laws can be a right pain in the arse. But they're all right. Father's a bit of a dickhead, but you can't have everything. I really like the mother. Wish you could meet Lucy. Really, you'd love her.'

I thought it unwise at this stage to tell him that the way this was going, I already knew, that I was in fact, *definitely* going to be meeting Lucy.

And soon.

I also failed to point out to him that I wasn't a fan of swearing. 'Sounds like you're on to a good thing.' Looking at my watch I stood up. 'Gotta go. Nice meeting you. Maybe see you again?'

He couldn't hide his disappointment, but said, keeping it oh-so casual, 'Yeah, great. That'd be good. I'm always here. Same time most nights. After work, you know. A drink and a bit of... well, you know.' He quickly scanned the room. 'Someone might be listening.'

And then he actually tapped the side of his nose. If I'd had a rip-roaring sense of humour I'd have ripped myself in two at the show he was putting on. But I didn't have one, so said, 'See you around then.'

Thus the die was cast. I'd left him wanting more. Always the way to leave anyone. But sometimes when they get more, they discover they don't really want it after all. Frank would be one of those. And he hadn't even bothered to buy me a drink. That irritated. It was the principle of the thing but showcased his innate selfishness. If it was free, he'd take it. Bad philosophy.

I spent several more *insanely* fun nights with the adorably amusing Frank. Saw an impossible-to-count batch of even *more* photos of Lucy, including selfies of herself. I didn't get the concept of the selfie. Surely you didn't need constant reminding and reassurance as to your very own existence? But then again, I rather thought, from the little I'd already seen of Lucy, that she might very well be in need of that constant reassurance. Tragic really. If you cared, I mean. Very sad. Lucy was very sad.

Having poured alcohol down the ungrateful Frank's mouth, he'd told me, with little prompting, all about the Twists. Where they lived, what they did, what they were like, but most of it centred around Lucy. How he loved her. Lived for her. A lot of it I knew anyway, but always best to clarify.

It hadn't taken long before he had offered up the Twists' family house for burglary. Nasty boy. He and the adorable Lucy had been living with them before getting their own flat, and there he'd sat, selling them down the river. Just to impress me. I'd said, 'I'll nick the stuff, and you, Frank, you can sell it on.'

No coercive control had been necessary with Frank. He'd betrayed the Twists with no overt persuasion from me – barely even any encouragement. He had done it all himself. Dug his own grave and jumped right in. He was so concentrated on impressing me, and striving to forever impress Lucy, he'd forgotten his manners. *Do not thieve from Lucy's parents' house: she won't be amused,* I wanted to shout at him. It was a big mistake. Frank should know that.

All those evenings spent together, Frank gabbled on about himself, (never once thinking to enquire about myself: He was all me, me, me). He thought I was his meal ticket to something bigger and better and that I was more exciting than he could imagine. Didn't think he'd ever met anyone quite as dangerous and exciting as me.

That was the only thing that he was right about. He'd never met anyone else like me. Not even close.

And he'd wish with all his heart that he had never met me.

I'd persevered with him longer than I'd strictly needed, but I had to be sure. I liked to give people the benefit of the doubt, but this boy was recalcitrant, obnoxious and without, as far as I could see, any obvious redeeming features. He was a big disappointment and a colossal failure.

I'd got as much as I'd needed from him. It was enough. I'd made my decision.

He gave me no choice but to move on to Roger Twist and the rest of the family.

All the Twists had been given a very cursory glance at this point. A general once-over. I had hoped that they wouldn't be needed, but that hope had died, the longer I'd spent with Frank. He had given me no choice.

And ultimately, that could only end one way.

Not well. For them. Not well at all.

9

ME

I n the kitchen, I made chicken sandwiches for five. I kept my ears peeled back to eavesdrop on the Twist family discussion. It had been rushed and hushed. Grappling for a solution to their problem. Which of course they hadn't come up with.

I'd recognised Frank's voice but hadn't heard what he'd said. I wasn't bothered. How could it possibly affect why I was here? Frank was an embarrassing idiot and I wrote him off accordingly. For the moment.

As I put together a little snack for all of us, I glanced over at the fridge where a single A4 piece of paper was held to the door by a ladybird magnet. I went closer in order to read it. *Had* to go in closer to read it: the writing was like flea-shit – peppered with a confetti of hysterical punctuation. It was headed:

Rebecca's To-Do List.

It said:

- *Make sure chicken today **IS NOT** as dry as last week!! It needs to be moist!!!*
- *Clean the house – it's bloody filthy: 'Disgusting'!!!*

- *Change the sheets and do the hoovering. Before I get home: - Do it NOW!!!*
- *Get your hair done. (Roots)!!!!*
- *Pick up my best suit from dry cleaners Monday!!!! IMPORTANT!!!!*
- *We're running out of Rice Crispies!!! Buy some!!!*

The minute stabs of Roger's pen on the paper looked as if they'd been fuelled with black ink and anger. Call it what you will but really no need to fancy it up any. Bullying was what it was. If I was being kinder, I might have said Roger's words were requests. But that was clearly farcical. They were orders. Instructions. *Demands*. Woe betide his wife if she ignored his list.

She clearly hadn't got round to doing her roots yet. I really hope that seriously annoyed old Roger.

But she had most definitely hoovered the downstairs: I could see the tracks that the vacuum had made in neat stripes on the dining and sitting room carpets. That was good. Always a plus to start off with a clean and tidy house.

From what I knew of Becky, I was surprised that she'd emotionally caved in quite so monumentally to her husband. But strange things happened in life. I do know that. And I also knew that I'd learn an awful lot more about her today. That was an undeniable truth.

It would be interesting to see how my appearance would affect each of their behaviours. But mostly I was interested in Becky. I thought her the nicest of the four.

I returned to the room carrying a large plate and four smaller ones; all of the sandwiches cut into identically shaped triangles. I'd added a little mayonnaise and some rocket for added texture. Then, irritated, I'd had to snip away at some green stems that had stuck out obscenely from the bread slices, but once done, they all looked origami perfect. The chicken was moist and garlicky and sumptuous. I expected no complaints from Rog about the chicken being too dry.

Sitting and not speaking, I placed the plates in front of the family, divvied up the sandwiches onto their individual plastic plates, saying 'S'cuse fingers' and then proceeded to devour my own snack. Felt four pairs of eyes on me. I made encouraging gestures with my hands, 'eat, eat,' and one by one they lifted the sandwiches to their mouths. As if the effort were killing them. I wasn't stupid. I was fairly certain that eating wasn't top of their priority list, but still... a little gratitude wouldn't go amiss.

I hadn't offered them drinks – glass, you know, can be a dangerous material. Broken shards and the like. So I delicately sipped from my own glass, savouring the pure and natural liquid as it rolled around in my mouth. And then I dipped my finger into the water, let it run, dripping, around the rim of the glass. It hummed. I shook my head, frustrated. Not the right tone. Drinking some more, just a little, I tried again. And this time the sound created was pitch perfect. It sounded like a pitiful scream. It screamed and screamed into the silence of the house, wailed out painfully in my head, matching and in perfect sync with my own internal keening.

Drinking some more, and repeating the process, I got a lower hum from the glass. More in keeping with the task at hand. I didn't want to drown in silent screams from my own past. It wasn't the right time for such self-indulgence.

Boosted by the food and water, I took out my wet wipes from my pocket and got rid of any edible detritus. I felt energised. Hot to trot, as my mother used to say. This was all turning into a fascinating social experiment. Over many, *many* months, I'd studied all four of them: individually. And also together, as a family unit. When possible. They actually spent very little time together in public. The picture-perfect family were neatly hidden away in their country house: rarely playing together in public spaces, nor joining in with others.

And hiding so many secrets and lies from each other.

Until now, I'd never really seen them interact together at such close quarters. Under pressure. It was proving to be a huge learning curve. And absolutely absorbing. Wiping my mouth carefully with a sheet of dry kitchen towel, I raised my head and addressed them all.

'I'm sure you're all wondering what I'm doing here. What I want.' This was met with glassy eyes and little expression from any of them, other than a strange, new gleam that appeared to flicker in Rebecca's eye. A new spark had appeared in her facial expressions that had not been there on my arrival. Being an observant person, I could pick up easily on visual cues. Probably came from years of watching other people. Watching them. Watching me. Watching out for myself.

Lucy was the first to speak. 'How did you get in?'

I saw Rebecca sigh as she said, 'I let him in. He tricked me. Told me your father knew him, had invited him for lunch today. Apparently we all met at your father's Christmas work's party. So... I let him in. It was a mistake. Mea culpa.' She bowed her head, embarrassed.

Lucy's face took on a look of complete incredulity. '*What?* Are you mad, Mum? For God's sake, how stupid are you? *Jesus.* We don't *know* him. He's a stranger.' Her eyes bulged with outrage at her mother's admission. 'What's wrong with you?'

'*I* might be what's wrong with your mother, Lucy. I do hope so. I should be wrong for all of you.'

Lucy's lip curled in anger when I spoke. I looked at her, eyeball-to-eyeball, and her lip uncurled immediately.

Holding my hand suddenly in the air, the family jumped as one, as if attached by a huge electrical cable, and not the more pedestrian cord that individually bound them. What did my movement herald? I smiled. 'Panic not. I'm just saying, because frankly someone has to stick up for Becky, I *was* at the Christmas party. Easy enough for me to slip in unnoticed, hidden amongst a group of drunken festive revellers. I wouldn't even consider it an audacious move. It was merely a question of looking like I was supposed to be there and knowing that people wouldn't question my presence. Because most of the human race are blind and stupid. Too consumed with their own pathetic existence to notice anyone else who should or shouldn't be there.

'I saw you all. Watched you all. Listened to your conversation. Saw you, Roger, making a waitress of your wife; waving your empty glass – waiting for her to fill it. And off she went, all demure and obeying, saying nothing. Nasty Roger. The fact is, not one of you saw me, although there I was, right in front of you. But visible to none of you. It's not important, but I'm just pointing out to you, Lucy, that you shouldn't be quite so quick to judge your mother.' I paused. Spoke to Lucy again: 'It's rude. You're rude. You'll learn.'

Brushing the crumbs from my mouth with a napkin, I addressed them all again. 'This is the dining room. Hence the sandwiches, the dining, if you will. Although "dining" is a grandiose term for a sandwich, but you get my drift. Eat. That's what you do in a dining room – you eat. In the same way that you bathe in the bathroom, go to bed in the bedroom. The clue is in the name. Each room has a purpose. We're now adjourning to the living room. What do you suppose that room is for?'

'It's for living,' Becky said. 'Living and talking and being – as a family or as oneself. It's also a sitting room. So it's for sitting.'

I think it's fair to say that Becky had found her voice. I'd like to think that it was my sudden and unexpected appearance into her life that had reignited her. Time would tell.

'Indeed,' I replied. 'And the living room is ‹
where we'll start living proper.'

I stood to release the ties that bound them,
stopped me.

'Thank God we got rid of the killing room. ~~~ ~~~~~
brightly at me, laughed out a shrill laugh – more of a controlled
scream: her face mocking, but the fear still leaking out of her,
despite her best efforts. But still I laughed along with her.
'Killing room.' Even I got the joke. Someone or something had
certainly brought Becky back from her previous habitat, stuck-
in-no-woman's land.

Rog, Frank and Lucy gaped at Becky's words. Silently
screaming, *Don't say the 'killing' word. Not in front of the bad
man.* Rebecca looked at her clan. 'For Christ's sake, it was a
joke. I assume John has a sense of humour. What do you want
me to do? Weep and wail and beg? What good would that do?'

'Shut up, Rebecca,' Roger spat. 'Just shut up.'

'No, Roger. *You* shut up!' She clamped her lips shut in
anger.

A shocked silence followed her words. Her show of
defiance. I liked her more and more.

Then Lucy bent forward, as far as she could, pushing away
her half-eaten sandwich, and thrust her bust at me. I was
horribly and instantly enveloped by the aroma of her cheap
perfume; more an odour of an up-market lavatory air freshener
than an expensive scent.

Licking her lips with her little pink tongue darting in and
out, she pushed out her chest at me, primping her hair with her
hands, preening and elongating her neck. She did something
strange with her mouth; pushing her lips out. I assumed it was a
pout. Was that meant to be attractive?

Leaning both heaving breasts on the table, she pressed down
on them to accentuate the very globe-ness of them, creating a

, more voluminous and inflated cleavage. She batted her
.vy eyelashes which opened and closed like shutters on a
window. She splayed her varnished fingers on the table. She
pouted again and licked her lips which she assumed was both
provocative and alluring. Was she really trying to seduce me?
Seriously? I mean, *really*?

'Thank you, John. For the sandwiches, I mean. Very nice.
Very nice indeed.'

Her voice had dropped an octave or two – husky, croaky. All
throat.

Why did women so often feel the need to debase
themselves? Lucy belittled herself and she belittled me. So she
certainly wasn't expecting the hand that slapped her face. Hard.
I hardly expected it. But it was a full-on swipe with a lot of heft
behind it: sending her face sideways and back across her
shoulders. My very big hand on her very small, fragile, face. Her
neck swung around, nearly swept off its moorings. I hoped she
wouldn't lose consciousness and prayed the worst she suffered
was a little whiplash.

Frank jumped up, his body still attached to the chair; the
four chair legs now horizontal, sticking out from his behind like
some kind of prostheses. 'Hey, hey – No. Stop, John. No. Stop.
Whoa.'

'Shut up, Frank. Just shut up and sit down,' I said.

He did, wringing his cuffed hands, looking tearful.

When Lucy slowly re-swivelled her neck and turned her
eyes to mine, they were blurred, unfocused. Stupid looking. A
line of tears rendered them ever more vacuous.

Where my fingers had slapped her, five bright red welts
showed on her white skin. Crimson on alabaster. A nice violent
colour swatch. I liked the visual technicolour display of the
slapping rainbow, portrayed so perfectly on her stupid face.

I threw the remnants of my water glass in her face. Her

head automatically recoiled, but she blinked, spluttered slightly, but life returned to her eyes. Her painted, normal facial expression made a reappearance. Whoop-dee doo. Little Miss Synthetic had returned.

I pushed her back in the chair so that she didn't drip onto her half-eaten sandwich. Water and bread just make a terrible mess.

So, there. Job done. That had shut her up. Reminded her who was in control. Dissuaded her from continuing to even think of playing further stupid and insulting games with me.

I proceeded to take them, one by one, into the living room.

10

REBECCA

They all sat on individual armchairs. Told where to sit by John – a mad choreography of unhappy, uncoordinated, steps. Gone were the cords binding them but still handcuffed, hands resting in their respective laps, their feet cable-tied. Rebecca's ankles already chafed. She thought that if they all decided to rush him, they'd have to take him by surprise by hopping at him – four abreast.

They had no chance.

Furious that he'd hit Lucy, Rebecca had had to force herself not to react. To say nothing. There was nothing she could do other than scream at him, which would have been pointless, and so she'd resisted saying anything at all. Had averted her eyes from her daughter's distress. Her mouth had emptied itself of saliva, leaving an arid hole; incapable of forming any words of distress. Maybe her silence was better. Rebecca felt intuitively that 'playing along' was the best course of action and her only hope of getting through this. Whatever *this* proved to be.

Burying the image of her daughter's slapped face, shocked and so horribly pale, Rebecca tried to focus. Forced herself to think. To be interested in what John was planning. Interested in why he was planning anything. She was terrified. Couldn't stop shaking. Couldn't think. Couldn't stop thinking.

Perching on the edge of the sofa, his rucksack beside him, John was holding his knife again. He rested his elbows on his knees, the blade hanging between his legs. She watched it swing like a pendulum. Hypnotic. 'Now, where shall we start?' he said. 'What do you think, Becky? Who's first?'

'I don't know what you've got in mind, so I can't comment.'

Keep the tone conversational, as if all this was everyday chit-chat.

'Fair enough,' John said. 'I'll tell you then. And then you can comment. We're going to go around the group, talking. Sharing. Sharing your secrets. You all have them. That's what I've got in mind. What could be simpler?' He grinned with his rodent-like shiny snappy little teeth. 'So, who in your opinion, should go first?'

'Me,' she said. 'I don't mind. I don't mind talking. About anything. I've even got secrets which I'll share. I don't mind. What's to lose? What's the worst that could possibly happen? My family might never speak to me again?' She shrugged, pretending really not to care too much about that particular prospect.

Panicking, she thought, *He could kill us, that's what could possibly happen. What should I do?*

John smiled. 'I like you, Becky. The only one with testosterone in abundance it seems. And for that reason, the fact that you're so apparently willing to reveal your deepest and darkest badness...' He shook his head. 'For that very reason, no. It's not you. The person who is first to tell all, is...' He turned and pointed the tip of his knife at Roger.

'Is you, Roger. Congratulations.'

Rebecca watched her husband's colour, already ashen, go an even more worrying graveyard grey. Even from a distance of six feet, she could see a line of sweat instantly appear on his upper lip, across his nose, dot his forehead. He looked as if he might throw up. Half of her hoped that Roger would projectile vomit across the room, splashing John's shiny shoes, but he just sat there, sheer terror paralysing him. She wondered what he'd say.

'What happens after we talk? Share out badness, as you put it. Share out secrets. What happens then?' she asked.

'Good question, Becky. But you'll have to wait for the answer. I think things will simply fall into place. We shall see.'

She tried to sound scathing as if the game were seriously flawed, or at worst, boring, as she said, 'We've all done things we might not be proud of, so what exactly is the point of this?'

'The whole point,' John said, 'is that I don't think you will forgive the secrets and lies of your loving family. I really don't think you will. *That's* the point, okay?' He looked irritated.

Good, Rebecca thought.

And then he said, 'Trust me. I believe we shall, for the moment, leave the resultant aftermath of our little chit-chat in the lap of the gods. And then, and only then, we shall take it from there.'

Not waiting for any response from her, John turned to Roger. 'Come on then, Rog – spill the beans. Tell us everything. I, naturally, already know everything about you, know more than you can imagine, but I don't think anyone else does, so come on. Go. The lies we weave, Rog. The tangled, tangled webs we find ourselves in. This is *your* untangling time.'

Rebecca watched as John shook his head in mock sympathy at Roger's plight, a quiet tutting coming from his lips. Her husband tried to steeple his fat fingers and couldn't: the handcuffs were too tight. Failing that, he sat. 'Stop calling me, Rog. It's Roger. And my wife is Rebecca, not Becky.'

Rebecca thought it a stupid thing to say. Ironically, at a time when as a family, they should be pulling together, she felt herself going off-piste. With the advent of real danger, she only truly cared for her daughter. She'd long ago ceased to even like Roger, let alone love him.

She jumped in quickly. 'Actually, if you remember, Roger, when we first met, everyone always called me, Becky. Becky Bee: that's who I was. I liked it then and I like it now. In fact I prefer it. I'm not Rebecca anymore. That's always been *your* name for me. Your first theft from me – my own name.'

Her husband's face showed bewilderment and indignation that she hadn't backed him up. Made him look a fool. He *was* a fool, Rebecca thought. Not liking to admit it, but unable not to, she realised that she was almost happy to see Roger the recipient of such condescension from John; that same patronising tone that John used now was identical to what she had heard so often come from Roger's own lips as he had berated her. Again and again. It was how he always spoke to her. And so she didn't help Roger as he waited in shock and terror – on his own. She felt no sympathy for him. She owed him nothing.

Roger's complexion was as colourless as the March landscape outside. Pallid and wishy-washy. Neither here nor there. She listened to John as he said to Roger, 'I prefer "Becky" as well. And I'll call you what I want, *Rog*. Your time starts...' John turned his wristwatch to his face. Allowed a few seconds to pass, and finally said, 'Now.'

11

ME

Roger remained silent. Unsurprisingly. He was boringly predictable. A coward. As all men who abuse women are. I hoped that at least his family would see that.

I said, 'Do you want me to start you off?'

Roger didn't move. Didn't speak. He barely breathed.

'Will you at least admit, Rog, that you have a secret, a *big* secret, that you'd like to share with us?'

A barely perceptible headshake.

'No? I'll give you a clue. Her name is Candi. Apparently and most specifically, spelled with an "I," and not a "Y." A small point but one worth respecting. For her. I don't think that's her real name of course, but that wouldn't have bothered you. Come on, Rog. Candi. Tell us about her.'

The whole family, plus me, sat waiting. And waiting. My temper, which I thought I'd kept relatively in check up until this point, finally threatened to spill over. And no one wanted that. I went and squatted at Roger's feet. 'If I was dealing with anyone other than you, Rog, I'd take my knife and threaten to hurt your family. Perhaps chop their fingers off one by one in order to make you speak. But I know you. I. Know. You. You don't care about anyone other than yourself. You're an "I'm-alright-Jack man". Which means that any risk to your family you'd ignore, as long as you were okay. As long as horrid little Rog was safe, any harm to your family wouldn't affect you, wouldn't make you talk. So, I'll start with *your* fingers. Ready?'

Grabbing his manacled hand within mine I placed his fingers on the arm of the chair. Rested the blade on the second knuckle of his third finger. Pressed down. Until a line of blood showed itself. Little droplets seeped up through his skin in bright red beads. A pretty crimson ring. Nice. I pressed down harder until we both heard the sound of knuckle breaking. Even nicer.

His face instantly went greyer. He gagged. I jumped up. 'No. No, absolutely not. No being sick. Not allowed. You throw up and I'll cut off your whole hand. Calm down.' I stood back, waiting for his nausea to pass. Let the minutes tick by. Finally... 'Better now, Rog? Breathe. Ready to talk? I'll start you off. "I went to see Candi, last Thursday, as I usually do." Do you want to carry it on from there?'

Roger just sat there. Incapable of speaking. I asked, politely, 'Would you like me to get the cling film out? Perhaps that would jog your memory.'

He looked up at me, a plaintive expression on his face, knowing and finally realising that he had no way out of this. 'I'll speak for myself.'

12

ROGER

R oger's gaze remained in his lap. Sweat continued to sweat. Tears weren't far off. He'd been frightened he might actually wet himself. Was worried that he still might. He'd been scared off from being physically sick by John's anger. But he got the message loud and clear. *Just be calm*, he told himself. *Don't piss John off any more than is necessary.*

He cupped his right fingers around his wounded left knuckle; squeezed it, trying to stop the blood. Fear seemed to wipe out any pain that his finger might be giving him. For now. Glancing up at John, really taking in the enormity of John's physical presence, Roger felt something inside himself give. A release of something. The warmth of urine leaking from him, staining his trousers, made him look down in confusion. Unable to process what he was seeing. What he'd *done*. He *had* pissed himself with fear.

Briefly, he closed his eyes in shame, and then without looking up again, he said, 'I visit prostitutes.' He briefly looked at Rebecca and was met with an expression showing neither surprise nor shock. Unreadable. Roger had been expecting at least disgust but not a cold indifference. He carried on.

'To be more precise, I visit *a* prostitute. Candi's her name. Nice girl. Young. Clean. Polite.'

'Vulnerable, you mean,' said Rebecca.

Roger ignored her interruption, chose not to look at his daughter, couldn't care less about silent, stupid Frank. But he was too scared to meet John's look.

But Roger's own reaction was one of outrage. *Why should I have to air my private life in such a public forum?* It wasn't fair. It was a grotesque ask. Too big an ask, but what choice did he have? And very obviously, he had no intention of telling the whole truth: was only willing to admit to a very sanitised version of his and Candi's relationship. A normal client/prostitute relationship: John couldn't possibly prove otherwise – whatever he might say or imply.

'I've been seeing Candi on and off for...' He shrugged. 'I couldn't say, but maybe two years? I'm loyal if nothing else.'

John shook his head. 'If you're waiting for a medal, I rather think you'll be waiting for ever. Get on with it. What do you do with this girl with whom you are so faithful? Why do you like her? What's she look like? Why her? Why not another girl? Why is Candi so special?'

Roger, forgetting momentarily that his feet were cable-tied, went to cross his legs – feeling more in control. He thought, *So what if I fuck prostitutes? Which red-blooded male wouldn't, given half a chance?* 'I make love to her. I like her because she's different, unique, her own woman. Doesn't pretend to be anything that she isn't. She knows her place. She's kind. And gentle. Blonde.'

He was warming to his subject; relaxing into the telling of it. Could forget the fact that he'd urinated himself. *So what.* He smiled. 'But there's no getting away from it – she's a tart. I pay her for her services. Forty pounds an hour. For whatever I want. She's grateful. Her little face lights up when she sees me. She likes me. Looks up to me. Does whatever I want. She definitely likes me. I *know* she likes me. She says I'm her favourite punter. I think I'm more of a friend really. She genuinely enjoys our time together. I know that's true.' He smiled, feeling like he should be congratulated for his honesty – and had passed some sort of test. If this was all that John needed, well... it wasn't so bad. He'd told his story and survived it. He dared anyone to prove his story incomplete. No one could possibly know any different. It was impossible.

Relaxing back into his chair, clasping his cuffed hands – his one hand still dripping blood, he positioned his tied feet so that his circulation wasn't entirely cut off, and angled his head towards John. 'Okay, John? Did I pass?' Of course he had. He beamed at everyone. Relieved. So relieved.

And then it hit him. How did John know about the cling film?

13

ME

Becky's first reaction to her husband's 'confession' to seeing a prostitute was a look of resignation. But as the telling went on, her eyes darkened. She was clearly waiting. Waiting for more. She was right to, for more there most definitely was. 'How old is Candi, Roger?' she asked. 'Just how old? Or more to the point, just how young?'

Rog bristled as if insulted. 'She told me she was nineteen. Nearly twenty. Next month is her birthday, so perfectly legal.' He smiled a smug smile.

'Nineteen,' said Becky. 'That's hardly old enough for big school. And that's *if* we believe you. Bloody big "if." She's probably underage, you're so stupid.' Her hands shackled together, her fingers were clenched so tight I winced at the pain she must be feeling. 'And do you think that I'm surprised by this revelation? This "kink" in your behaviour? Don't you think I already know you use prostitutes? Have always known you've used them for most of our married life? Am I meant to be impressed? Shocked? Horrified? Well, I tell you what, you nasty little man...'

She leant forward, her neck straining, her throat muscles

contorting and pulsing with anger. 'I couldn't be *less* surprised. You shit. You absolute shit. Yet again, you cease to amaze me.'

Roger's face contracted into his neck as if he'd been slapped: genuinely shocked by Becky's reaction.

Lucy, on the other hand, just looked sick and pale and very young. Of course that might have been the after-effects of the slap to her face, but I didn't think so.

And Frank continued to pretend he wasn't there. Hoping, no, *praying* to God that I wouldn't speak to him. Rat him out to his in-laws. I smiled. He'd wait.

Turning to Roger, I said, 'But you've left out all the good bits, Rog. All the gory details. But before we go into them, and we will, how *is* Candi? Seen her this Thursday, have you? How was she?'

'I didn't meet her this Thursday. Busy. At the office, running late – you get the picture.'

'But that's not true, Rog. Come on. You can't kid a kidder. You *did* go to her flat. I saw you. You're a creature of habit. Not like you to change your routine. Thursday is Candi-day. So why pretend you didn't go this last Thursday?' I smiled. 'I filmed you on my mobile.'

Roger slumped further into his armchair, trying to make himself invisible. Hoping I'd move on. No chance of that. 'Okay, I did go, but she didn't answer. Okay? Satisfied?'

'No, I'm definitely not satisfied, Rog. But credit where credit is due. You at least told the truth there. Candi didn't answer your knock on her door, nor your impatient little eager-beaver taps at her window.' I put my knife down on the sofa, sat back and folded my arms. 'Perhaps you wondered why? You must have. It was a set date in both of your diaries. Didn't you wonder just a little why she failed to open the door?'

Roger just sat there, like an amorphous lump. Face trying oh-so hard not to give away his fear. I let the silence settle, let his family look at him, let them watch him, let them see him for what he was.

Eventually, I couldn't bear the suspense any longer. 'Do you want me to tell the rest of it? Would that be easier? Tell it *all*? I think your family deserves to know everything, don't you?'

In a pathetic attempt to challenge me, Roger said, 'You can't know what went on between me and Candi. You weren't there. Thank God for small mercies.' He smiled and rolled his eyes. But we all knew that it had been a most ineffectual attempt at a joke. But I played along, just because I'm a nice man.

'Yes, I agree, Rog. Thank God for small mercies that I wasn't there to see you. Thank God for that very small mercy. But I know Candi. I know her well. Very well. She told me all about you. And your little... likes and dislikes.'

'You don't know anything. I don't believe you. Candi wouldn't tell you anything about me. Nothing bad.'

But worry showed on his florid, flaccid, face. After his initial editorialised telling, relief had temporarily swamped him. Thinking it all over. Thinking himself safe. His relief had been so very palpable I'd felt like leaning forward and stroking it. Now that relief had been washed rudely away. I think Rog finally got that I knew the punchline to the Candi-saga. He guessed I might in fact know more than he did.

And I did. 'She told me something very bad about you. Wanted me to know everything.' I held my first two fingers up, crossed. 'We were like that, me and Candi. Close. Close as close could be.'

He smiled a very unsure smile.

'You killed Candi, Rog. I know you did. I found her. After you'd left the previous Thursday. That's why she didn't answer the door to you *this* Thursday. She was dead. And you killed her.'

The atmosphere in the room gasped to a full stop. Not

actual, audible gasps: more a collective and appalled muted intake of breath.

His whole body deflated like a burst balloon, disregarded and forgotten at a child's tea party.

Doomed.

14

ME

And then Roger's head jerked up. I saw a flash of inspiration, a ray of hope cross stupid, nasty old Rog's face. In a rare display of intelligence, he said, 'If she's dead, then how did you know about the cling film?'

'Because I've known Candi for a long time. I told you. You should listen more. I repeat, she told me all about you. You disgusting little man. If I did spitting, I'd spit on you. But I don't like saliva outside the mouth. It's a repellent habit. Lucky you.'

Becky shouted. Suddenly. Making even me jump. 'You *killed* a woman, Roger? How could you? What did you do to her? You've always been a complete bastard. But *killing* someone? A young girl? What did you do? How did you kill her? Have you been to the police? Do they know? Do Candi's family know? Her parents? Does *any*one know?'

'*I* know, Becky. I know that your husband is a murderer,' I said gently and with very real sympathy. As real as it gets for me, anyway.

Becky sucked in air as if she were drowning. And suddenly stood up. Her movement took me by surprise. I watched with fascination as she bunny-hopped across to Roger's chair, falling into his lap as she reached him. Raising her cuffed hands, she swiped at his face and then, getting a better purchase, leant on her elbows, and rained down her fists-in-metal onto his head. Again and again and again.

And then she stopped. Breathing hard. 'You bastard,' she said. Slowly she went back to her chair on her knees, dragging herself by her forearms; wanting and needing physical distance from him. Reseated, she tried to gather herself, tried to stop the tears that ran down her face. Attempting to wipe them away with her hands, she only managed to smear her face with her husband's blood. And still the tears fell. Tears of anger, pure anger – not of sadness. Well, perhaps there was sadness for Candi mixed in there somewhere. But mostly there was fury. Absolute fury, fuelled with a lot of hatred for her husband. I liked her purity of emotion.

I did *not* like the snot that trickled from one nostril. She sniffed and the stream of snot snapped quickly upward and thankfully out of sight, as if it were something on elastic.

Roger sat stunned; blood trickling from tiny cuts made by the handcuffs: across his brow, his cheeks and his nose. *Well done, Becky*, I thought. *Well done. And about time.*

Lucy made whimpering little noises, whilst managing simultaneously to look angry and frightened. And sad. So very sad. She was a positive kaleidoscope of facial emotions. Her skin was bleached white with shock, but also a pink, angry rash mottled her neck as if to add a final and insulting dash of unnatural hues to her body on learning the news that Daddy was a killer.

Frank, very unexpectedly, stood, wobbling at first as he got his balance with his two feet tethered together. 'You're filthy, Roger. Disgusting. You killed a woman. *Killed* her. For God's sake. You should be locked up. You're...' I could see his brain grappling for a suitable adjective. Lamely, he finished with 'You should be locked up.' Then he sat down.

Hark. It's a miracle. Frank speaks. In whole joined-up sentences. He *is* alive after all. A definite improvement on his former monosyllabic protests at me hitting his wife. At least he now sounded a bit like a grown-up. He was a fledgling man; even the stubble on his chin was like the fluff of an embryonic newborn chick. I couldn't believe what a drip he was.

I chose not to comment on either Becky's nor Frank's displays of anger towards old Rog. I think he got it. Wanting to move things on, I bent forward from the sofa. 'Don't you all want to know how Rog did it? How he killed poor Candi?'

'Of course I want to know,' said Becky. 'Tell me exactly what happened.'

So this is what I told them about Roger and his exploits.

15

ME

I started following Roger on a Monday. With little enthusiasm. It required no skill nor any sophisticated technique. I simply had to be patient and stave off the tedium of watching and trailing Roger's very repetitious life. It wasn't razzle-dazzle excitement. It was the epitome of mundane.

I began by waiting outside his office building until he arrived early on that first Monday morning.

Over the coming days, weeks and months, as I got to know him and his routine, I was amazed at how quickly I discovered that he was an absolute bastard. It was clear from day one. (And yes, I do swear. But only internally. When it's really warranted. That's allowed. Better in than out, in this case.)

Every single night, upon leaving work – rain or shine – he'd come out from the front of the building in order to preen and shine before his adoring flock: the public. Of course they didn't know that Roger Cometh, but all the same, he'd follow the same ridiculous ritual of looking down upon the commoners from the top step of a short flight of stairs down to the pavement. He'd tug down on his jacket importantly. Make it creaseless. Then he'd readjust his tie. Smooth his hair. His I'm-the-king-of-the-castle routine finished, he'd offer up a little swagger, perhaps for his own benefit, and then with an about-face he'd backtrack around the side of the building and disappear.

Only to emerge in his I've-got-a-big-penis shiny silver Porsche.

That first day, it had been easy enough, as it continued to be, to follow him to work, in my own I've-got-a-penis-but-don't-feel-the-need-to-brag-about-it car, (a Ford Fiesta). After work, he'd drive to a pub off the high street, and then home. It was hardly a rock 'n' roll lifestyle, but I knew that everyone had their stories, and I suspected, from his more than obvious unpleasantness, that his story might be worth learning.

I trailed him into the pub on day one: Monday, and then the following Tuesday, Wednesday and Thursday evenings. It all fell into place as easily as a priceless timepiece – never missing a beat: neither Roger's friends, nor his drinks and amount thereof, nor the seats in which they sat – none of that ever changed. Precision, replication and sticking to a routine was key for Roger. His life was all very orchestrated and buttoned up: anal, displaying an almost ritualistic behaviour, never veering off the path of pre-organised decisions. And boring old Rog left the pub at precisely half past seven on the dot. For the first three nights: without fail.

Early evening, that first Thursday, the red leatherette booths were mostly empty, as always, but overflowing with Roger and his three loud friends. The three sidekicks were all on the fat side, although, like a trio of Russian dolls, they decreased in size. From obese, to fat, to chubby.

Always the same embarrassingly school-boyish braying laughter, coming from a group of male want-to-be-somethings, but who remained, sadly, a group of very ordinary male nothing-specials. Nothing ever changed. That grinding regularity kept their group safe and strong. A unit.

I listened in to their conversations, sitting as I always did, in the next booth with my back to them, pretend-reading the daily paper. That fourth evening that I joined them, I followed Roger up to the bar as he got a round in. An extra pint for him. A break in his routine. I could hardly contain my excitement.

I let him order first. After he'd asked for four more pints, I hooked one foot around the strut of the stool, keeping my balance. We were shoulder to shoulder. He ignored me. I don't think he even registered my presence. I stood at an angle to him, resting my ankle on my stool and presenting him with most of my back. I kept his reflection in sight in the mirror behind the optics. Bent my head to my paper, pen in hand, crossword at the ready. Ears flapping, eyes swivelling: all senses at the ready.

A young girl, perhaps mid-twenties or thereabouts, walked in and up to the bar. Strutting across the pub, her stride was strong and true. She oozed confidence. A good-looking girl: striking, vibrant, independent. And perhaps a little pissed off. Possibly a bad day at the office? Who knew? But you couldn't fail but pick up on her mood. Unless you were Roger.

Roger turned to his pack of mates and did a not-so-discreet fist-pump, and then pantomimed big breasts as he held his grubby, stumpy little fingers in front of his chest. Getting his oh-so-macho gentlemen-in-waiting's attention with their idiot sheep mentality. He turned his magnificence to the girl.

'Hello,' he said.

I was sure the girl would fall for that startlingly original opener. My eyes couldn't help themselves: they rolled in disbelief at Roger's crassness.

She glanced at him and did a very mini smile in polite acknowledgement but failed to answer him verbally.

'Can I buy you a drink?' Roger said.

'No, thank you – really, there's no need.'

'Oh, but there's every need. What's your fancy?'

'No. Really. You don't have to buy me a drink. I'm fine. Thank you.'

Her smile was getting thinner by the second, and Roger's sloppier and wetter. He ignored her courteous rejection and pushed it. 'But I insist.'

'And I *de*sist. I don't want a drink from you. I'm buying my own. Thanks anyway.'

Roger laughed; too loudly, too brashly – turning and grandstanding to his pals who couldn't quite hear the conversation and were relying on Roger's body language for their cues. Trying to keep up the pretence that he was a true leader in his very small world, egged on by his merry little band of arse-lickers, Roger waggled his eyebrows theatrically. If I could see his reflected grandiosity from my limited position, then the girl most certainly could. She leaned forward as the barman approached. 'A gin and tonic, please. Ice and lemon.'

'Make it a double,' Roger said.

Finally the girl faced him square on. 'Why don't you take a hint, mate. I don't want a drink from you, so if you wouldn't mind, could you please leave me alone and fuck off back where you came from.'

This was most unexpected. I'd already labelled Roger as a bully, and correctly so. All bullies, like any predator, hone in on victims who themselves give off a pulsing siren call of 'Come-get-me-I'm-yours.' They screamed 'victim' – it might as well have been etched upon their foreheads. And thus their distress signal was picked up by their attackers. Like a shared radar, they emitted a strange mating call to each other. The vulnerable crying out to be exploited by the weak-seeking predator. A match made in hell.

But this girl absolutely did not scream 'victim' or anything else. She just looked quietly at Roger, not bothering to hide her disdain.

And yet, here he remained, angry but not giving up, apparently not recognising the error of his selection. He'd picked a tiger and not a mouse. His wires weren't merely crossed – they were hopelessly tangled. I could have told him that this was not a girl to be messed with: she shone with self-assurance, would and could and absolutely should make mincemeat of this wispy haired middle-aged man who dared to stand in her space. And yet, he'd persevered. Perhaps it was that one extra pint that he'd had, that had skewed his judgement.

I watched in the mirror as his reflection coloured: his face purpled in indignation, at being rebuffed. By a *woman*, no less. His back was firmly blocking out his friends' view. He leant into the girl. 'Don't you dare fuck with me, young lady. Don't. You. Dare.'

'I dare,' she said. 'Why wouldn't I? Who do you think I am? What if I let you buy me a drink? What then? What would you expect? I recognise men like you. You stick out like a turd in a baby's bath. Your attitude stinks. If I accepted a drink from you, you'd think me beholden to you, and that sure as shit isn't going to happen.' She smiled at him; flashy perfect white teeth splitting her pretty face. 'Is it?'

'If you were so fucking lucky that I actually had bought you a drink, you'd owe me, bitch. You'd owe me.'

The girl looked around the bar, laughing at Roger, wanting an audience to witness her annihilation of him. 'What would I owe you?'

He whispered, his voice hissing as he spat out: 'You'd owe me, full stop. For the pleasure of my company. Who do you think *you* are?'

'I know I'm not for sale.'

'Just as well,' Roger said. 'I'm not buying.'

She laughed. 'You could never afford me anyway, you pathetic little man. Piss off.'

She paid for her drink, took it from the bar in one hand, book in another, and headed for a table and chair where she sat and sipped from her drink and turned to a page in her book. I swivelled on my stool, and peered over my paper, eyes still pretending to crossword. It was fascinating. His colour was high, alarmingly so, and his teeth clamped together, biting down in fury. Breathing slowly, he gathered himself, unbuttoned his face, de-coloured and turned, laughing and rolling his eyes at his chums. Nothing to see here.

Why had he got it all so wrong? Was it that one extra pint? Or was he just a really inefficient prowler; seeing prey in front of him instead of an alpha female. I couldn't understand such a basic mistake.

As he left the pub, I saw that it was quarter to seven: a whole forty-five minutes earlier than usual. He really was mixing it up this evening.

He got into his macho car and drove off. I pootled along behind him in sedate fashion in my positively girly and dainty car by comparison, and proceeded to follow him in tepid pursuit to his destination.

Another detour from the norm. He wasn't headed home as usual. This was turning out to be a real night to remember.

He pulled up and parked his penis-on-wheels in a side street off the main drag in the redder lit side of town. I followed in my boring unnoticeable car, drove like an old lady. Didn't want any unwarranted attention. False number plates. But real me. As real as it gets, anyway.

I parked behind one of those dreadful people carriers on the main high street and watched with interest as Roger approached a door, between a chicken shop and a launderette, his hands in his pockets. He was unaccountably wearing a trilby – going for perky-man-about-town. Failing miserably.

It was a sorry looking building, uncared for. Knackered. He

rang the bell and waited. Clearly it was a place familiar to him. He smoothed down his hair, replaced his hat, and waited. He rang the doorbell, leaned on it, and then rapped the letter box handle – making his presence felt. Mainly to himself.

I couldn't help but notice that his hands were now gloved. And that was definitely a bad sign for whoever the occupant was. It suggested something ominous, something that shouldn't be. It was September: one of those warm, late summer evenings – temperature in the late teens. Certainly not cold.

Not cold enough for gloves.

And they weren't *gloves* gloves. They were latex, finger-hugging gloves that even from this distance looked out of place. A weird mixture of transparent opaqueness. These particular gloves, outside of a medical setting, were *never* good. They didn't scream out *Fun*.

Roger waited, tapping his foot impatiently. Walked to the window facing onto the street and knocked on it. Back to the door – which finally opened. And there it was, the reason for Roger's juvenile mistake with the girl in the pub. His terrible error of judgement. It hadn't been the alcohol after all.

He'd been looking forward to *this* meeting. Sexually overexcited. That had been his mistake. Thinking with his dick in the pub; his behaviour penis-led. And still being led by it, he pushed past the lank-haired girl who'd opened the door. She cowered, cringed and flinched all in one motion but stood back to allow him entry: clearly expecting him.

With her head bowed, she appeared to do a little bobbing at the knees and possibly said something to him. I was too far away to see. What I could see was that she dreaded him. Needed him. Hated him. As he passed her, he swivelled back suddenly, making her jump as he cupped his hand to his ear, as if he hadn't heard her properly. She spoke again, her eyes lowered. Roger, seemingly satisfied, breezed past her.

I knew from one glance that she was both a prostitute and a junkie.

And Roger was her client. Naughty Roger. But no surprises there.

Poor girl.

Now please don't confuse me with a caped crusader. I'm not in the habit of saving damsels in distress. It's simply that I'm a believer in what's right and what's wrong, what's good and what's bad.

And Mr Roger Twist was most definitely bad.

I had no reason to think that the girl was not good.

But I recognised the set-up. Had seen it a million times.

And I knew she had to be saved from big bad Roger.

16

ME

A red glow was illuminated in the bottom right window on the ground floor. A redder light than it had been. I imagined an extra lamp had been switched on. I saw the silhouettes of the trilbyed Roger and the young prostitute cross behind the net curtains. Shadows only but hauntingly sad all the same. Roger's outline took its hat off.

Settling in for a wait, I sat in my car and feared for the girl. Thirty minutes crawled by. And another. I was getting bored and more than a little irritated. Used the time to practice my one-hand-tying of my double safety knot shoelace. Strong fingers were key and of course a manual dexterity borne from years of practice.

What was Roger doing to the woman? I shuddered at the thought as I was pretty sure he wasn't being nice to her. From what I'd seen of him, *niceness* didn't come into it – wasn't in his nature.

At nine on the dot, Roger reappeared on the doorstep. Still gloved. Just under two hours with the girl. He pulled the collar on his light jacket around him as a September chill had shown itself, put his hat back on and slammed the door. Made a point of slamming it. Hard. He smirked as he walked away. The door bounced back on its hinges, and hit the wall and finally came to rest, a couple of feet ajar.

Roger didn't even notice. Didn't care. Walked off smiling. Not the tenderest of departures. More an adieu of victory. I was surprised he wasn't whistling in triumph.

I waited for the girl to appear. Waited and waited. Wondered just what she was doing. Not coming to the door. Uncaring as to it being open, or unable to close it herself? Hoping that she was indeed capable of doing *some*thing, I worried that anyone could simply walk in. Damn it. I wasn't overly pleased to be cleaning up after Roger but I felt needs must.

Tired of doing nothing, and despite myself, nervous for the girl, I got out of my car and crossed the road. Stood at the open doorway. Glanced at the doorbells. Far too many for a three-storey building. There must be a bell for every room. Bedsit land.

Having seen her, however fleetingly, I recognised the type and knew that it was unlikely that the girl had a pimp in tow. There was no one watching out for this prostitute. She was way too far down on the ladder. She was barely worthy of living, let alone having someone who pretended to watch out for her safety, and then who only would take her money from her. She was barely reaching the bottom rung of *any* ladder.

Barely existing.

Even if there had been a lurking pimp, I was confident that I'd win in any fight. Hadn't lost a fight since I was eleven. Didn't plan to start now. I was big and big on violence. A winning combination.

Politely, I rang the bell for 1A and waited. Waited some more. No response.

Pushing the already-open door with my elbow, I walked in,

closing it quietly behind me with a soft foot shove. I stopped outside the door on my right. Cheap plywood showed a thin coating of paint; a shout of respectability, with visible brush strokes and all. A splat of emulsion stained the doorknob, but hey – who cared? I knocked gently. Put my ear to the wood. Heard nothing. Deciding on one of those stupid 'Coo-ee' noises, I knocked again, receiving no answering birdcall. Silence.

I pushed on the door and turned the knob. It swung open; the lock not locked. The red light had been turned off, and the shadows murked and lurked around, making it difficult to make out shapes or movement. I swept my hand over the wall until I found the main light switch and turned it on.

As a precautionary measure, I did a quick scan of the small room, taking everything in at one glance. Definitely no pimp. Nowhere to hide. No help at all for the poor unfortunate.

It was a square room with a window. No carpet, no curtains and yellowish lino with a burnt scarred rectangle in the middle of the floor. It didn't actually smell particularly bad, but equally I felt my nostrils quiver in distaste at a vague but indefinable odour. It might have been sadness.

As I stepped further into the girl's home, the net curtains fell like sheets of thin membrane; holes dotting the lower half of the curtain. I felt and heard the leather soles of my shoes stick to the flooring. Sweat filled the space with its tangy aroma, with an added tinge of everything that is old and dirty. An all-encompassing smell. I crept softly into the centre of the room: about three paces. 'Hello?' I said to the form on the bed, stepping a little closer. I hoped the chick was still alive in her filthy nest: her chest panting with gasps, her tiny mouth open, hungry for help. That's what she looked like; a newly born bird, parentless and forlorn.

And that's precisely what she was doing. Panting. Short out-of-breath inhalations; jagged, her cheeks pink from the stress of simply continuing to live.

She was lying on her side on a single mattress; curled in a foetal position, bony knees drawn up tight to her chin, her hands cupping her ankles. Hearing me, her face didn't move but her eyes rolled slowly around until they landed on mine. Or more specifically, one eye rolled around. The other was too swollen for the exotic movement of eye-swivelling. Her one good eye took in my big body as it approached her. I must have seemed huge from her vantage point. She was hurting too much to move in order to protect herself from a stranger walking into her space. Her face, her trembling lips, her one good eye, her one bad swollen eye: they all just silently pleaded with me, *please, not more. Please go away.*

Clumps of her hair had been pulled out and lay on a grey and greasy-looking pillow; her face was bruised and her mouth cut.

I held my hands up in a show of surrender, indicating no intent to harm. My body language gentle. My nice-boy act. A bit of charm and a whole lot of kindness was called for as I invited her into my world. And strangely – or not – it was no act. I meant it. I think I even made shushing noises as if she were a baby laying in swaddling. Her big round flat and empty good eye filled with tears. The damaged eye, big and black. A slit. A tear still managed its escape. I wanted to tell her not to give up. Not now. Not now I was there to help.

Apparently, this wreck of a girl was what Roger did. What he did for fun.

'Who are you?' she said, her voice weak; barely audible. 'How did you get in?' Her breath was breathy like she'd forgotten how to inhale and exhale properly.

I gestured at the bed, silently asking if I might sit at the end. She nodded, unable to stop me and believing, I think, that any extra hurt I could cause wouldn't even touch the sides. She was all hurted-out. I turned my knees away, not wanting to encroach further on her space. 'The front door was open: I let myself in. Don't worry. I'm not here to hurt you,' I said. 'What's your name?'

'Candi,' she said – her voice childlike. 'Spelled with an "I." Not a 'Y.''

Really? I mean, really? Candi? I didn't think so but didn't think it was important. What did a name matter after all? I'm hardly a stickler for such things. I said, 'My name's Paul. Paul Bettering. I'm a copper. Vice squad.'

I flashed a fake police ID at her – again, I'm the man who knows a man who knows a woman. The woman was a veritable treasure trove. Fixed me up with anything I needed; especially very specific and more exotic bespoke items that were sometimes required. It's all about who you know.

I actually had a fake card and/or documents for many different identities for myself: covering every eventuality – all completely authentic looking. The woman was the best of the best when it came to supplying fraudulent accreditation. Pick a card, any card. A card for every season: stashed for all occasions in a discreet panel on the underside of my Ford Fiesta dashboard. Nowhere a real copper would search if stopping me for a routine traffic violation, which was highly unlikely, taking into account my very tame driving habits.

I had a similar panel in all of my very boring and highly missable vehicles.

Candi's little black button eyes widened as far as they could, bearing in mind the puffiness of one, and I was quick to explain: 'I'm not here to nick you. Relax. I just want to know about the man who just left. The man with the hat.' I cocked my head to the side and added, 'Why are you breathing like that?'

'It's nothing. Out of breath.'

That was her first lie. I was sure there were many more to come. 'Was your last client into strangling?'

'Are you really a copper?'

'Really, truly.'

'And you don't want to nick me?'

'No, again, really, truly – all I want to know about is the man who just left.'

'He's a fucking psycho. Likes to use cling film. Over my mouth, you know? When he's finishing off. You know – he likes it when I nearly stop breathing. It's the only way he can get his rocks off. Fucking psycho.'

I made more soothing noises. And Candi was right. I suspected that Roger was indeed a psycho. Still in the closet in that regard. But it takes one to know one. At least I'd had the grace to out myself in that regard, and as a common courtesy to all, was prepared to acknowledge that I might be on the 'ab' side of normal. Had been for years. Perhaps since I was a boy. 'How about we get you fixed up, before we chat?'

'What do you mean "fixed up"?'

'Cleaned up.' I stood and went over to the little kitchen area: a two-burner ring, a sink and a fridge. The fridge was virtually bare: apart from one very old-looking saveloy looking obscene in its dusky pinkness: a strangely lewd food item sitting all on its lonesome. There was something else I couldn't immediately identify on a chipped blue saucer.

I opened drawers, one after the other, looked under the sink, and came up with an unused J-cloth. Taking the cleanest dirty glass, I filled it with water and dunked the cloth. Reapproached Candi with my makeshift medical supplies and set about making her more human. I leant over her and tended to her; wiped away her unshed tears, the blood, but failed to wipe away her desperation. Her expression of resignation. I wasn't a magician. There was no bunny a-leaping from my hat, nor were there any tricks up my sleeves.

'So what did he do to you, this man? What's he call himself anyway?' She looked a little vague: confused, as if she'd lost the thread of the conversation. I smiled encouragingly. 'Your last client? The man with the hat?'

She pulled away. Maybe an inch or so. Fear filled her face. 'Why are you asking?'

The spilt blood cleaned from her face, her skin looked doughy, like uncooked pastry. I doubted she had the best diet, probably no diet at all. Instead I imagined she dined on daily syringes of heroin and not a lot else. No nutritional value there.

I didn't bother asking if she had any plasters or antiseptic – bit like asking Roger if he had a conscience.

Having made her presentable, more comfortable, I said, 'Are you sick?'

Her eyes squinted, thinking. Assessing the situation. Was I an easy touch? Copper or no? But I could see from the one eye that her pupils were like pin pricks, her irises showing green. Still stoned. 'You're not sick,' I said. 'So let's chat.' I rested my hand on the thin duvet between my legs and her body – a decent distance away: non-threatening. 'As I said, I'm not interested in what you're doing: drugs, sex, rock 'n' roll, who gives a fuck?' I smiled like a good copper would, using the appropriate lingo. 'But I do want to know about your last client. What's the John's name?'

'What's it to you?'

I sighed. Deep from my belly. 'He's a nasty shit. I want to get him. I don't want anything from you, except information. I can help.'

'Help how?'

'What do you want?'

Her good eye squinted to match her existing slit-eye, and a

sly look came over her. She was as easy to read as a child's comic. 'Food? Money for food?' She smiled. A cutesy smile, trying to trick me the only way she knew how. Presuming that I might fall for her feminine wiles, her luscious sexual body still apparently up for sale.

Kill me now.

'Let's not play games, Candi. I'm a copper, and you're a prostitute and a junkie. I assume you don't want to be the former but would like something to feed the latter? Yes?' I waited for the nod. 'I can help you. Get you what you want. In exchange for information. So, I'll happily get you food and anything else your little heart desires. Even drugs, if you want. Do we have a deal?'

A really stupid question to ask a junkie, *Do you want drugs*, but I waited politely for her answer.

'What? You'll get me drugs?'

'Amongst other things. Whatever it takes. But don't take the piss. I actually do want to help you. So, come on. You tell me everything that your last client did to you, and I'll sort you out. Proper sort you out. Trust me.'

She struggled to sit. I gently supported her from her elbows, pushing her up the bed. Unable to miss the fresh cigarette burns along her forearms. An extreme dot-to-dot, strictly for the more mature adult. They were pink and pulsing from their recent application. Roger really hadn't played fair.

Candi smiled. Held out her hand, palm up. 'Come on then. Fair dos. Give me the dosh and I'll give you the information. Can't say fairer than that.'

I told her to hang on. Just wait. I'd go and get supplies. I'd be back in about an hour. Maximum. I'm a man of my word and our verbal agreement was one to which I'd adhere. Just call me a psycho with a heart.

Plus, she was right. Fair dos and all that.

17

BECKY

Becky could hardly fail to notice that during John's telling, both Lucy and Frank had sat forward in their chairs. As she herself had done. As if they were all listening to a monologue on stage. The damning denouement. The final reveal.

Only Roger sat, his posture unchanged. His back pressed hard against a cushion. Wanting to disappear. Rigid. Looking at him, Becky realised just how much she hated him. Had hated him for years. She *despised* him.

She had also delighted in the fact that Roger had wet himself. Shown his fear to all. Pathetic, horrid little man.

And the worst of it was, she hadn't, not for one moment, not even for a split second, doubted the story that John was telling. Her husband had very early on in their sexual relationship, before their marriage, shown a tendency to delighting in her pain. At first, Becky had welcomed it, had thought, *yay, bring it on – exciting. I'm game: up for anything new and fun.* Before it wasn't exciting. Before it wasn't new and fun anymore. When it just hurt. But by then, of course, it was too late and she'd married him.

He'd effectively trapped her. Charmed her trapped her. God, how stupid had she been?

She'd effectively and swiftly put an end to his violent tendencies in the bedroom by moving into one of the spare rooms after their honeymoon. Locking the door; a chair wedged under the doorknob.

But every week, every Thursday, Roger would come home, a bit more pissed than normal, a bit angrier, and a bit more violent. Thursdays, and Thursdays only, he was always more sexually demanding. Now she knew why. She'd learnt quickly to diffuse his anger by leaving food out for him. Food after alcohol had always made him sleepy, and she'd always been sure that he passed out before his anger could blossom into anything else. And before he could force his way into her bedroom.

Roger had actually killed someone. He'd always been a sadist. And now he'd *killed* someone. A young girl. Jesus bloody Christ. She couldn't get her head round it. Didn't know how to act, what to say, how to feel.

Anger was the easiest emotion for her at the moment. Strange, as it was the one emotion that Roger had stripped her of for so many years. She found that a little part of her was still relishing John's arrival, his presence. It had, if nothing else, brought her alive again. She was like a bloody born-again woman. *I hope it's not too late*, she thought.

She was alive, sitting in the chair that Roger had chosen, the set of uncomfortable chairs with matching sofa, and looked at Lucy. How best to keep her and Lucy alive? It went without saying that she wanted neither Roger nor Frank to die – of course not – but Lucy remained her priority. And for Lucy to live, Becky had to live.

What she needed was a real, proper plan. And quick. 'Lucy. Lucy, look at me. Are you all right?'

A sneer threatened Lucy's lips, but it wasn't really heartfelt.

More of an act. Just like Lucy. Superficial. Going through life, never really getting it. 'Come on, Lucy,' Becky said. This time her voice was harder. She needed a reaction. A real one. Not a bloody rehearsed phrase that meant diddley-squat. 'I know this is difficult, hearing about your father, but hang in there. I've got this.'

I've got this. Becky almost laughed. How pathetic was that? Of course she hadn't got this. She hadn't got this at all. But she could at least lie to Lucy. Give her hope. Becky smiled at Lucy. A tentative smile came back. Becky nodded at her, not quite knowing what she was trying to communicate, but trying anyway. Lucy just smiled again.

They both, for the moment, visually held on to each other, and ignored John who watched them keenly.

What Becky needed was a plan. All she really knew about John was that he was a little hysterical about physical human waste, like sweat, any form of regurgitation, or anything dirty or messy. Could she use that knowledge as a weapon against him? How strong was his aversion? If spat and dribbled on from a great height, would he run screaming from the house, or would he kill them instead? She could do nothing until she knew the answer to what seemed a very pedestrian and odd question.

Would vomiting over John save the family, or be the death of them?

Fuck it, she thought, the idea was laughable. She needed a better plan than that. It wasn't even a plan. It was just an observation. He was a neat freak. How could she possibly use that against him? Frankly, her diagnosis of him got her precisely nowhere.

Her predicament was that she and her family were all tied up. John wasn't. She was unarmed, John had a knife. He had a plan. She did not.

She was sane. John was not.

Becky turned to him. 'Is that it? Roger's story? Or do we have to guess the end?'

Watching John's face smile, she wanted to hit it. Hit it and scratch it and make it bleed. She wanted to destroy him.

Before he destroyed her and her family.

And then she caught sight of the pile of correspondence still in their envelopes on the side table next to her, strewn as she'd left them, in a sprawling mess. She knew the letter opener was underneath. It was within easy reach.

Letter opener against real knife.

It was better than nothing.

18

LUCY

Dad's killed a whore.

She didn't know whether to laugh or cry. To believe or to not believe. Part of Lucy couldn't wait for John to carry on the story. But it wasn't a *story* story. It was real. A real, live account about the day in the life of her father. A lot of days of his life. Days and months and years of his life she could do without hearing.

Instinctively, as she'd listened to John speaking, she'd felt for Candi. Related to her in some strange way. Didn't know why, but she did. Felt sorry for her. Her shit of a father was apparently just the same as all men. Sex: it was all they wanted. Give men sex, and they were happy.

She wished she knew what it was that someone could give her that would make her happy. If only life was as simple as being satisfied with a fuck. Her father really was a five-star shit. A shit with knobs on, as it turned out. Had sex with other women. Had sex with a real prostitute.

And he was a murderer.

Lucy felt numb.

Placing her hand in front of her mouth, she mouthed out the

words again to herself: *Daddy killed a whore.* Tried to taste the truth on her lips but she knew that truth didn't have a flavour. Not like mint, or chocolate. The words felt like sawdust on her tongue – was that the taste of an ugly truth? She didn't know.

Looking at her mother, it was clear that *she* had no problem in believing the story. None at all. What did her mother know that Lucy didn't? Or that Lucy refused to acknowledge herself?

Who was she kidding? Lucy had been the recipient of her father's cruelty first-hand. She wasn't sure why she was even thinking of defending him. She knew what sort of man he was.

John had sat back, a sort of dreamy, remembering, look on his face, as if his words had transported him back to that crappy little room on the high street, and sad little Candi. Lucy wanted to blame Candi but couldn't find any reason to. However hard she tried. She found that deep down she did believe. Believed everything that John had told them. Her father had even admitted to knowing and seeing Candi in the first place, so the rest of it must be true, right?

Her father – a killer. *Shit.* But she knew he wasn't a nice man. He was cold. He was cruel. He was a bully. And he had a very nasty temper. Usually directed at her mother, sometimes at her, but he definitely had a temper. Never physical; there'd never been any physical violence, just words. And humiliation. A lot of humiliation.

Could that translate into murder? At the thought of her father actually killing Candi, burning her, doing something with cling film which Lucy didn't linger on, made her flesh crawl. Literally. She glanced down at her arm and watched as goose pimples, like an advancing army of tiny little foot soldiers, popped up. Having no control over them, she carried on watching in mute horror as they speckled her skin, raising the hairs along her forearms so that they stood to attention.

Her mother said something, interrupting Lucy's goose

pimple exhibition. 'Lucy. Lucy, look at me. Are you all right?' And then a smile and a head nod. *Which meant what exactly?* She knew her mother was trying, but what the fuck?

'I know this is difficult, hearing about your father, but just hang in there. I've got this.'

She spoke as if John wasn't there. *Good for her*, Lucy thought. Then she thought about her mother's words and failed to hide her derision: *'I've got this.' Yeah, right, course you do, Mum. You've got this like I've got this. Which means we've got diddley. We're both lying.*

She had a father who she hated for his cruelty. She had a husband who she hated for his weakness.

She wasn't good at picking men.

She hated men.

Daddy's a murderer.

And then it hit her, like a punch to the stomach. What was her mother's secret? Surely it couldn't be as bad.

And her own secret. How could John know about that? He couldn't. He really couldn't know.

19

FRANK

Frank couldn't take it all in. He'd never been over-fond of Lucy's father, but this... this was unthinkable. He couldn't get to grips with it. The whole situation made him feel totally bewildered.

When he'd married Lucy, he'd been more than happy to be part of Rebecca's family. *Becky*, as it now turned out.

And as it also turned out, Lucy's father was a murderer.

According to John, Roger had paid a girl, Candi, for sex. Beaten her, burned her, smothered her with cling film, strangled her and killed her. He'd tortured the girl, for Christ's sake. Strangely, Frank was more upset by the pulling out of the girl's hair: it seemed such an intimate cruelty – spiteful. Frank felt sick at the thought. Didn't know what to do with the information. And yet he believed it. Had no problem believing that Roger could kill.

Feeling sad, he turned to look at Lucy. She looked numb and blank-faced. And she ignored him. He couldn't really blame her: it wasn't as if he'd covered himself in glory so far in this situation. He never really did as well as he might. Always underachieved. That's why he always tried far too hard.

Pretended that he was a small-time petty criminal; but only ever really flirting with danger, a little dealing in drugs here and there. But very small scale. So small it hardly registered as real bad-boy behaviour. He'd sold a couple of spliffs here and there, and once a wrap of cocaine (which had felt far too white-knuckle for him; his innards had turned to liquid at fear of getting caught). So, since then, he never actually put himself in any real nor immediate danger. A wannabe hands-off criminal. Because he just didn't have it in him.

Frank was embarrassed that he could only mimic being a 'tough guy; a hard man'. Knew that he couldn't really pull it off. When people asked him what he did, he'd say, *oh, you know, this and that*. Giving it large. Going for the mysterious don't-mess-with-me look. Never getting it quite right. Never quite achieving his aim. It meant fuck-all really. He'd waggle his hand, palm down in the air, to imply his 'job' was something dodgy, exciting and bad. Then he'd tap the side of his nose. Like a character out of a cheap B movie. He *was* a cheap B movie. Would never be on the A list for anything. A bit-actor. A bit of a man, if truth be known.

And all his lines were delivered with a phoney working-class accent. He'd add the word, 'mate' onto the end of every sentence. Like it meant something. Something chummy but tough. To make him anyone other than himself. To give a little credence to his bad-guy persona.

But the desperate disguise of the real nice boy that he was, was coated by such a thin veneer of pretence, that Frank knew that it didn't even need chipping away at, before it gave way. It just needed a little scrape, a scratch even, and his true, imbecilic self would be on display to all. He would be naked to the world at the merest of glances. And he didn't want people seeing his weaknesses. There were too many to number.

Now he was sitting in a room with a murdering father, and a

sinister, and very disturbing man. Who was much more frightening than Roger; John was terrifyingly bad. There was something very wrong with him, but Frank wasn't sure what it was or how to deal with it. As well as terrified, Frank felt deeply concerned. Had no idea what was coming next. And whatever *did* happen, as it surely would, he wasn't sure how he'd react to it.

He wished he could call his mother for advice.

That's how hard he was. Wanting and needing his mother's support.

He was drowning in self-defeat and loathing.

And then he was struck by an obvious question. His only secret was knowing John. Telling him about the Twist family. How big a crime was that? It was more shameful than anything. But would that be all that John could expose about him? Lucy already knew he pretended at a life of crime, so that wouldn't warrant a revelation with any great shock value to her, and in the grand scheme of things, it wasn't in the same league as what Roger had done. It certainly wasn't *murder*.

And Frank knew Lucy's secret. He thought he was the only person in the world who did, and that made him feel a little better. A little closer to her.

A little more important.

20

ME

I was enjoying myself. Was enjoying the telling. Was enjoying having an audience. They all hung on my every word. All agog with the horror of it all. I don't like to be cruel, but I didn't think I was being outrageously so. I was just being myself. Demonstrating my right to mete out justice to those in need of my particular brand of moral correction. However *off* my own moral compass may or may not be. It's possible it needed a little tweaking here and there, but I was confident that I was right. I was happy with my own code of conduct. Rights and wrongs, truths and lies; often a fine line between them. But not for me and what I knew of Roger. For me, it couldn't have been more straightforward when it came to Roger and his crimes.

He sat, nursing his injured hand, covering it with the other, unable to stop the steady drip, drip, drip of blood that pooled in an ever-increasing crimson circle on his thigh, merging with the halo of damp made by his own urine. *That* particular sight I could well do without.

But he couldn't tear his gaze from mine.

Lucy, busily avoiding the fact that her father had been proved to not only use prostitutes, but tortured them and had killed one of them for sport, said, 'Why were you so kind to Candi? Did you go and get her drugs?'

'Why are you so interested in Candi?' I asked.

'I feel for her. Why shouldn't I? Dad certainly didn't. Someone has to give a shit about what happened to her.'

I put my hand to my chest and nodded. 'That's it, precisely, Lucy. And I did my best to look after her.'

Becky leant forward. 'So why didn't you report Roger to the police, or better still, threaten Roger, tell him you knew what he was doing? Why didn't you stop my husband from killing the girl? You could have stopped him.' She glared at me, her eyes angry. 'You could have saved her.'

'Don't even entertain the notion of blaming me, Becky. Your husband is wholly responsible. I had to let things play out naturally. Because in the end, life has a way of working itself out. It always does – que sera and all that. And telling Roger that I knew what he was doing, well, that just didn't fit in with my plans. But don't worry, his actions will have serious repercussions.' I turned to the man of the moment. 'You do understand that, don't you, Rog? That you are accountable and that you will pay?'

'Who made you judge and jury?' Roger said in a rare display of confrontation.

'Who made you God of your own tiny world?'

'I didn't kill her.'

'You did, Rog, you did. And someone had to stop you. Consider yourself stopped.'

'You're mad,' said Roger. 'No one believes what you're saying, you know. I certainly know it's all rubbish. She was alive when I left her two Thursdays ago. You're just playing mind games with us all. Trying to turn everyone against me. What do you really want? If it's money, I can give you my bank card. I'll even give you the pin. Take what you want. Just take it and go.'

'Firstly, don't kid yourself. I, in no way, have turned anyone against you. You did that all by yourself. Big pat on the back to you. As for money? Consider me as financially rich as I wish to be. And more to the point, I haven't got what I want from you, Rog. Not yet. Not by a long shot. I suggest you all accept my presence here and settle in for a long day.' I beamed at them all. 'And well into the night I suspect. Shall I carry on?'

Becky waved her hands in the air, the bands of steel around her plump little wrists reddening her skin, demonstrating that that was precisely what I should do. 'Go ahead,' she said. 'How much worse can it get?'

I smiled again. Couldn't stop smiling. I was having the time of my life and it wasn't even teatime yet. The rest of the afternoon stretched happily and languidly in front of me, like an as-yet untravelled path upon which anything could happen along the way. I had a good idea about upcoming events, but people were odd and surprising things, and this family was no exception. It was always wise to expect the unexpected. You just never knew.

'To answer your question, Lucy, yes I did buy her drugs. And a lot of food,' I said. 'Filled her cupboards and tiny fridge with all sorts of wholesome treats: full of nutrition and vitamins and all-round goodness. It was the least I could do. I genuinely wanted to help her. As you so rightly say, why wouldn't I care about her safety?'

I looked around this mismatched family. 'I'll give you a quick summary of what happened to Candi. I hope you're all sitting comfortably.' I waited.

A tight nod from Becky and Frank. A more reluctant one

from Lucy. A predictable scowl from Roger. I sat back and placed a cushion behind my back and crossed my ankles, my long legs stretched out in front of me.

21

ME

Having bought drugs, food and water, soft drinks, four plates, bowls, cutlery, new saucepans, medical supplies, new sheets and a duvet (with matching cover), I was pleased with my purchases. However, there are limits. I was not prepared to clean Candi's bedsit, (time was pressing. I had places to be), so we both watched as two silent, burly, surly women came around and cleaned and scrubbed Candi's little world, put on the new bedding and left. As I say, I know a lot of people and the two cleaners had been paid handsomely. They didn't have to smile about it, while they cleaned – displaying merriment hadn't been included in the price.

After their departure, both Candi and I sat on the bed, looking around the room in amicable silence. Finally, she spoke. 'Bloody hell. I wouldn't recognise the place. Thanks. Really, I mean it.' She screwed up her battered little face. 'What's your game, anyway? What do you want from me? Just info on that perv who comes round? Is that it? Is that all?'

I nodded, smiling. She deserved a smile. I didn't suppose she encountered a lot of that particular facial movement. I held my hands out, palms up. 'That's all.'

'Got the drugs then?'

I patted my breast pocket. 'I have the drugs. And you don't. And you won't until you've eaten.'

She shook her head. 'I want them now. Where'd you score anyway? Who'd you get it from?'

I held my hand up, stopping her from speaking as her mouth remained open, quick to carry on the protest. 'Don't bother arguing, Candi. You'll get the gear, as promised. And to answer your question, I have my sources. Don't worry, it's good stuff. Not too pure. Don't want you overdosing, do we? But right now, you're not sick, you don't *need* heroin at this very moment. You want it, but you don't need it. Okay? So, first we'll eat.'

'You're kidding me, right?'

'I kid you not. You remember what food is. You cook it, put it on plates, shovel it into your mouth. Do it enough and you'll grow up into a big and healthy girl.' I smiled. 'Hope you like pasta. You just sit there and relax.'

'You're not a perv, are you?'

'No. Are you?'

She laughed. It was nice to hear and looking at her, she looked surprised at hearing the noise coming from her own mouth. As if she couldn't remember the last time she'd made that sound.

For a moment, I allowed a strange feeling to ripple through me. I thought it was a genuine paternal feeling towards the girl. Perhaps not a *genuine* fatherly emotion because I've never had children. But I understood and recognised the need to protect her and diagnosed it as paternalistic. In an academic way only though. I'm very good at aping the emotions of others. It comes from my almost obsessive observation of people, so much watching of others, and consequently copious amounts of mimicking on my part. I am a mirror. Everyone else's emotions so easily shared and put on public display for me to copy.

could almost pass for normal.

Concentrating now, I tied a bought-that-day pinny around my waist – one of those blue cotton things with white stripes, ala chef-mode, and laid out my ingredients in a neat row; everything precision and no mess. The worktop gleamed and I smiled again.

It was my one grand passion, cooking, and I became wholly absorbed. Enjoying the process. Lost in the creation. Revelling in the aromas that I manufactured. I was making a simple pasta dish with fresh tagliatelle, cooked al dente naturally, with a sauce of asparagus (lightly steamed), pan-fried lardons, button mushrooms, lemon juice, a little white wine and crème fraiche. To be accompanied by a side salad of avocado, spring onions, lettuce and cherry tomatoes. I focused quickly on creating a piquant vinaigrette dressing; hardly stretching my culinary talents but always fun to get right. Having already grated the parmesan, I put the water on for the pasta to boil. Heard Candi's voice behind me.

'What are those long, green stick things?'

'These?' I said, holding an asparagus in my hand. 'It's a vegetable. Asparagus.'

A small silence. And then, 'I've never seen one before. But it's a vegetable? So they grow on trees, then?'

'Yes, Candi, asparagus grows on trees. Just like money.'

More silence, then a bark of laughter. 'Now I know you're taking the piss.'

We ate on our knees, and after a suspicious start from her, prodding and smelling the food, she finally bent her head and started eating, cramming it in as fast as she could swallow. 'Breathe,' I said. 'You'll choke.'

'Don't care. It's hurting my bloody lip, but I couldn't care less. Best meal I've ever had.'

I was delighted and flattered. It's always nice to be appreciated. I finished my food at a more sedate pace, refilled Candi's plate and sat back, waiting for her to be ready to talk.

After a less than lady-like burp, she said, 'Thanks for that, really. Fucking great.' She wiped her hand across her mouth and put her plate on the floor.

'In the sink. Leave to soak in hot soapy water.'

She looked at me as if I were mad, but got up slowly, painfully, and did as asked. She leant back on the sink and crossed her arms. I got up, walked up to her and handed her a wet wipe. I never shared them, but if I was going to give one to anyone, she was most deserving, I thought. She took it, smiling, and used it like a flannel on her face; rubbing softy over the sore bits.

'So, now you want to ask me questions about that client. The one who did this.' Looking down at her own skinny and battered frame, she held her hands out to the sides to indicate the magnitude of her injuries. 'What do you want to know?'

'What's his name?'

I was interested to understand how Roger's brain ticked. *If* it ticked at all.

'He's never told me his name. He makes me call him "Sir."'

Original Roger.

'And what does Sir do when he visits you? How's it play out normally? I assume he leads the way every time?'

She hugged herself, wincing at the pain. 'It's always exactly the same. Every bloody Thursday. He walks in wearing his plastic gloves, you know, like what doctors' wear. He makes me greet him with a bow and I have to say, "Sir," like he's a king or something. The second time he came, ages ago, a couple of years maybe? – something like that – I forgot to say it, and he punched me in the face. I haven't forgotten again.'

I grimaced. Master Roger and his slave, Candi. I could weep. Theoretically.

'And then what?'

Sighing, she said, 'It never changes. As soon as we're in the room, he hits me in the face, pulls me by the hair and pushes his face close to mine. He says, "Say it, you bitch, say it." So I say, "Thank you for visiting me, Sir." Then he says, "Don't look at me. You're not worthy." So I look away and he pushes me to the floor, kicks me, sometimes he pisses on me and laughs and I stay on all-fours. Like a bloody dog. Which is what he likes. "What are you?" he asks, and I say, "A dog, Sir." He always finds that funny. I don't know why, but he always does. Laughs every time. I've got to say, I'm a bit sick of the joke myself.'

'He's a control freak. Enjoys hurting you.'

'Oh, yeah. He just loves that. And sometimes he... you know.' She huffed and bounced her shoulders in revulsion at the memory. 'Sometimes he makes me drink his piss. From the floor. Like I really am a dog. Disgusting bastard.'

She goes quiet for a bit and I sit it out. Letting her tell it in her own time. Not looking at me, but glancing at the curtained window, she said, 'It goes on for what... hours? A couple of hours. Feels like a bloody lifetime. Him saying how great and powerful he is, how weak and stupid and useless I am, and every time he speaks I have to say, "Yes, Sir, you're right."'

'And the longer it goes on, the more sexually excited he gets?'

'Yeah, exactly. That's the bit he enjoys most. The warm-up. His idea of foreplay. Not that I need foreplay with punters. I prefer the ones who just come in, drop their trousers and stick it in. And then they're gone. *That's* how it should be. But that's not how it is with "Sir."'

'And after you've crawled around like a dog, been beaten, urinated on, how does he move on to the sex part of it? Or doesn't he? Can he get it up?'

She snorted with a well-practised snort. 'Blink and you'd bloody miss it. He's got a dick the size of...' I watched her face furrow in concentration as she tried to come up with an appropriately offensive simile. And then she smiled, a proper grin. 'He's got a dick the size of an asparagus stick thing.'

I copied her facial expression showing derision and disgust. It wasn't too difficult. I sat in silence, wondering how men like that could possibly get any enjoyment out of physically and mentally hurting women like Candi. Where was the fun? I'd never understand it.

'Anyway,' she said, 'after he's got bored with the dog thing, and calling me names, and pissing on me, and hitting me, he finally throws me onto the bed and gets on top. Gets his asparagus out and sticks it in, and at the same time, he takes cling film from his pocket and puts it over my mouth. I hate that part. I can't breathe. It makes me panic. It makes him orgasm.'

Shrugging, she said, 'And that's it, really. Same old, same old.' She went for another laugh but this time, she couldn't pull it off. Looking over at her bed, I assumed she was picturing Roger on top of her, smothering her, violating her. Nearly killing her. She said, 'Thanks for the new sheets and stuff. Clean. Nice and clean.'

Candi liked clean. I liked that she appreciated the new bed linen. I said, 'You're most welcome. But tell me this, why do you still let him in? He's dangerous. He'll kill you one day. You must have other punters. More normal ones.'

'Not that many, no. Look at me. It's not like I have money pouring out of my knickers, is it? We're not talking high-end, top-notch prostitution here. I can't afford to be choosy. I need the money. Talking of which... Can I have my drugs now?'

I stood up. 'Do you have a spare key to your door?'

'No.'

'I'll sort it out, get a copy made and I'll come and visit every week. Whenever I can. I'll bring food and cook, we'll eat, talk and I'll bring you drugs. Enough to make it worth your while. If you're not in, I'll just get cracking on the food and cleaning up.' I looked around the for-now still clean room. 'And *you* can make an effort to keep things from getting dirty again. Okay? It won't kill you. Nothing in life is free, Candi, you know that.'

'Yeah, I know that. But you need to give me the drugs now. I've done what you wanted.'

I took out a wrap and passed it to her. She turned to the worktop and opened it up. Got a spoon to cook the heroin and filled a glass with cold water from the tap. She was distracted, impatient for me to go. 'Key,' I said, holding out my hand. Sliding her fingers into her back pocket she gave it to me. I watched as she automatically went to her drawer where she kept her old syringes. Tapping her on the shoulder, I pointed to the cupboard above: a brand-new packet of 10ml syringes. I left her to it. I didn't need to watch. Standing at the door, facing her I said, 'Take care, Candi. See you later. I'll bring your key back in a minute after I've made myself a copy.'

'Yeah, mate, thanks.' She stopped for a minute from her task and turned. Really looked at me. 'I mean it. Thanks for everything you've done. Life almost felt normal there for a moment. *I* felt normal.'

'You *are* normal. *Sir* is not normal. Bye.'

I walked out without waiting for her reply.

22

BECKY

An eerie hush fell as John stopped talking. I don't think any of us knew what to do or say. I decided I had to say *some*thing. 'You're a strange man, John. Such kindness to Candi. Why not just give her enough money so that she could stop being a prostitute? Wouldn't that have been easier?'

He laughed. 'There's never enough money if you're a junkie. Whatever I did, I knew I couldn't make her stop using, but I could at least make sure she had a good meal on a regular basis.' He shrugged, and if I didn't know better, I'd have said he was almost embarrassed at admitting the generosity he'd shown Candi. Almost weakened by his own kindness – in his eyes. He was almost everything. Nice in a funny way. Right about his philosophy on life, about right and wrong. Normal.

But 'almost' wasn't good enough.

And he was far from normal. A long, long way away from real *normal*.

Becky turned to look at her husband. Roger sat, staring straight ahead, his face uncharacteristically difficult to read. It was like he'd switched himself off, not caring to have his sexual perversions shared en famille. 'How could you, Roger?' Becky said to him. 'Really, I mean that as a serious question. How could you do that to a young girl? To any girl? What's wrong with you?'

He shook his head. 'Nothing's wrong with me. I didn't kill her.'

'But I have the evidence right here,' John said, and pulled out his mobile. 'You tap, tap, tapping on Candi's window, knocking on the door, back to the window. Impatient to get in. You peering in again through the open window when she didn't come to the door. You clearly seeing her legs lying there on the bed, as you pulled aside the net curtains – the only part of her body visible from the window. But you definitely got the smell, didn't you? I've got your physical recoil right here.' John held his mobile aloft. 'Care to see?'

'That doesn't prove that I killed her,' Roger said. 'It proves only that someone killed her. And it wasn't me. I swear to God, it wasn't me.'

'But I know it was you, because I watched you arrive two Thursdays ago, I recorded that as well, if you'd like to see it. Filmed you arrive, filmed you leaving. And then I went in and found her. She was dead. You got carried away and you killed her. I have the proof. Want to take it to court?'

Becky said, 'But why didn't you call the authorities when you found her, John? Why leave her lying there, dead, for another week. That's disgusting.'

John jumped from the sofa. 'That's rich. I'm disgusting? Roger's the disgusting one. I gave him the opportunity to make amends, to do the right thing. To call it in. But he chose to kill her, leave her and run, like the craven little man that he is.'

Becky sank further down into her chair. Frightened by John's anger. He turned to her husband. 'Get up, Roger. Stand up now.'

Roger didn't waste any time in following the order. John's

words were to be obeyed. Not considered casually. Even from here, Becky could see Roger's body shake as he stood. She knew something was going to happen.

Something big.

Something bad.

'How do we know *you* didn't kill her?' Roger asked. 'Your fingerprints must be all over her flat.'

'I'm not on the system. I have no criminal record. Because I'm very good at what I do. I also clean up wherever I've been because I like all things tidy. Clean is good. Clean is safe. *I* didn't kill her. Why would I? I would have had no reason to murder her. She was my friend.'

He turned towards his rucksack and pivoting back on his heels, John suddenly and inexplicably had a gun in his hand. A large heavy-looking gun. He pointed it at Roger's face. 'You humiliated and abused a young girl. You murdered her with your sexual perversions. You killed a girl who had only just discovered asparagus. You can't buy that kind of purity. And yet you destroyed it. For that, you cannot be forgiven.'

Then he stepped forward and pulled the trigger.

23

FRANK

Ohmygod, ohmygod, ohmygod, ohmygod, ohmygod, ohmygod, ohmygod, ohmygod, ohmygod, ohmygod...

24

LUCY

Red. The room exploded into red. Red covered everything. She closed her eyes but could still see red. Her ears rang and automatically she raised her hands to cover her ears but could only reach both of them if she bowed her head and then used both her middle fingers to press against her ear canals.

Keeping her head between her knees, she just sat there. Eyes tight shut. Paralysed. Still her ears rang but the silence was deafening. Red and deafening. She didn't want to look up. But couldn't help herself. A quick raise of the head, a rapid eye open.

Red.

Daddy's missing most of his head.

She lowered her head back down, her eyes shut and continued to see red.

Felt nothing. Or maybe she felt everything. She wasn't sure of the difference. The physical and emotional numbness wasn't *nothing*. It was *some*thing. But mostly it was red.

Red. She felt red.

The red of violence.

25

BECKY

Becky sat in her chair. Wet *something* dripped from her face. She let it drip, not wanting to touch it. Imagining what it was. And wanting it off her. But not wanting to know *exactly* what it was. But she knew. Wasn't an idiot. It was Roger. Bits of Roger.

After the blast from the gun, the contrast of the sudden profound silence was total. Complete non-noise engulfed her. Her brain momentarily stuttered to a halt, and all she could do was sit there.

The smell of blood had creeped uninvited into her olfactory senses, tainting it with the whiff of copper and rust. Unpleasant and distressingly strong.

Roger had been thrown into his chair, his body falling backwards, and now he slumped with his legs splayed out in front of him. The top half of his head was missing. But not missing. It was clear where most of it was; on the walls, the ceiling, the carpet. On her. The bottom half of his face remained, on a ragged fleshy stump, looking surreal, keeping in place what looked like a laughing jawline. She closed her eyes – it was too much to take in.

Hearing John's voice, she kept her eyes shut. 'Sorry about that, Becky. It's always that big old exit wound that makes such a mess – far worse than the entry point. You got the worst of it, I'm afraid. Although, it has to be said, I rather think Roger has the most to complain about.'

John said nothing further. Silence again. Blessed silence. Until it went on for too long. But still she refused to open her eyes. She heard John's voice: 'Look at me. Now.'

Knowing he was addressing her, she opened her eyes and stared flatly at him. She felt stupidly empty and watched as he smiled a soft smile at her. He looked almost beatific. Calm. As if he had blossomed amid the carnage which he had created. The shooting, the murder, had made him cosmically serene. Surrounded by blood, John appeared truly *at home*.

'Consider yourself liberated. I've freed you from Roger. You can be your own woman again. A relief for you, I'm sure.' He held up his hand. 'No need to thank me. Really. But be careful with control. It's a powerful thing. Use it wisely now that I've returned it to you.'

He grinned. Grinned quietly and maniacally at her, as if he hadn't just obliterated her husband. Virtually blown his head off. 'But really,' John said, 'a little thank-you *wouldn't* go amiss. I know you've been planning on this day for months and months. Probably years. And now I've made it possible for you. *I've given you back your control.* Take it and welcome it. Enjoy it.'

Fight or flight?

Neither, she realised. Shock of a life taken had slapped her around the face and rendered her immobile. Trauma didn't seem a big enough word. Thankfully she could still relate to the here and now of her child. She would save Lucy if she died trying.

And grief for Roger? Not yet. Not possible. Definitely not

yet. And probably not ever. Why would she grieve for a man who had tortured her for years?

But *murder*? His still body lying destroyed next to her – that just wasn't right. She'd never wanted him dead.

Her body felt crippled, both physically and emotionally. She was covered in blood spatter and worse, chunks of her husband's flesh. Looking over at Lucy, her heart pulsed erratically as she watched her daughter sitting with her head between her knees. 'Lucy?' she said. 'Lucy, speak to me.'

Lucy's head remained bent but a tiny voice from far, far away said, 'Leave me alone.'

'Come on, Luce. Sit up. Do you want to use the lavatory? Get out of this room for a minute? I'll ask John to cover up Daddy.' Becky glared at John, who shrugged in agreement – a why-not gesture. Happy for the moment to oblige. 'Untie her,' Becky said to him. 'Take her to the downstairs bathroom and get a towel. To cover... to cover...' She wanted to say, 'This mess' but thought it sounded too callous. 'To cover Roger. Please.'

'Okay. I can do that. Come on, Lucy.'

Becky watched as he picked up his knife, strode over to her daughter and cut her cable ties. The blade sliced through the shackles as easily and effortlessly as it might have spread jam on the morning toast. 'Up you get.' He put his hands under her elbows and walked her across the room.

Turning, he said, 'And to let you all know, I've already decluttered the bathroom of everything possibly weapon-like. The bleach has gone, nail clippers, razors – they are things of the past. Even the loofah – in case any one of you decided to secrete it about your person and loofah me to death, is now not there. It's an empty room. You can each use the loo, wash your face and hands and come straight out again.'

He waited for nods that didn't come. 'Lucy first, Frank, and then, you, Becky. Come on. Chop chop.' He clapped his hands and Lucy cowered away from him and Frank jumped in his chair.

Lucy allowed herself to be led across the room, head still hanging and her body broken-looking. Becky could tell that Lucy had disassociated from her surroundings and now was barely aware of being escorted and chaperoned away from her father's dead body by a lunatic.

The sight of her baby, so defeated, frightened, cut-off, galvanised Becky to action. Instinct kicked in. *Survival. Now,* she thought, *now's my chance.* She waited until she was sure that John wasn't coming back and then lurched to her left, and in her haste, knocked the pile of letters from the side table to the floor. 'Fuck,' she hissed. Glanced up. Was met with Frank's face: changed by terror, smaller – consumed by overly large and bulging eyes. He stared at Roger. Not blinking. 'Frank,' Becky whispered. There was no obvious response. She tried again. 'Keep a lookout, Frank. Tell me when they're coming back.' She didn't wait for his nod. Suspected it wouldn't be coming quickly enough. If at all.

Flipping the top envelope aside with her fingers, screaming silently at the weight of a piece of Roger's flesh that sat on the paper, she swept the entire pile from the table, panicking, heart thumping, pulse racing. Trying not to gag.

Where was it? It wasn't there. The letter opener wasn't there. Shocked by its absence, she could only sit and stupidly stare at where it should have been. Uncaring at the mess of envelopes she'd strewn across the floor. The evidence of her search for it.

Then she heard a tutting noise, followed by a gentle laugh.

'Come now, Becky. How stupid do you think I am? When I came in here, after tying you up, waiting for Rog to come home, I couldn't help but notice the disarray of correspondence on the table. It's against my nature to leave such mess, just sitting there... *on show*: for everyone to see. Such slovenliness. *Obviously* I started to tidy them. And there it was. Your little weapon. I took it. I have it. And I simply left your gross lack of housekeeping on display – and wondered how long it would take you to go for the letter opener.'

Gently, John sat a compliant Lucy back in her chair, and walked towards Becky, a large bath towel hanging neatly over his forearm. Like a butler ready to buttle. He said, 'I'm liking your shocked disappointment, Becky, but equally disappointed that you thought me that careless that I wouldn't have checked the room for sharp objects before bringing you all in here. Shame on you.'

He covered Roger with the white towel. Almost dainty in his movement as he tucked in the corners, cocooning Roger in a neat package. Her husband, the pupa. Only his feet stuck out from the bottom of the towel. John looked at her and pulled a stupid, childish face – conveying an apology. 'Sorry about the towel – could only find a white one. It will stain. You'll never get the blood out of it. Sorry.'

She sat back and closed her eyes. Bit down on the inside of her cheek to generate saliva. Heard Frank being taken from the room and thought, *He's going to kill us all. How can I stop him?*

Act like a mother.

Opening her eyes, she smiled at Lucy. Lucy responded with what could have been a smile, but which Becky really thought was more of a grimace. A rictus grin on her ridiculously overpainted face.

26

ME

Becky had remained tight-lipped on her trip to the bathroom. I'd waited outside whilst she used the lavatory, and then had politely waited some more as I'd heard the basin taps running as she'd washed her face. From the wetness of her top when she'd come out, she'd evidently attempted to clean and scrub her husband's blood from her clothes as well. With little success. I hadn't pushed her for conversation at that point. More than happy to give her time to take in her new life.

As a widow.

Once she'd got over the initial shock at the gruesomeness of her husband's death and warmed to the brighter prospect of her now-single life, I knew she'd be pleased. It was what she'd wanted for so long.

Independence.

Before the day was out, I was pretty sure she'd be thanking me. She'd realise what I'd given her and would relish it. She'd consume it, quickly and greedily.

All back in our designated places, the trio retied and still handcuffed, and now thankfully squeaky clean, I sat in silence.

Wondering who'd be the first to break it. I was surprised that it was Frank.

Again he stood to deliver his words. Unable to tear his eyes from the bloodied towel that covered his father-in-law. He spoke facing the dead man, watching as large crimson blobs grew and spread like a fungus in a petri dish. As if Roger still breathed, his death seeped through the material. Completely and forever ruining the soft cotton fluff of the Egyptian white towel.

'It was me, Becky,' Frank said to the corpse, not daring to look her in the eye, directing his speech to the dead. He turned briefly to include his wife in what was apparently going to be his confession, and then as quickly turned back to Roger. 'It was me who told John about you all. About this house. About where you keep the spare key, Becky. Where your jewellery is. When you'd all be out. It was me. But I was only joking. None of this should have happened. But it's all my fault. I'm so sorry.' Then he burst into tears. 'How can you forgive me? I'm so, so sorry. Really sorry. I know John. From the pub. I thought we were friends. I brought him here. God, oh God. I'm sorry.'

His pitiful reveal came out in a rushed monotone. There was no inflection in his voice, no cadence nor natural rhythm. Just words heavy and thick with guilt. He fell back into his armchair and held his head in his hands. Crying like a baby.

'For God's sake, Frank. Shut up,' I said. 'That's not your secret. And there are worse things than knowing me.'

'What? What do you mean? That *is* my secret.'

I didn't answer. What was the point. He'd get it. Later.

But joy of joys, Lucy seemed to react to something other than her now-deceased father. She brought her head up from between her knees, spat out the one word, 'Judas,' and then leant back and stared at the ceiling.

'I met him in the pub. He tricked me. I didn't know what he was going to do. Didn't know he was going to hurt you. That he was going to be so... violent. I'm sorry, Lucy. Rebecca – Becky. Really sorry. What can I say? What can I do?'

Glancing at Becky I saw only resignation on her face at his betrayal, but at the same time, not really all that surprised at this turn of events. She did a teeth-gritting, jaw-clamping thing. 'John tricked me too, Frank. It's what he does. It doesn't matter. It's done now. I don't blame you.'

Silence again. Well, *what* an anticlimax. Now Frank had gone back to looking the familiar fool that he was and everyone knew that he was. He'd accomplished nothing. But perhaps I wasn't being fair.

'Your intention was true, Frank, so congratulations on that,' I said. 'But equally, as I also said, you're telling the wrong secret and it's not time for your confession anyway, so please be quiet.'

Obediently, he did so. The three of them appeared trapped in their own little individual hells. And their hells were oddly silent. I waited for them to show a little enthusiasm for the hearing of new revelations, a little positivity, a little *some*thing, but they seemed more than a little subdued.

I shouted and jumped up violently from the sofa. 'Pull yourselves together. I will not have this. You *will* listen to each other's secrets. Yes, I killed Roger. So, sue me. He deserved it. You all know it, and I know it. Candi knew it. You will *not* forget what Roger did to her.'

Relaxing slightly, I retook my seat. 'You'll get over it. It's not the end of your lives. Only his. The world hasn't stopped turning on its axle. Roger was a cruel man. You should be thanking me.' I inhaled deeply and regained control.

My raised voice and unexpectedly violent eruption from sitting to standing had the desired effect. They woke up. With a jolt. I breathed in slowly again. I wasn't a cruel man and so I made the effort to apologise to Lucy. 'I'm sorry I shot your father. But you must understand why it had to be done. You'll recover. It's called "life." Or in your language, "Shit happens." So, come on. This isn't a funeral. It's time for Becky to tell all.'

'Will you let me make my daughter some tea first?' she said.

'No need for you to trouble yourself.' I patted my rucksack. 'I have a flask for this very occasion. Reaching into my bag of goodies, I brought out a flask and four little plastic cups. Poured them each a cup and passed them round. 'There's sugar if you want. Hope you all take milk in your tea? Shall I pour?'

Becky ignored me and I watched as she watched Lucy. Waited until she saw her daughter start sipping from her cup. Waited for the colour to come back into Lucy's face. And it did come back. Just a soft pink. But better. Good. I was pleased. Lucy took little sparrow sips, quickly and frequently. And then she looked at me, upended the thankfully empty cup. 'Give me a brandy and cover my father with something else. Something dark. The linen closet is down the hall.'

'Use Roger's black towelling dressing gown,' said Becky. 'It's on the top shelf.'

'I know where it is, and I'm more than happy to oblige. See, ask and you shall receive. I shall be gone for approximately ten seconds. During which time, Roger is in charge.'

I took the brandy bottle with me: adding my knife and gun to the rucksack which I slipped on over my shoulders. Leaving nothing to chance. Glass, as I've said, is a potentially nasty material. Best kept out of the hands of the frightened and desperate.

Back in the sitting room again, having quickly washed the plastic cups in the bathroom en route to the linen closet, Rog was now indeed covered with something admittedly far more suitable, something that covered the colourful visuals of his killing. The hood of his dressing gown had been ironed flat, making a peak at what should have been the back of his head.

Inverted over Roger's body, it covered his once-face and came to an empty point where his face no longer filled it.

I poured out two hefty snifters of brandy into the previously used, but now washed, plastic beakers, for both mother and daughter, (Frank declined the offer), and then I sat. Ready and eager to continue.

And then, yet another interruption which I could hardly ignore. Lucy burst into tears. Not a genteel, lady-like sniffing, but a full-on torrent of snot-ridden tears. I now had to bite my inner cheek to keep my patience in check and listened to Becky soothing her daughter, comforting her, calming her. Time passed. I turned on the lights and closed the curtains, letting Lucy excrete her eyeball and nasal cavity fluids; her tears of... shock? Grief? Anger? Who knew? Not me. But I let it run its course.

Sucking at her glass, draining the very last drop of alcohol available, satisfied that Lucy had returned to a vaguely recognisable normal, Becky spoke.

'I can talk for myself. Unlike my husband, I don't need your voice. Shall I start?'

Relieved and grateful that we were all back on track, I said, 'Yes, off you go.'

But Lucy interrupted the flow. 'Mum, please don't say you're a paedophile. I couldn't bear it. If you are, I might personally ask John to shoot me.'

And then she started laughing. Really laughing. Until she doubled over, and like a contagion, this howling hysteria spread to Becky, who joined in. They sat opposite each other, tears of mania rolling down their respective cheeks. Roaring with a desperate and, frankly, slightly frightening non-hilarity. Stamping their feet to match the rhythm of their laughter. I didn't suppose they really thought the situation in the least amusing, but it was fun to watch.

If you were mad.

It was the shock. Hitting them hard. Human beings are such complex and curious creatures. Their emotions so convoluted and abrasive. Dirty and such messy emoting from the two women. Such an unnecessary expenditure of energy: so tiring and so totally and wholly pointless.

Needless to say, Frank didn't join in with the laughter. Just sat there with his eyes all forlorn and confused. Bewildered by life.

I'd seen this reaction to shock before, this hysterical laughing, when I'd frightened others. It was strange, but even as I child I can't remember ever laughing that hard at *any*thing. Can't remember laughing at all. I never got the joke nor thought life was ever that funny. And I don't think I cried either, not even as a child. Although I must have. But the memory eluded me.

I smiled now to show willing, and to try to really feel something of what they were both experiencing. It was intriguing, but completely beyond me. And I thanked God for that. I'm all for pretending to be a member of the human race, but really, I couldn't be more pleased that I didn't have to do all these emotions. I was a clean slate in that respect. And glad of it.

There were some of these odd feelings that I was better with; like sympathy. I could feign that in spades. For sympathy was the same as kindness, and kindness was but a step away from acknowledging right and wrong and being able to tell the difference between the two. Wrong, was, by definition, not right; and the giveaway was that it was often unkind, so I could pull off a passable impression of compassion. Candi being a case in point.

I'd connected with her purely because of her simplicity. It had been refreshing to see someone unencumbered with endless suitcases and bags-for-life, overflowing with emotional baggage.

She hadn't been awash with self-indulgent emotion but had accepted what life threw at her and got on with it. Without complaint. It was how I liked it. But I only really understood the *concept* of kindness, on an academic level, not actually connecting in any truthful way.

Lucky me, I thought. Really. Lucky, lucky me.

I was an empty man – devoid of all the trappings of angst, hatred, guilt, shame, love, et cetera, et cetera, that so plagued those amongst whom I lived. If that made me only a flesh-covered mannequin, then so be it. I was grateful for it.

Although I did want to feel *some*thing. At some time in the future. Something real. Just so I could say I knew how whatever it was made me *feel*.

Just for once.

Eventually, *Praise Be*, their spittles and gobbets of laughter sputtered to an end with much hiccuping from Lucy. She brought me out of my internal meanderings, by saying, 'It doesn't matter what you say or do, Mum. John's going to kill us all. You know it and I know it. So, none of it matters, does it?'

'Of course he's not going to kill us, Lucy. Don't say that. Don't even think it. He's not.'

Lucy slid off her chair and legs still bound, hands cuffed and resting on her chest, she lay on her back and closed her eyes. 'I'm listening, Mum. Tell me your bad.'

27

BECKY

Yes, Becky thought. *Lucy's right. John is going to kill us all.*
It was clear that John couldn't murder Roger and then simply leave the house. Becky knew that made no sense. The question was: what could she do to change his mind?

What did they really know about John, anyway? Nothing. He was almost certainly using a false name and if, and it was a big if, *if* they were left alive, any description they could give the police would be vague at best. There was nothing stand-out about John. An extraordinarily ordinary looking man, with no distinguishing features. Totally forgettable.

And now it turns out he has a gun. As well as a knife. I don't have a weapon. Not even a silly letter opener.

Maybe he would be happy if she openly and honestly revealed her secret, unlike Roger who'd had to have his ripped from him, word by painful word. But realistically, Becky knew that wasn't enough. How could it be? What did John really want?

Bizarrely, Becky felt ridiculously calm. *Insane.* Lucy had thankfully and finally fallen silent after a last strange bark of a laugh, and a 'Fuck, sorry. *God.*'

'That's okay, darling. If we didn't laugh, God knows what we'd do. Are you ready to hear my story?'

Lucy nodded. She still had a worryingly berserk aura floating around her, mania still lurking – but at least she was engaging with Becky's words.

'Right,' Becky said. 'Listen carefully to me, Lucy. Concentrate on everything I tell you. Not because it's madly important, but because it'll give you something else to focus on. Okay? Ready?'

She waited for her daughter's nod from the supine, and then said, 'I'm a blackmailer.'

What was the use of any preamble? What would be the point of tiptoeing around the subject? She felt no need to wrap her words up in twinkly, glittering paper and present them on a platter, ready to be relished and enjoyed like delicious little sweetmeats. Why the bloody hell should she? Much better to dole her words out like unwanted but necessary medication: bitter pills, hard to swallow.

She was sitting next to her dead husband, his brains all over her, looking at her fragile daughter and her weak but sweet son-in-law. That sweetness, however, now somewhat dubious. But this wasn't the time to be overly saccharine in her word choice. She'd tell it exactly how it was.

And maybe, just maybe, score some brownie points from John. For her veracity. A gold star for effort.

'I don't mean I blackmail just *any*one. There's three of them. Three men. But I've only blackmailed one of them. So far. One complete bastard. The other two are equally shitty. And I feel neither shame nor guilt for gunning for any of them.'

'*Mum*,' said Lucy, her voice incredulous, her head now turned on the floor to face her mother. 'Who knew? What a family. You're a *blackmailer*?' And then she smiled at Becky – a more normal smile. Probably relief, under the circumstances, Becky thought, that it wasn't a worse secret.

'Lucy, this man, John...' She pointed at him, sitting oh-so smug on the sofa. 'This man, John, or whatever his real name is, has just killed my husband and your father. I appreciate you don't need reminding of that. None of us do.' An involuntary shudder worked its way through her body. 'And there's nothing I can do about that. But I will not be made to feel guilty for a little harmless revenge. Because that's what it was for me. Revenge. And then there was the money of course. There was that as well, and that was what started it. I mean, my need for money. But Roger started it really. And after what he did to me, my actions pale into insignificance. And remember what he did to Candi – it makes my crime inconsequential.'

Lucy had calmed down considerably but still a titter escaped her, although the sound was more like the tinkling shards of fragmenting glass, instead of the full-blown delirium of frenzied madness. 'I'm almost relieved it's just blackmail,' Lucy said. 'If it wasn't so awful it would be really funny.' She giggled again, and it sounded so shrill and fractured, Becky worried that Lucy would crack like an old vase, splintering into a crazed mosaic pattern.

Becky unexpectedly caught sight of Roger's brown shoes which peaked out from the bottom of his dressing gown, each neatly tied in a bow. They were scuffed. *They need a clean*, she thought absurdly. And then realised, *And now it's not my responsibility. Not anymore.*

'What I did,' Becky said. 'I did for a very good reason. The men deserved it. They really did.'

There was a blob of something on her thigh: she couldn't believe she'd missed it when she was cleaning herself in the bathroom. Breathing deeply, she swallowed, keeping her gag reflex in check, stopping the automatic pitch and toss of her stomach, and swatted it off her leg. Didn't wonder too closely at what particular piece of her husband it was. 'And of course obtaining money by deception, the definition of blackmail, *is* a crime,' she said. 'But it's not crime of the bloody century, is it?'

'I've most certainly heard worse,' John said. 'Nothing to be ashamed of, Becky.'

Thank you, John. I feel so much better now that I have your approval.

'Maybe I need to explain *why* I blackmailed them. Then you'll understand better.'

She was primarily talking to Lucy because she loved her and wanted her to understand. But to Frank as well because he was there and was her daughter's husband. But she knew that John's reaction to her story was key. Perhaps crucial to the survival of her family. The truth was all she had. She hoped it was enough.

'The three Russian dolls?' John said.

Becky turned from Lucy to him. 'What? Who? What do you mean?'

'Roger's friends: Charlie, Phillip and Simon. The three fatties. That's who you're talking about.'

Irritated that he knew, but unsurprised, Becky nodded. 'Yes, the three little piggies. All of them bastards.'

No one said anything, so she carried on.

'I'm not going to sit here and itemise every little cruelty perpetrated by Roger. You don't need to know his every mental perversion detailed and catalogued by me, the psychological mind games that he subjected me to. Just believe what I do tell you. I'll condense it for you. In a nutshell tied prettily with a ribbon. Although there was nothing pretty about it.' She gathered herself internally, cleared her mind, and clasped her hands in her lap.

'Before I married Roger, I was a happy, fun and

independent woman. Twenty-one. Becky Bee. Thought I was the best thing going.' She laughed at the arrogance of the statement. 'I was young, and that's the beauty of youth; blissful and sometimes misplaced arrogance. Carried away by my own brilliance, and my own self-belief.

'I couldn't have been happier. I was known as Queen Bee by all my friends. And I had plenty of them. I was the belle of the ball. More striking than good looking, but I had a presence. You couldn't miss me. I was too gobby to miss. But in a nice way.

'If there was a party, I was there. I *was* the party.' She smiled at the memory. 'I even used to wear a figure-hugging cotton dress – more like a tight long top – with black and yellow horizontal stripes. You know, like a bumblebee. God, I was happy. Popular. I thought I had everything. I *did* have everything.'

Becky felt her surroundings, and the people in it, diminish as she spoke. Lucy, Frank and even John seemed to get smaller and smaller, further and further away as she basked momentarily in her past.

'And then I met Roger. He was different from all my other boyfriends. More grown up. He was only a couple of years older than me, and I mistakenly thought that made him a man. Not a boy, like my previous lovers, but a real, grown-up *man*. And so charming. He had oodles of charm. Hard to believe now.'

A laugh escaped her and she was shocked at the vitriol it contained. Its hatred. It wasn't a laugh at all. It was a tightly restrained scream of fury.

She bit down quickly on her lip and continued to spit out her life in words frosted with a deep and joyless chill.

'Roger made me laugh and I was flattered by his attention. He seemed sophisticated and worldly. Took me to fine restaurants, dined me on rich food and expensive wine, bought me beautiful jewellery. Made me feel special.' Becky cocked her head at her daughter. 'Difficult to imagine him like that, isn't it?'

'Bloody impossible,' Lucy said. 'I'd love to see what you looked like back then. Before Dad. Why haven't you ever shown me photographs of you when you were my age?'

'Roger burnt them all. All of my photographs. Every last one of them.' Becky tried to run her paired hands through her hair. 'God, he was a shit. He took everything from me. He even took my bumblebee top. I loved that dress. And he took it. He said, "You're a Twist now, and the Twists don't do novelty clothes." I know it sounds like a little thing, him taking my dress, stupid really, but it really upset me. But it was only one of many, many cruel acts.'

Lucy said, 'Like what? What did he do, that you hate him so much?'

'Everything changed the day after we got married. He picked where we were going on honeymoon. I was ecstatic at that stage: thinking it all terribly romantic. A mystery destination. Turned out we were going to the Maldives. Great, you might think. As did I. We had one of those little beach shacks, stupidly expensive, and totally cut-off from anyone else. And that's precisely why Roger chose it. Except for a lovely little man who was our personal chef, I didn't see anyone else. Roger would bugger off every day to God knows where. I didn't see anyone. No one at all.

'Roger stopped talking to me. Completely ignored me. Day one of our honeymoon, it was as if I didn't exist. I couldn't understand it. I was crushed and felt silly. Thought he was joking, that he'd suddenly laugh and say, "Ha, got you." But he never did. I didn't know what I'd done wrong. He literally wouldn't speak to me. At all. Not one word. I spent those two weeks on my own, going for hot long walks along the beach. I can't tell you how confused I was.

Completely abandoned. He still expected sex. It was different than it had been before: brutal and clinical. It certainly wasn't making love. He fucked me. No, that's not true either. He raped me. And then he just rolled over. With not a word spoken.

'When we returned to London, the day after in fact, he started talking to me again. As if it had never happened, as if I'd imagined the whole thing. And the awful thing was, I was so grateful that he was speaking to me again, I simply accepted it. I forgot to be angry because I was so bloody relieved and bewildered and humiliated. All at the same time.

'Roger informed me that we were moving out of the city and moving into this house. *This* house.' She swept her handcuffed arms in an arc, encompassing the whole of their home. 'This... this... *monstrosity* isn't me. I like colour, rugs, books, music, throws – *Life*. Not this antiseptic house. It's more like a doctor's waiting room. Anal. Uptight. All angular, hard lines – heavy dark furniture. No softness. The interior has been totally Rogered.

'I had to leave all my friends in London, he confiscated my mobile, telling me that as we'd moved away, my friends weren't interested in me anymore. I was out of sight, out of mind, was how he put it. He closed down my bank account, saying that he'd look after the family finances. I was given cash every week, for which I'd have to provide receipts. And give him change if there was any.

'Very quickly, I was told which clothes to wear, which clothes not to wear, how to cut my hair, what colour my hair should be. Over the years, he systematically stripped me of everything. My whole personality was taken away. I was no longer Becky Bee, the Bee's Knees. I was simply, Roger's wife. The mother of his child. Mrs Roger Twist.'

'But why didn't you leave?' John asked. 'You're not stupid.

How could you let that happen? For such a strong woman, you were frighteningly obliging to his every whim.'

'They weren't whims, you fool. Roger wasn't *whim*sical. Don't you understand? It was all about control. He had it. He took it away from me. Which bit of that don't you get?'

John did one of his meaningless laughs again. 'Oh, I get it, all right. Just wanted to make sure you did.'

Becky wanted to shoot John. Right there and right then. Shoot him with his own gun. But she reined in her anger, aware that John was goading her.

Fuck him.

Still angry, her shame now out there for all to see, she said, 'I *let it happen,* as John said, because Roger was a professional. A professional controller. It started on our honeymoon, but the subtle taking-over of my entire life developed slowly, day by day, week by week. The months and then the years all merged into one long and embarrassing eradication of me. But I didn't see it happening. It was so painfully gradual, but simultaneously so painfully quick, that I didn't realise I was lost because no one was looking for me. Not even myself. It was too late. *I* was too late to save myself.'

Becky held up her empty plastic beaker. 'More brandy, please.'

Show no fear.

He refilled it and, taking the drink, not bothering to thank him, she said, 'Roger stole my life without me even noticing. And by the time I *did* notice, I was too ground down to do anything about it. I wasn't here anymore. I was gone. Roger had deleted me.'

'So then what happened?' Lucy asked. 'How did it come to blackmail?'

'Because I decided to escape. To leave Roger. You were old enough. I planned to get away and contact you later. But if you want to know exactly why I did it, I'll tell you. It was all really very simple. It started about two years ago.'

Involuntarily, she put her hands to her mouth in unexpected recognition of the timeframe. 'Of course. Bloody Roger. That'll be the time, as we now all know, that he began his "relationship" with Candi. No wonder his revolting treatment of her spilled out into our marriage. He must have been basking in the brilliance of his own sexual sadism. Bastard.'

She stopped, temporarily thrown by being able to suddenly understand Roger's introduction of the buddy-scheme to his psychological torture of her.

'He decided to involve his three fat little friends in one of his depraved games. With me, obviously, as the butt of the joke. And it was one step too far. Even for me, in my pathetically depleted state. There's always a line that's a line too far. Or so it seems. And he crossed it. Stepped right over it, in cavalier fashion.'

'The straw that broke the camel's back,' said Frank, his voice reedy with angst.

'You could put it like that. But to me, it felt like a very deliberate and emphatic step that Roger had taken. I prefer to think of it as a step too far. Felt more like a bloody great giant *stride* too far. And that's when I thought, enough. Fuck you, Roger. No more. I'm fighting back.'

She looked to John and then realised that she was as good as asking for permission to speak. Immediately she refocused on Lucy and Frank. 'Do you want to know what happened?'

'Yeah, Mum. Course. You can't stop now. Just speak to me. Ignore shit-face John. Pretend it's just you and me.'

Becky smiled. 'Right, this is what happened.'

28

BECKY

Becky took a breath. Hers was a secret that stuck in her throat, but she found herself glad to be able to clear it: like coughing out the badness, the shame, the degradation. Now was the time to speak and by doing so, cleanse and release her internal clogged-up emotions: like unblocking a drain. It was time that Lucy knew.

She clasped her fingers together. 'It was another Saturday evening: the first of the month. Which meant the regular cooking of a meal, by me, for Roger's three work colleagues: his subordinates. The dinners had been a date in the diary for about four years. But about two years ago, the already dreaded Saturday took on another twist. A depraved and shaming twist. A *Roger* Twist if you like. That's how I always thought of those nights. Roger Twisted night.

'The first Saturday of every month always followed the same rigid routine. Roger would invite his friends: Charlie, Phillip and Simon. Roger was their boss and they, sycophantic lambs to the slaughter, were invited along for the ride. For the show. To watch me. To watch Roger shame me. Nothing overt.

Ignoring my existence was as bad as it got. At the beginning. As if I really wasn't there. And they followed Roger's lead.

'It was an easy enough game for them to play, without getting too involved, without getting their chubby little hands too *too* dirty. They could convince themselves that they were merely doing as their host did, which *is* the correct etiquette. They weren't actively hurting me, they told themselves. So no harm done.

'For them. No harm done.'

Lucy said, 'I was still living at home, wasn't I? I must have been eighteen. Just started working at the pub. I met them all once because I got home early one Saturday night. I remember because they were slaughtered. You hurried me upstairs. You always tried to get rid of me on Saturday nights. That's who you're talking about, isn't it, those disgusting, fat drunks. Right?'

'Yes, that's them. Unforgettable men, aren't they?'

'Unforgettably revolting, yeah.'

'Anyway, it was my job to prepare and serve the dinner. Of course I wasn't invited to sit at the table and eat with them. Instead, I'd sit in the kitchen and wait for Roger's summoning handclap – when more drinks would be demanded, the starter, the main, the pudding, the coffee, the port. More alcohol.

'Following Roger's lead, as I carried in whatever was required, the three men all dropped their gaze. As if I was invisible. Or if I was visible, I was merely a servant, not worthy of looking in the eye. One of them, Charlie, the fattest of the trio, was initially embarrassed by Roger's behaviour, and had, on the first night all those years ago, attempted to smile and speak to me. Had even stood up as I'd first entered the room, carrying the first course.

'Roger glared at him. Stony-faced. Glared into a frozen icy silence. My husband had thrown his cutlery down and they'd cluttered noisily against the as-yet empty side plates. "No,"

Roger said. "Do. Not. Look. At. Her." Charlie had blushed, muttered something, quickly sat again, and pretended to be suddenly fascinated with the tablecloth. Embarrassed and unsure of the rules.

'Having put the food in front of them all, I was abruptly dismissed with an unnecessarily dismissive flap of Roger's hand, and Charlie never looked me in the eye again. Not then, anyway.'

Becky paused her story and she and Lucy looked at each other. Lucy shook her head. 'God, Mum, I can't believe it. I had no idea. Really. Wow. *God*. It sounds really dreadful. No, that's a stupid word. It's much worse than simply dreadful. It's bloody diabolical.'

Becky shrugged. 'Good word. That's precisely what it was. Diabolical. Anyway...' She shuffled herself forward in her uncomfortable chair. 'This particular Saturday, I was resigned to another evening of the same. I sat at the kitchen table and swallowed down a second glass of wine. The alcohol blurred my reality. It was enough to take the edge off but it never made me drunk. I was always on such a high level of alert on those nights that any amount of alcohol couldn't make me even merry. It just made things that little bit softer.

'And there was nothing to be merry about anyway. I'd just served the main course so had settled into relative relaxation for the length of time I knew it took for the piggies to scoff from their trough.

'And then, shattering my quiet little sanctuary, Roger clapped his hands. Right behind me. He must have crept along the hall, making sure I didn't hear him. The two claps of his hands were so close to my ear that I felt the rush of air as his palms slapped together. The suddenness of the noise made me jump up from my chair. The vibration of the after-clap rang in my ears like a forever-echo. Putting my hand to my ear, I staggered to standing and spilt some of the wine on my dress as my heart pounded in my throat like a wrecking ball. I looked at him. Waiting instruction.

"'Follow me, dearest wife. Your presence is required.'"

'This was a new game. A deviation from all the preceding Saturdays and I knew that I wouldn't enjoy it.

'In I went. Behind Roger who led me in like I was the village idiot. He held his arms out expansively, as if introducing the next act. I didn't smile. Neither did the piggies. None of us was sure what was happening, but each of us I believe, realising that whatever it was, it wasn't going to end well for me. Might, at worse, be awkward for them.

"'Rebecca," Roger said, by way of announcement; his smile as wide as wide could be. So broad was his smile, I hoped his face might actually split in half. He sat back down at the table. His eyes shone and I realised how drunk he was. "Rebecca, this roast beef is shite. It's 1) cold..." He held his index finger aloft to show that there was a list of my failures yet to come. "2) overdone. You know that I like it pink. 3) the potatoes are *under*done; like bloody bullets and 4) you look like shit. What the hell are you wearing? That dress makes you look as cheap as chips. It's even stained with the wine you've been knocking back. You look worse than the beef, and that's saying something."

'I was wearing the dress that he'd instructed me to wear. Red, plunging neckline and figure hugging. Not knowing where the courage came from, I answered him back. For the first time in years. Perhaps it was the publicness of it all that emboldened me. I said, "I'm sorry if the food is substandard, but if you remember, *you* picked this dress. *You* made me wear it, so if it looks cheap, remember who chose it."'

Becky now pulled herself back from the shockingly vivid reliving of her memory of that evening and the delight which she'd felt when she'd finally managed to undermine Roger. 'It was great, Lucy. Seeing the shock on his face gave me a fleeting feeling of power. He looked like I'd slapped him around the face. He couldn't believe it. And inside I'd smiled to myself. Such a little thing, Lucy, but it really had made my day. Made my *year*.'

'God, Mum. Well done you. I can't believe my father treated you like that. Can't get my head round it.'

'Yes, we were both unfortunately far too attached to him in the very physical sense: we all lived together me, as his wife, and you, as his daughter. He had no idea how great we really were, Lucy. Don't forget that. He didn't know how lucky he was to have us.'

Lucy smiled. 'Yeah, but forget him. Go on with your story. It's *your* story. Not his. Don't make it about him. It's about you.'

Becky nodded. 'After I'd embarrassed him, by pointing out his mistake, Roger covered his loss of control quickly, not wanting to appear stupid in front of his entourage of adoring piggies. So whooping with laughter he slapped Charlie on the shoulder. "What do you think, chaps? Am I wrong?" His voice was slurred, his movements were wild and uncoordinated. "Or is it my imagination? What do you think, Charlie? Simon, Phillip? Come on. You may speak the truth. I won't bite. And she needs to hear it. Does she, or does she not, look cheap?"'

Strangely, having anticipated feeling shame recounting this particular evening, Becky didn't feel any shame as she retold it, and was actually starting to enjoy her own narrative. Becky wanted everything out in the open. Every last shameful and mortifying detail. 'Where have I got up to? Oh, yes, of course – how could I forget? My cheapness had been called into question. An awkward silence fell at the table. Plates were stared at. Knives and forks laid down. Glasses lifted and drank from to give the three fatties time to think how best to respond.

'And I stood there with my eyes focused over Roger's left shoulder. Like a frightened child being told off by the headmaster, I wished myself somewhere else. *Any*where else would do. I simply stood there, limp and defeated like an old washed-out rag.

'And those three fat guests sat in silence. Taken aback by the unexpected turn of events, they'd temporarily forgotten how to move. How to speak. How to escape with their head held high.

'It was apparently okay to ignore me, but to blatantly verbally abuse me, was perhaps a bit too much to ask of them. Roger was not a happy man. "What's wrong with you, men? I said, *come on*. Speak freely. Let's play a game, as this shite isn't worth eating. Let's amuse ourselves. Rebecca, you'll play, won't you? Tell the nice gentleman that you'll join in. They need a little encouragement." He threw back his head and laughed. Repeated my name, "Rebeccaaa." Elongated. Drunk. Mocking. Wet sounding.'

Lucy said, 'God, gross, Mum. Give me a break. What are they like? Men? They're all arseholes. All of them.' Becky inclined her head in vague agreement, not committing herself, choosing to ignore the vicious bitterness of her daughter's words, not wanting to engage in Lucy's anger at the world.

Becky continued. 'Instinctively, I crossed my arms. A pathetic shield against Roger and useless against being played with like a toy. I knew how Roger's mind worked. Bracing myself, I waited. Watched as he clasped his hands behind his neck and looked up at the ceiling. Pretending to think. I knew of course he'd already decided my fate, and this was him showboating. Charlie, Phillip and Simon watched him too. All of them florid, fat and weak. Such pathetic, imbecilic men – so eager to please the boss, and terrified of falling out of favour.

'"Right," said Roger, banging his hands on the table. He picked up the tall, wooden pepper grinder, tapped it on the edge of the table as if testing it, and then tossed it in the air. Caught it. "Perfect. This is what's going to happen. This..." He held the grinder aloft in the air. "Is my gavel. And this is an auction. Of my wife. Can't pretend she's in mint condition, definitely been used. *Very* second-hand. So, I'll start off the bidding – just to get the ball rolling. Do I hear a penny? Just one penny for my wife. It's a bargain. Can't say fairer than that. Any advance on a penny?"

'All the fatties reddened, their eyes skittering with nerves, unsure where to settle their gaze. Unsure if they should play. Roger turned to Simon, the least morbidly obese but still a disgusting ball of perspiring lard. "Simon. What's your offer?"

'He laughed nervously and drank some more wine. Needing the extra thinking time. Finally, he said, "A fiver?" Blushing, he avoided looking at me. Avoided looking at Roger. At any of them. Not sure if he'd played a blinder or had overstepped the mark.

'Roger beamed with satisfaction. "Do you hear that, Rebecca? A whole fiver? And other bids are *still* welcome. This Lot is still up for grabs." Phillip said, "A tenner." Charlie said, "I don't want to play. It's cruel." "Oh, come now, Charlie. Don't be so fucking wet," Roger said. "And just you remember whose food you are eating, whose drink you are drinking and who's your fucking boss. You *have* to play. So, I repeat, how much for my wife?"

'"Three hundred pounds."

'Laughing with childish delight, Roger held the grinder over the table, ready to bring it down. "Any other bids? No? Last chance. Are we done? Right then. Going, going..." He eked out the suspense, looking to each of the men in turn. No response. He raised his voice in excitement: "... gone."

John interrupted. 'How very Roger-like. The misuse of control and so unnecessarily cruel. A very depraved man.'

Becky had almost forgotten that John was there. She didn't care what he thought. This story was for Lucy. And for herself. Ignoring John as if he hadn't spoken, Becky said, 'Roger brought the pepper mill crashing down again and an awkward silence fell. Broken by Roger's ever-drunker laugh. "Boom. The little lady will be going to a good home I'm sure. And I'm equally sure, Charlie, that your wife will enjoy having a new pet around the house."

'Phillip and Simon tittered, glad to be out of the running. Charlie smiled at me. I stared right through him.

'"But of course," said Roger. "I can't *really* sell my wife to you, Charlie old boy. Can't even lend her out on a daily basis. Because she's my property. I *own* her. But as you are, for this evening only, partial owner, tell me what you'd do to her. If she were really yours. I mean sexually, what would you do to her? No holds barred. Because there's frankly not a lot else to do with the unwanted baggage that is my wife. What would you do with her? For fun? Just because you could. Any of you? I want you each to tell me your secret sexual fantasies that you could perpetrate against my sweet Rebecca." He held his hand in the air. "Go."

'My teeth were so tightly clamped together, my jaws ached. I glared at them all. Hating them all. Wanting to kill them all. If I'd had the nerve I would have gone to the table and picked up the carving knife and slit their throats. One by one. And I would have enjoyed it.

'Simon was slumped in his chair, almost too drunk to talk. But he managed to slobber out, "I'd fuck her till she bled."

'Roger applauded and said, "Good one, Simon. I like it. Phillip? Can you better that?"

'I saw various options go through his head as he deliberated on his answer. Wanting to get it just right. Wanting to please Roger, but not wanting to offend. I didn't really see how much more offensive *I'd fuck her till she bled* could get, but I patiently awaited Phillip's response. "I'd fuck her in front of my wife and then make my wife do her."

'He sat back in his chair, delighted with his answer. Roger patted him on his back and Phillip laughed loudly. Thinking promotion, in whatever form, was now a sure-fire thing. "And Charlie. How about you?" Roger said.

"'I'd take her out to dinner and then I'd escort her home. If she was amenable, we'd make love. I'd stay the night with her and make her breakfast in bed the following morning. And I wouldn't tell my wife. That's what I'd do."

'Roger gaped at him like an idiot goldfish. "You kid me, right?"

"'I kid you not."'

Frank coughed, as if he needed physical permission to say something. Becky nodded at him, irritated that he was stopping her, mid-flow. He said, 'You mean, Roger expected you to stand there and just suck it up? All this sickness from his mates?'

Becky looked at Frank and realised what an idiot her daughter had married. He seemed to be awash with an unfathomable inability to empathise, and most definitely lacked the art of showing, or feeling, *any* sensitivity. She didn't answer him, but instead carried on relentlessly.

'That evening, at that very moment, listening to Charlie's attempts to be chivalrous, I could feel the heavy quietness of the room wrap itself around all of us. The two men, Roger and Charlie, continued to stare at each other, both of them unwilling to budge. "You do know there's a vacancy coming up, don't you, Charlie, as assistant partner? The post is my right-hand man. That means working alongside me, not under me. That job could be yours. It could still be yours. It could be any of yours." He looked to his right and left to include Phillip and Simon. "It's up to you of course, Charlie. No pressure. But I really think you should change your views on what you'd do with my wife. If you were given the chance."

'And just like that, Charlie's hunger for promotion, hungrier still for Roger's acceptance, won the day. He joined in. He bloody *dived* in, flippers and all, to quickly accelerate himself back into the light that was Roger. Out of the potential darkness of Roger and back into the glorious light that he saw in Roger, with his myopic porcine eyes.

'Taking a breath, he turned to me and said, "I'd wait for her in the dark, wearing a balaclava, and I'd rape her. Again and again. And she'd never know it was me."

'Roger slapped him on the back. "Bravo, Charlie. Good one. Pity it's all a game, isn't it? Now let's eat the rest of this shit. Rebecca, the food needs heating up and bring in some more wine while you're at it. You can leave."

'I left. Feeling so physically small, I wondered at my very existence. Thought I might have disappeared without me noticing. I pinched my arm. Just to check.

'My final duty of those Saturday nights was to see the guests out. To thank them for coming. To hand them their coats and to make sure their taxis were waiting before showing them the door. This part of the Saturday-dinner-party routine didn't change that night. Roger and his three appendages all stood in the road, giggling, swaying and trying to get into their respective taxis. Roger tried to oversee proceedings but was too drunk to do anything other than stagger uselessly around. I saw Charlie pat his pockets and then point back up at the house. *Shit.* He was doing the old *I have to go back for something I've forgotten* trick.

'Stepping passed me, he said, "My hat. Forgotten it." And he had. There it was on the hook. When I was pretty certain I'd taken it off and given it to him. He bent in close and stage-whispered in my ear. "I'm really sorry, Rebecca. I didn't mean any of those things. It was cruel. And I'm a weak man. Greedy. I need the promotion and the extra money. So, I'm sorry. Really, I am." Blank-faced, I didn't react. What was there to say? Instead I watched him as he fumbled inside his coat and taking out a card, he gave it to me. "There. If you ever need anything, ring me. We'll meet. I'm not like your husband. I like women. You can trust me." He squeezed my hand. "Call me." And then he too left.'

Becky stopped talking. Although mentally tired from the telling, she found herself oddly at peace, as if she'd taken off a too-tight fitting dress and could now breathe more normally: her lungs unincumbered. A lightness and buoyancy filled her and she closed her eyes and smiled.

29

LUCY

John looked at his watch. 'Shall we take a break? Now seems like a good time for one, don't you all think? How about some food? And some more tea to wash it all down with? We've a lot to get through.'

John flashed his teeth at them all: annoying in their neatness. *He* was annoyingly neat.

Lucy sat up and, staying on the floor, tilted forward at the waist and leant her back against the front of the armchair. Jutted her chin up so that she could look John in the eye. 'Are you being serious? How fucking mad are you? Haven't you got anything to say about Mum's story? You could at least acknowledge her honesty.' She paused, and then added, 'And also the fact that my father is now officially the biggest shit in the world.'

John held his hand to his chest as if mortally wounded. 'But I do acknowledge her frankness. Refreshing that someone can be so open about their behaviour. I feel this is a moment. An important moment. For all of us. And we all know already that Roger was a *very bad* man. Already acknowledged I think you'll find. And dealt with accordingly. But as I say, I think it's time to eat now.'

'I couldn't,' Lucy said. 'And I probably won't be eating tomorrow, because you'll have killed us all by then. If you're hungry, help yourself, you arsewipe. Knobhead. Fuckwit.'

'There really is no need to swear like that, Lucy. You have what is commonly known as a potty mouth. Shows a great paucity of language. But I concede that you might be feeling more than a little testy at the turn of events today. Not your usual Sunday lunch, is it?'

Lucy tuned him out. For reasons she couldn't truly understand, she was furious. Seething. So angry that she could kill someone. John. She could easily kill John and feel nothing. She wasn't sure why anger had taken such a hold, but it was a damn sight better than the crying and way better than the manic laughing.

And a real plus – if you could call it that – she was getting used to the dead body of her father sitting in the chair. It had been horrific, his killing, was *still* horrific, but it was bearable. Sort of. Well, of course it wasn't. How could it be? But she had to pretend. Mostly because there was nothing she nor any of them could do to change it. The shooting of her father was something she *had* to accept. Because it meant survival. The possibility at least, that they could all survive this.

The one great bonus: she couldn't *see* Dad anymore. She just had to ignore the covered towelling lump that he'd become. She tried to think of him as more of a carcass: impersonal bones and flesh that were no longer her father. But she thought that brutal. Then again, her father *had* been brutal. Very brutal. So much worse a man to her mother than she'd ever imagined. As bad, if not worse to Mum than he had been to her. *Definitely* worse to Mum, Lucy thought sadly. Perhaps that was the source of her fury: the sheer disgusting *violation* of her mother by her father. She shook her head, not wanting to dwell on it. It had been told now. Lucy wished she'd known at the time, but what could she have done?

The knowledge of her mother's abuse made it far easier for Lucy to finally settle on thinking of the mound that had been her father as a pile of dirty washing. Impersonal. Completely dehumanised and not a part of her.

Not much of a stretch.

She also felt much closer to her mother than she ever had before. They'd never been close: all this 'we're like sisters, me and Mum' she'd heard people say – mostly from spoilt little princesses – it had never washed with her. Lucy's mother hadn't done cosy, warm mothering. Lucy hadn't done cosy, warm daughtering.

Perhaps they were more alike than she'd previously supposed. Although in her state of an all-consuming fury, she was very aware that she had managed to find and put on a pair of rose-tinted spectacles in terms of her relationship with her mother. Suddenly it was 'Me and Mum'. *Pfft*, she thought. It was ridiculous and sentimental. But that didn't stop it from being true. She *did* love her mother. More so now, having just listened to her secret. And she'd happily go with that realisation. Not a lot else to happily go with.

To back up her newly found knowledge, she said, 'Are you all right, Mum? You don't want a break, do you?'

'No. I want to get on with it. What's the point of delaying anything?'

'Sustenance,' said John. 'That's the point. What's wrong with you people? You can't survive on nervous energy alone. Food is needed. And we're going to eat if I have to force-feed you. And I'm sure none of you want that.'

He opened his rucksack and took out a Tupperware dish

and opening it up, he delicately and carefully picked up a tin-foiled, perfectly wrapped block. 'Sandwiches.'

Lucy snorted. 'What *is* your rucksack? A fucking Tardis?'

His smile this time seemed more genuine as he nodded happily, taking her comment as a compliment. 'Actually, it's all about the packing. Packed right, you can fit so much more into a confined space than you might imagine. Tidiness. It's key. As well as precision and execution. And practise obviously.'

He put his knees together, with ankles out, in a girly way, and balancing the sandwiches on them, he slowly and precisely unfolded the tinfoil. Not wanting to rip it. Lucy thought that the packaged stack of sandwiches looked as if they'd been gift wrapped for a special occasion – perhaps Christmas. The tinfoil had been expertly used as a covering; each and every fold sharp, pointed and unwrinkled. Delving into his bag again he brought out five plastic plates.

'I hope everyone likes cheese and ham and salad. Not very exciting, but most people like the combination,' he said.

John frightened Lucy. He was behaving so normally in such an abnormal situation. It freaked her out. Back here on Planet Earth, it was just herself, Frank and her mother.

And dead Daddy.

Frank finally spoke. 'So what did you blackmail Charlie with, Rebecca? It was him, wasn't it, and not one of the other two?'

A guttural sound escaped Lucy's throat – again, anger. 'Who do you think it was, Frank? *Of course* it was Charlie. It wasn't some bloody random milkman who was just passing by, was it? And what do you think she did? She slept with Charlie, *had bloody sex with him*, because he was gagging for it. Just like all fucking men are. God, Frank, just shut up, will you?'

Without thinking, still trembling with anger, she accepted from a plate a sandwich cut into quarters from John and began eating. Strange, but she was hungry. Even stranger, they were all hungry it seemed as one by one they wolfed down the food. She watched her mother take a huge bite, chew and swallow.

Catching a crumb with her still-cuffed hands, Rebecca said, 'Yes. I had sex with Charlie. Twice. I contacted him. Finally. It took me a year to think of the idea, and a further six months to get the courage up to actually do it. But I did it. Rang him up. Made him book a room in a respectable hotel, agreed on a date and a time. I arrived early, telling the receptionist that my work colleague would be joining me. I don't know why I bothered with that particular subterfuge, really. I certainly couldn't have cared less what the woman thought, and because I'm middle-class and dress relatively well, I knew the cover story was unnecessary. But I pretended anyway.

'I'd managed to save some money over the months and had bought a small video camera. I hid it in the room, facing the bed, hidden behind a pile of ring-binder files, filled with obscure rubbish printed from the internet at the library. I'd brought some notebooks with me as well, and lots of pens, to support my cover story that Charlie and I would be working. I pointed them out to him when he arrived, knowing that he wouldn't inspect the side table too closely. He was eager to get down to business.

'It was a disgusting and demeaning five minutes. All sweaty fumbles, grunts and snorts from him. I didn't even bother pretending that I was enjoying it. He wouldn't have cared anyway. It was truly hideous. But I'd captured it on film. That was all that mattered. I met him once again. For sex. Just for added insurance. With one act of infidelity I thought it conceivable that his wife might forgive him. But twice? I thought not. And anyway, I suspected Charlie was more frightened of Roger finding out than his wife. And I was right.

'I asked for a thousand pounds the first time. And then upped it to two thousand. A month. And into my new bank account it went. Gathering interest, getting larger. I felt giddy with the power. I'd taken back control of my life and I didn't feel guilty in the slightest. I felt bloody great. He was a shit. All the little fatties and Roger were complete shits. And I'm not sorry Roger's dead. There...'

She dabbed at her mouth with a napkin provided by John. 'I've said it. I'm glad Roger's dead, and I only wish I could have gone on to blackmail Phillip and Simon as well, because they'd have been just as easy prey.'

Lucy watched as her mother de-crumbed her fingers over the plate and sat back smiling. Her secret told. And Mum was proud of it.

Lucy didn't blame her. How could she? Her mother's life had been dreadful. And her father... she couldn't believe she hadn't known the lengths and depths he'd gone to in order to torture and destroy her mother. 'Well done, Mum. Really, well done you.'

'But, Rebecca. I mean, Becky, sorry,' said Frank. 'What about your family all this time? Your friends? When you were married to Roger, why couldn't you go to them for help? Why did it have to come to this? Having sex with a man and then blackmailing him? Why didn't you just leave Roger?'

Becky laughed, although the sound of her laughter wasn't exactly overflowing with humour. Instead, there was a slight edge to it. 'God, you're an innocent, Frank. You haven't understood. By the time we got back from our honeymoon in the Maldives, or my honeymoon in Coventry, as I prefer to think of it, Roger had convinced me that my friends had moved on, weren't interested in me anymore because I'd moved out of London. Roger could have convinced me that I was a banana after only a few months of marriage: I'd have believed anything – I was a woman with absolutely no self-worth. I wasn't a person. I wasn't a person *at all*. I was wholly alone. That's how quick my destruction was and how good Roger was. A real old pro.'

Becky put the plate down on the carpet and spoke directly to Frank. Tried to make him understand. 'My mother died when she gave birth to me. Something my father could never see beyond; I was the cause of his wife's death – I was to blame and thereafter everything was my fault. He brought me up alone. A cold and cruel man – we just lived in the same house, shared the same living quarters, breathed the same air, ate the same food. That was it. My grandparents had emigrated years before the birth of you, Lucy. They came back for my mother's funeral, but soon returned to Australia. I've never really known them.

'My relationship with my father is now, and had been for years before my marriage, one of polite acknowledgement. Cards at Christmas and birthdays. Nothing more.'

John said, 'God, Freud would have a field day. You essentially married a replica of your father. There's originality for you.'

Becky carried on speaking, as if John wasn't there. 'I never met Roger's parents. I was apparently okay to marry, but not okay to introduce to his parents. So my only potential point of contact was my best friend, Lara. Roger took away my mobile before our honeymoon, saying it would be romantic to be cut off from everyone, for it to just be me and him. Of course I believed it at the time, that it was a loving gesture. Didn't realise that that was as far as Lara went. No doubt Roger texted her on my mobile saying that I no longer wanted to mix with her – made up some flimsy but plausible-sounding reason. He was spiteful because he could be. It amused him. He told *me* that Lara had texted saying she was no longer interested in keeping in touch. Chalk it up to another huge thing that Roger took from me. My best friend. No doubt, Lara is married now, so I wouldn't know how to find her anyway. Wouldn't know where to begin. *I was completely alone.'*

'Did the Saturday night dinner parties with the fatties and Dad continue, after that night? The abuse? Did that carry on?' Lucy asked.

Becky laughed. 'No. Roger's not stupid. He knew that just the *threat* of it happening again, the merest hint at something similar happening, was almost as bad as it *actually* happening. I literally shook with the constant fear of being summoned. Of Roger sneaking up on me in the kitchen again. I never sat down on that bloody chair with a glass of wine again. Always stood facing the door, so he couldn't catch me unawares.

'But the fear of the same game being played made my legs tremble, to the point that I had to lean on the worktop for support. I was terrified, waiting, every first Saturday of the month, not knowing what was coming. *Every single bloody first Saturday of the month.* He was clever, Roger. And the others – they just followed on. It was never mentioned again. I think the fatties were as relieved as I was and continued to ignore me. Easier for them. Pretending it never happened. But I never knew it wouldn't happen again. I just hoped. That's what got to me. The not knowing.'

She stopped talking and sat there. Lost in thought. But weirdly other-worldly. Like the telling of her secret had freed her of something. She came to with a sort of jerk.

'Charlie would often loiter behind, when your father and Phillip and Simon were more pissed than he was. He always made it clear that the offer was still there for me to take up.' She tossed her head. 'Horrid man.'

'I'm so glad you got him, Mum,' Lucy said. 'Good for you. But why did you stop there? Why not move on to one of the other two fatties? After Charlie?'

'If it ain't broke, don't fix it. And anyway, it's only been six

143

months. Funnily enough, I was aiming to start on Simon this month, but things have changed. Haven't they, John?'

'Indeed they have. But time is fluid. What will be will be and all that. If it was meant, it would have been done already.'

'Oh, puh-lease,' Lucy said. 'That's just cosmic bullshit and you know it.'

John smiled his vapid, stupid smile and slightly dipped his head: possibly in acknowledgement.

'Look. None of you are getting it,' Becky said. 'It's not rocket science. I was no longer me. Hadn't been me since I married Roger. I'd forgotten who I was, because I'd ceased to be anyone. For fucking years.'

Lucy nodded encouragingly. 'I understand, Mum. It's the men who aren't getting it.'

'I'm well up on the story, Lucy, thank you,' John said. 'I know exactly of what your mother speaks. I really do. It would frighten you what I know.'

Frank remained silent.

Becky continued. 'Since marrying bloody Roger, I was instantly and completely unhappy from that point onward. But my role as quiet, subservient wife became so familiar so quickly, that it began to feel normal. I'd stopped begging, stopped pleading, stopped crying. I'd stopped doing anything because what was the point? If there ever had been a point to my life, I'd forgotten it. I got through each and every day, breathing. In and out. Going through the motions. Even thinking seemed far too complicated and futile. I'd become complicit in my own destruction.

'I had no control over my life. Roger had it. He had all the control. And there was nothing I could do. I had no friends to save me. I was totally cut off from the outside world. Even had I been part of the living, I felt such shame. How could I admit to anyone what my life had become?' Her voice had risen, stronger and angrier. 'What part of that don't any of you understand? I couldn't have been more alone had I been the last person on this bloody planet. Roger annihilated me. End of.'

Lucy was stunned into silence at her mother's sudden flare and pulse of anger and flinched when John stood and turned to her. 'Do *you* understand now, Lucy? You're not the only one who's angry. And your mother has a lot more to be angry about than you. Give her a little credit. She deserves plaudits and accolades for her actions – she certainly shouldn't be expected to apologise for them. I, for one, am extremely proud of you, Becky.' He turned towards her. 'I'm glad you got a little taste of that control that you so fiercely won back for yourself. Now, have you all finished eating? I'll just pop out and give the plates a quick rinse and then I'll be back. Okay? And when I say "rinse," I mean *wash*. Thoroughly – with soap and water. Cleanliness is next to godliness. Although I don't believe in the latter. Why would I? But just so you know.'

Lucy had to ask, 'Are you going to shoot my mother through the head now? Like Dad?'

Despite her anger, Lucy was thrown by the fear that made her voice wobble and made her breath hitch in her chest as she asked the question. John glanced at her as if she'd asked what time it was. His expression bland, his voice neutral. 'No, Lucy. I am not going to shoot your mother.'

He turned to Frank. 'Your ankles are bleeding. You've got blood on your natty little deck shoes. And that's just stupid. Stop wriggling your feet would be my advice.'

And then he left the room.

30

FRANK

In a rare show of courage, Frank shouted after John, surprising even himself. 'Yeah thanks, John. *Mate*. Thanks for pointing out the bleedin' obvious. Thanks a bunch.'

Frank knew he had blood on his ankles. Didn't need telling. He wasn't wearing any socks, which hadn't helped. Both of his lower legs were killing him. He was uncomfortably aware that both his wife and his mother-in-law were also eyeing the bloody mess he'd made of himself. Frank hadn't appreciated John pointing out what was plain to see.

'Oh, Frank,' Lucy said. 'You idiot. Stop moving your legs. You're making it worse. You can't escape from the ties.' She paused as he looked down at her.

'Get up,' he said. 'Sit in your chair. You're too vulnerable on the floor. John could walk past you and kick you in the head. You need to be on the same level as him. Go on, get up.'

He didn't want her pity. Pity was for the weak, and he refused to admit that he was in any way lacking. So he continued to internally lie to himself. Kept on doggedly persuading himself that he could do this. Get through this. *Live* through this.

On the bright side, Lucy had been clearly surprised by the tone he'd just used, and had teetered to her feet, dutifully falling back onto her chair. She smiled at him. He didn't smile back. 'And I'm not an idiot, okay. I know you both think I am, but I'm not.'

Lucy raised her eyebrows. Still doubtful, but at least she'd done what he'd asked.

Rebecca said, 'God, Frank. What have you done? Your ankles, they're so swollen. Ask John for some ice. Lucy's right. There's no hope of escaping these bloody cable ties. They're too tight. You're just making it worse.' She tipped her head to one side. 'No one thinks you're an idiot. You're doing your best. We all are.'

'I'm not asking John for ice or anything. Okay? And no, we're not all doing our best. We're not *doing* anything. We're just sitting here, telling our secrets. And for what? Like Lucy said, is John going to shoot you now? How do we stop him? We have to *do* something.'

It was the nearest he'd ever come to being rude to Rebecca and he felt his cheeks colour at his own audacity. And he'd stopped trying to call her Becky – it felt too intimate and casual. She was his mother-in-law for God's sake – not a *friend*.

Both women shrugged in tandem; neither having an answer for him. And they were right. What *could* they do? There was no way out. He felt like screaming with rage. Impotence washed over him.

All the while that Rebecca had been telling her story, her secret, he'd sat and listened intently. Horrified but strangely fascinated. He couldn't get his head around how badly Roger had treated her, what he'd put her through. A man he'd known, had lived with. And he'd never even guessed at the atrocities the man was capable of.

More to the point, he couldn't grasp why Rebecca hadn't

just left. What had stopped her? She could still walk, couldn't she? There was nothing wrong with her legs. Her confidence had been knocked, that's all. She'd just proved that Roger was a bastard, and everyone knew *that*. It was her fault that she'd stayed. She should have had more courage and escaped. With Lucy.

He had found himself oddly dumbfounded by Rebecca's words. He hadn't been sure what to say to her, nor how to say it. Couldn't convey to her his sympathy, perhaps because it was diluted somehow by his incomprehension that she hadn't simply left Roger. But Frank wasn't stupid. He knew that sympathy was the last thing Rebecca wanted. For all the shit she'd been through, in this situation now, in this very moment, Rebecca seemed to him to be remarkably calm. In control. As if she'd reached some sort of inner peace. But of course she wasn't in control. She couldn't be. Like Roger had taken control from her, so John had ripped control from all of them. It was unthinkable. The whole thing.

John had gone strangely still as he'd listened to Rebecca's secret. The only thing that moved had been his fingers with their incessant tying and untying of his shoelaces one-handedly. But his face had been intent – he'd barely interrupted Rebecca as her words had fallen over themselves, fluent and articulate. He knew his expression had been hard to read.

Giving John surreptitious glances as he'd tried to uncable his feet, Frank saw that John had been completely focused on the story, as if internally taking down her statement in his head. Verbatim.

Trying not to further frighten himself by concentrating too much on John, a laughable notion had occurred to Frank when Rebecca had started talking. His notion had been a noble, and ultimately, as it turned out, stupid one. He'd thought that with

Roger now dead, it was up to him to save the two women. He was, after all, the only sane man left standing.

And so, listening all the time to Rebecca, he'd decided that someone had to actually *physically* do something. At least attempt to escape. Bound and cuffed as he was, he'd had to get over his feeling of shame that John was even here. That it was his responsibility that he'd brought John to the house. Found it hard to move on from that. His inability to get anything right. But this was his opportunity.

Everything that he'd done since meeting Lucy had been a pathetic attempt to impress her. He loved her so much. And now this situation with John – it was all his fault. Guilt nibbled away in Frank's gut.

And worse still, Lucy wasn't even impressed by his bravado, the dipping of his toe into crime. She knew all about it. Just let him get on with his stupid falsehood. That just made his whole charade sadder. She saw straight through him. Knew how gentle he really was. How soft. A complete pushover.

Always a pushover for Lucy. And she knew that. Knew that he'd do anything for her. Knew he was hopelessly in love with her.

Maybe, now, this was his chance. To prove his worth. To save her. *Carpe diem and all that.*

Genuine fear of John had kept Frank relatively silent throughout the afternoon. Speaking out loud had terrified him. But now he realised that this was his chance to really make a difference. To make his parents proud of him. To be the man they'd brought him up to be.

And so, he'd wondered. Listened and wondered. What could he *do*?

Was he a coward?

No, he wasn't. He was just a boring, and very unremarkable

young man: a twenty-two year-old mechanic. Pure and simple. That's all he was.

But he thought he could do this. He could save Lucy. And her mother.

Having placed a cushion over his hands, he'd narrowed his fingers and tried pulling them through the handcuffs. No give at all. Knowing it was a waste of time, he'd instead concentrated on his feet. Flexing his thighs, he'd widened his legs as far as he could without drawing attention to himself. And pushed his ankles out as far as possible. Pushed against the cable ties. Pushed again. And again.

Nothing. After thirty minutes of discretely flexing, if anything, the ties had felt a little tighter.

He'd ignored the pain. Flexed and pushed again, moving his ankles up and down as well as horizontally.

And realised that the cable ties had *definitely* tightened. It wasn't his imagination. He'd been shocked to see a little blood trickle from his swollen ankles and onto his canvas deck shoes. Bending down with his cuffed hands, he'd attempted to slide his fingers in between the cable tie and his flesh. The gap was tighter – no question about it – his fingers couldn't even squeeze past the plastic which now cut into his leg. Both ankles and calves were red and inflamed. From all that pushing and pulling and squirming, he'd not only made his ankles bleed, but worse, all he'd managed to achieve was to engorge his calves with blood and aggravate the skin. Swelling his ankles. Tightening the ties. He'd felt like shouting in frustration. Wiggling his toes, his feet had tingled with pins and needles.

And that's when he'd really realised, perhaps for the first time, quite what a pathetic and useless twat he really was.

Made all the worse when it turned out that John had been aware the whole time of his efforts to escape. Had embarrassed him by bringing attention to the blood on his shoes. "You've got blood on your natty little deck shoes." *Bloody bastard.*

Fuck it.

What to do now?

And would John shoot Rebecca?

The thought made Frank ill with fear.

And the question still remained, *what the hell was his own secret?* He honestly didn't know, and the not knowing was making it worse. It truly frightened him.

31

ME

It had started raining. Hard. As I quickly washed and dried the plates, I looked out of the kitchen window and watched the drops fall and bounce outside; highlighted by the glow of the light from inside. The rainfall was sudden and unexpected.

A bit like me.

March. In like a lion, out like a lamb, is how people describe the month. That would be the opposite of me. I'd come into the Twists' house like a lamb. I hadn't quite decided on what animal I'd be leaving as. Not yet. Normally, it wasn't something I had to think about – it just happened.

But this time, this job, I didn't feel as wholly confident as I otherwise would have.

Because things weren't necessarily going to plan. On the surface they were. All was moving seamlessly, without any obvious derailment: everything was how and where it should be. But there was something I couldn't quite put my finger on. Perhaps it was me that was wrong. My head was full. Too full. Full with thoughts that I hadn't anticipated and definitely not experienced before. They'd caught me off-guard. An oddity in itself. Not something I was used to and I'm not overfond of the unfamiliar.

I was fairly sure that I'd identified my thoughts as well I could with the term 'confusion'. Confusion never happened when I was in professional mode. Or even when I wasn't. It led inevitably to chaos.

I didn't like chaos.

Chaos made me nervous, and this family wouldn't like me nervous. I didn't like me nervous, so I wouldn't wish it upon anyone else.

I heard the central heating click on with a satisfying whirr. Immediately, the radiators gurgled to life. It was a comforting and welcoming sound. I was fairly certain that Roger had strict rules as to when and even *if* the heating was allowed on. Couldn't imagine him embracing warmth from anyone or anything. I, therefore, assumed the heating would only be on for an hour. Maximum. Walking over to the boiler, I turned the knob to 'continuous', hoping against hope that Rog, with a lot of his face missing, somewhere up there in the heavenly ether, would be angry at the sheer profligacy of my actions. That made me smile. But there was a definite nip to the air and I thought it best if everyone was at least as comfortable as they could be. I wasn't here to be unduly unkind purely because I had the power to be so.

Before leaving the kitchen, I surveyed the worktops for mess. Couldn't help but notice the toaster wasn't aligned with the back of the wall; its shiny surface sat at an unseemly angle. I pulled it square, preparatory to pushing it back flush against the tiled wall, when out scuttled a small spider. Becky – definitely not a domestic goddess even with, I suspected, a lot of training in that area of expertise from Rog. A small but perfect web nestled underneath the lip of the tray on which the toaster stood.

I laid my hand down gently next to the spider and waited for it to crawl aboard. For a few seconds, I enjoyed playing with it, letting it run around my fingers. Finally, it settled on the end of one my well-manicured nails, and I opened the window – *off you trot, little chap.* I could never understand people who so nonchalantly killed spiders. They did no wrong, harmed no one. Why were people so nasty? What was *wrong* with them?

Leaving everything as it should be, I crept down the hall, as I imagine Roger had, stealth-like in his attempt to unknowingly creep up on his wife, ready to clap loudly in her ear. I heard nothing at first from the captured and endangered Twists. I stood halfway down the hall. Eavesdropping like a schoolgirl.

I heard Lucy say, 'Quick, Mum. He'll be back in a minute. But I swear to you, he doesn't know my secret. I know for a fact he doesn't. He might know some stuff about me which I'd prefer to stay private, but he doesn't know my real secret. No one does. Except Frank. And he wouldn't say. Would you, Frank?'

I could imagine the look Frank must have given Lucy. I heard his outraged voice: 'Of course I wouldn't. How could you even think that? Christ. No one knows your secret, Luce. I'd never tell.'

It was the same old stuff I'd heard a million times before. People rarely surprised me, and that was a shame. But because of the looming threat of my own confusion, I was careful not to linger on the subtle but slightly worrying state of my own thinking. Realised that if I gave it real space in my head, I might make it come true. Just by worrying about it. Crazy, I know. But still.

So, I deleted the unpleasant and replaced it with renewed vigour for the good things to come. The revelations and the repercussions. Good triumphing over bad. As it always did if I had my way. And most days, that's precisely what I had. My way.

I'd had to make a note-to-self whilst Becky was unburdening herself: shut up and let her speak. Don't interrupt her. Just enjoy her freedom of speech, the boldness of her veracity. I'd noted with satisfaction that Becky couldn't help but look proud when she'd announced her crime as a blackmailer. Even Lucy had looked a little impressed, albeit surprised.

Just before entering the sitting room, Becky's voice stopped me. I listened.

'*What can we do?* We have to face the fact that he might, at some point, kill us all. So I repeat, *what can we do?*'

'For fuck's sake, Mum. Don't give up. Not after everything. And everything Dad did to you. You've got to carry on. We've got to survive.'

'I've no intention of giving up without a fight. I'll happily kill John. Just give me the chance. The bastard.'

'Good for you, Mum. And I'm sorry.'

'What for?'

'For everything Dad did to you. I'm really sorry.'

Perhaps Becky shrugged or smiled at Lucy. I didn't know. But I heard her say, 'I just don't know what to do,' sounding frustrated with herself. And me, I suspected.

I walked back in then, taking them by surprise. 'Good to know I've at least got you all thinking and talking.'

Despite Becky's words, I seriously doubted she was anything other than supremely confident that I wouldn't be sitting there, with hand poised on the trigger. She exuded a strange confidence and had been more than erudite in her narrative, detailing the many and varied punishments perpetrated by her husband. She radiated an inner calm. *Not* fitting for the occasion. But I thought that her confession had released her, and Becky the Bee had put in an appearance. And *that* in itself was something to keep an eye on.

She made me slightly nervous – nothing on a scale to

seriously worry me, but enough to keep me on my toes. And for that, I warmed to her.

Upon my reappearance, she had adopted a very contrived, bored, expression which she wore with defiance. She carried it well, but it didn't fool me. She was following everything, missing nothing: her brain was working overtime, tick, tick, ticking away. Trying to out-think me.

Other than Becky, I knew the emotional stage Lucy and Frank were in. A certain amount of relaxation had kicked in. Even though they'd seen me kill Roger, they'd got used to me being there. Their acceptance wouldn't have made their terror of me dissipate any, but it had made them simply more resigned to their fate. Unfortunately for them, they had no idea what was coming.

I needed to up the pace. Get all their little hearts a-hammering again.

Putting the rucksack back on the sofa next to me, I faced them all. 'I rather think it's time for the kiddywinks to join in, don't you, Becky? The grown-ups have had their say, now would be fitting for the children to play.'

Becky said, 'John, don't. Please. Just leave them. Let them go. Please. They're not guilty of anything.'

'And how are you so sure of that?'

'Maybe I'm not, but I *am* sure that I don't care what either of them have done. It doesn't matter. Let them go and you can keep me. Do whatever you want. Please, John. Please.'

'Don't beg, Becky. It doesn't become you and is a return to the bad old Rog days of total submission. That is categorically *not* what I want.'

Frank shrugged. 'I don't even have a secret, so I don't mind going next.'

Lucy shook her head. 'No, I'll go next. John doesn't know my secret, do you, John? You can't know it. So, I'll go next.'

'Yes,' I said. 'Let's listen to what Lucy has to confess. Off you go.' Smiling, I tried to convey encouragement. She needed a little shove to get her started so I said, 'Would you like me to start you off? Like I did for Daddy?'

Again, Becky said, 'Please, John. I am *begging* you. I don't care if I am. Stop this right now.'

Ignoring her, I continued to stare at Lucy. Felt the others' eyes join me in my gaze. Her bravado deserted her and sitting there, abandoned with the reality of having to reveal herself in words, she might as well have been naked under the eyes of us all. The poor girl seemed as if she were teetering on a precipice. Edgy wasn't a big enough word to describe her plight.

Knowing she was next to tell her secret, she was already close to disintegration. She hadn't seriously expected me to pick her for first-in-line and the brutal truth of her situation took hold, catching her off-guard. She was genuinely taken aback by the turn of events. I didn't enjoy watching the vulnerability ooze out of her: desperate, childlike, needy. Like a tangible thing, it gushed from her, and Lucy sat, mute, her eyes filled with tears.

Frank shuffled in his seat. 'For Christ's sake, John. Leave her alone.'

'Shut up, Frank. She has to speak. She'll feel all the better for it, won't she, Becky? Tell your daughter that admission of her behaviour is better out than in.'

Becky said, 'Fuck you, John. Seriously, *fuck you.*'

'I've told Lucy, so I'll tell you – less of the swearing please. Now, Lucy. I'm happy to help you start. Everyone here has already witnessed you trying, in a very clumsy way, to flirt with me, to try to coerce me into some sort of allegiance with you, by your not-so-discreet offer of sex. And that's what you do, isn't it? It's your automatic response to men. You think that's what they all want from you. That sex is *all* they want from you.'

Her chin came up, going for defiance, and getting nowhere close.

'I'm sure your behaviour and attitude to men was shaped by good old Rog. What did he do to you? Tell you that you were a cheap tart, nothing better than a whore? Sounds Roger-like to me. Is that where your hatred of yourself stems from?'

'For God's sake, John,' Becky said. 'Stop with the amateur armchair psychobabble. You're not a therapist. I'm not even sure that you're really a human being. Not in any real sense of the word. You're talking rubbish and you know nothing about what drives my daughter.' She leant forward. 'And stop fiddling with your bloody shoelaces. What is it, a nervous tic? You're not even aware you're doing it.'

'I'm aware, Becky. I'm always aware. And don't even try to stop me grilling Lucy. She shouldn't need grilling anyway – she should know that she can cook on gas all by herself. You know that, don't you, Lucy? Speak. Tell us all.'

Like an angry little girl, Lucy had clammed up, her lips tightly shut. She closed her eyes to stop tears falling, leaving her wobbling chin the only indicator of her distress.

'Please, John. Let's do me instead. I'll talk,' Frank said. 'You're bullying her. It's not fair.'

'What *is* fair, Frank? Life? Nah. Definitely not that. We have to proceed. It's *the law*. My law. I'll say it for you, Lucy, and you can nod along and stop me if I get anything wrong. Now, that's what I call fair.'

I got up quickly and felt the radiator. Satisfied that the warmth was spilling into the room, I said, 'Really, I don't think that what you do will come as any great shock to those assembled here today. Perhaps to Frank, but even he, deep down, must know. You do know, don't you, Frank?'

'Know what?' Frank's words were so full of doubt and misery, his very existence was called into question. He seemed to mist over, became almost translucent, his light for Lucy flickering and dimming. But the light wouldn't go out. I knew that. As did Lucy.

'You know that Lucy sleeps her way around the masses,' I said. 'Sex is how she gets around. A bit like a bus, but cheaper. Quicker as well, I suspect, although I'm not a fan of public transport. For Lucy, sex is simply a way of getting from A to B with the least effort and the greatest reward. A reward, as she perceives it, anyway. Not a reward I'd want, but each to their own. It's not a big secret, Lucy. Frank will be upset, perhaps cry, but ultimately he will still profess his undying love for you, and he will forgive. And then we can all move on. So just admit it.'

Frank, no surprises, jumped up, outraged. His impossible-to-hide silly and swollen bloody ankles were displayed like an art installation: a visual depiction of his current failings to date. And that was only counting today. He sat down just as quickly. There. How easy was that? He knew.

Lucy looked at him. 'I'm sorry, Frank. Really, I am. I don't know why I do it. Especially now I've got you. But none of the men mean anything, and the sex means even less. It means nothing. Completely nothing. I swear.'

'I suspected,' Frank said. 'Couldn't really believe my luck when you said you'd marry me. Thought I'd won the bloody jackpot. And I have won it. It doesn't matter.' He trailed off, unhappy and defeated but oh-so familiarly wet in his self-made jelly mould. Too quick to forgive, in my opinion, but I expected nothing less from him. A constant bloody disappointment.

'But that's not really how it is, is it, Lucy?' I said.

'What do you mean?'

'The sex. With men. Is it under duress?'

'Course it bloody isn't. What are you talking about? *Of course* men want to have sex with me. And I let them. They're

159

not *raping* me. Course they're not. How stupid do you think I am? Fuck.'

'I'm sure that's true,' I said. 'You just keep telling yourself that. But would you like to hear the truth. The real, unexpurgated, unedited, gloriously full-to-brimming truth of it all? Would you?' I didn't wait for her answer.

I just started talking.

32

ME

It had been almost relaxing following the life and times of Lucy Twist, after witnessing the horrors of Roger's nocturnal habits. She, in comparison to her father, the sexual sadist, was more of a walk in the park. Stupid, but normal.

She worked full-time in a pub. Easy enough for me to finish up watching Rog's exploits, and then move on seamlessly to Lucy's pub. Unoriginally named The Cock.

The more I got to know Lucy, understood what she was about, I thought that perhaps, on some level, she'd subconsciously picked the pub for its name only. But I didn't think her that intelligent, if I'm being perfectly honest.

Frank, perhaps wisely, chose to drink in a local pub closer to his work. She, therefore, greedily took the opportunity to, in her eyes, hold court: to mesmerise and then ensnare the men. To entrance and titillate them. Any man would do, it quickly became apparent. As if she were feeding on them; would starve and wither without their adoration. I didn't enjoy watching the show that she put on every night.

I'd watch her most nights, bustling and blonde behind the bar, bubbly and brash simultaneously. She certainly knew how to work it. Well, to be more accurate, she *thought* she knew how to work it. How to work men.

But she'd made a schoolgirl error. She'd been unappealingly unsubtle about what she wanted. Had made it too painfully obvious that it was she who was the one desperate for the attention, desperate for any man to notice her. Desperate for them to ask her for sex. Desperate to get picked up, to be chosen. Desperate.

It was not dissimilar to watching a slow-motion car crash. It could only ever have one outcome. Lucy might think that she always came out the undisputed winner, the number one woman, but always, by the very act of her sleeping with any of her conquests, these *animals*, she'd already lost the game.

One night, funnily enough I think it was a Thursday, so a night that I'd had to bear witness to the psychopathic behaviour of Roger and complete the ensuing after-care that was my duty to Candi, I eventually and gratefully found myself heading, tired, into The Cock.

Here, my name was Tim. Big Tim. Who'd sit and sup his one pint, nursing it, making it last, but not a bother to anyone. Quite a laugh if you got him in the right mood. It was a persona I found easy to slip into – nothing loud nor overt, just a bloke. I sat amongst the beer-swilling crowds, camouflaged so well that I frequently had to remind myself that I wasn't actually Tim. It was a good and easy disguise which required absolutely no finesse nor subtlety. Just being there, big, male and with a pint, ticked all the relevant boxes.

I *was* aware, however, that alcohol had never agreed with me. And I was surrounded by men who drank. I didn't drink a lot because I didn't like the feeling of being drunk and I had a very low tolerance for any alcohol. Drunk meant danger as it meant the possibility of me forgetting who I was. And that wouldn't do. It was the sort of thing that could end in tears if I fell out of character and into another. So I just gently and slowly supped quietly from my pint of weak lager, and laughed when appropriate. Which was harder than one might imagine, as the group of lads who I allowed to believe had befriended me, were excruciatingly unamusing. But so used and well versed in the art of pre-empting others' facial expressions and actions, I carried Tim off easily and consequently laughed in all the right places.

The group of young men in their twenties who frequented the pub, were your bog-standard morons. Most of them perfectly harmless, as far as I knew.

But predatory. Sexually, all up for it. As all men are. *That*, Lucy had got right. Show a man a vagina, and I'd defy any of them to turn it down. In normal circumstances. The male: a disgusting filthy example of a most unpleasant species. They showed no appreciation nor genuine liking of women at all. It had baffled me all my life: this vicious circle of wanting sex, getting sex, then demeaning whoever had given you sex. It rarely deviated from this course, and it was an easy trap for Lucy to fall into. And she so blatantly lost at her attempts to play the game. Was instead constantly trapped by the games men played. She'd unknowingly embarrass herself: again and again and again. Would she never learn? It depressed me.

'All right, Tim, mate. How're you doing? Pull up a stool,' David said. He of the tattooed woman on his forearm, and the monobrow. His eyes were glazed that night, and he weaved a private and meaningless swaying dance to a tune only he could hear. He clapped me on the back and I nodded back, pretending gratitude at being included.

'None of the other blokes in tonight?' I asked.

'Yeah, sure. They're all in the bogs at the mo. Look, here's Teddy and Chris.' He pointed as two very dull and distinctly uninteresting looking young men staggered their way through the throng. They in turn held aloft their pints of beer in salutation and we all sat, like big black crows at the bar – on our perches, ready. They were all slaughtered, whilst I was simply thirsty and tired.

Someone cuffed me around the head. Hard, inadvertently unbalancing me. I nearly, inadvertently, smashed his teeth in. But I righted myself and saw Danial – another male who appeared only one step up from a primate. 'All right, Danial. How goes it?' I said, with a chirpy pitch to my voice that I wasn't really connecting with.

'Great, mate. I'm great. Fucking gasping for a pint. Get the old slag's attention will you. Lucy's her name. That one there. The blonde tart with the big knockers.'

My little gang of new-found friends all laughed uproariously as if Danial had said something funny. I failed to see the humour in it, but went along, playing the game, holding my hand in the air, and waving a twenty-pound note at Lucy. For good measure I added, 'Yes, certainly couldn't miss those melons. They'd take your eye out if you weren't careful.' This sophisticated line was delivered with toe-curling distaste but received with beer spurts of laughter and much waist-bending, knee-sagging and heads thrown back.

Eventually, she turned her attention to us. Danial ripped the twenty-pound note out of my upraised hand and rolled it into a tube shape as he saw Lucy approach. 'Hello, darling. How are you tonight? Look amazing, as per,' Danial said.

Of course, Lucy responded in the only way she knew how. She fluttered her ludicrously long eyelashes and thrust her bosom at him. Being presented as he was with Lucy's breasts, as he had correctly predicted, Danial slipped the tubed shaped twenty-pound note straight down and into her cleavage. 'Make mine a pint of the usual, would you, Lucy-Loo. Thanks, babe.'

He turned round and did an eye-roll to his three friends. I

was reminded uncannily of Roger grandstanding to his Russian doll trio, the three fat piggies. Remembered how Roger had pulled lewd and leering faces at them, making reference to the girl who'd dismissed him at the bar when he'd insisted on buying her a drink.

Here, it was the same eye-rolling, big-bazooka jokes, bawdy laughter. I felt like I definitely didn't belong in tribes like this. I certainly entertained no desire to be one-of-the-lads. I despised their idiocy, the brains-in-their-genitalia mentality. They were gormless, and yet one of them would be Lucy's potential prize for the night. In her eyes.

In her eyes only as it turned out.

'Right,' said Danial. 'How about a game of rock, paper, scissors? Are you all in?'

Much hilarity and fist-pumping followed. I was relieved that at least I knew the game. I asked, 'What's the prize?'

One-browed David, the drunkest of them all, said, 'Come on, Tim. Don't be daft. I'll give you a clue. It ain't Lucy.'

I confess I was confused. As she brought Danial's pint over, I bent my head down and retied my shoelaces. Didn't actually have to look down to do so, but just to be on the safe side, I averted my face and eyes. Didn't want Lucy to really look at me. Needn't have worried. I knew I wasn't her type. But caution was never a bad thing.

They all leered at her and crowded around her when she delivered Danial's pint. Some of the froth slopped over the rim of the glass onto an already-sodden beermat. 'Lick that off for me, would you, babe,' said Danial. He ran his own tongue around his lips in exaggerated fashion, and Lucy, bless her, dipped her finger into his pint, and drawing it out, she sucked it slowly, essentially giving her own digit a blow job. A lot of hollering and metaphoric chest-beating followed and I simply smiled. She airily-fairyly walked away, with an added wiggle of her buttocks.

I said again, 'So if not Lucy, what are we playing for?'

Teddy and Chris giggled. 'You'll see. You up for it?'

Shrugging, I said, 'Yeah, course – count me in. But rock, paper, scissors; it's a game for two players, not a group game.'

'Well spotted, mate,' said Danial, his voice heavily laden with sarcasm – as if he were dealing with an imbecile. 'That's why we play it in rounds. First you and me, okay?'

'Okay. I think I've got it now. Tricky,' I said for good measure.

'One, two, three,' Danial said. Now remember, I have a natural dexterity of hand and the ability to pre-empt others' physical gestures, so it was easy for me to win or lose. I was always one rock, paper or scissor ahead of anyone.

I turned to face him, and on the count of three, held out my hand, showed scissors. Danial presented paper. My victory.

Quickly glancing up, I saw Lucy watching, knowing and recognising the game that us macho chaps were playing. She wasn't really interested in me as a candidate – I was too old and boring looking. But I'm sure she was happy that I was there to make up the numbers.

Danial was out and did a thumbs-up and an exaggerated phew of relief. That was a clue. A pretty humongously big, obvious clue. Apparently, for reasons as yet unknown to me, winning wasn't the aim here. Losing was. Or to be pedantic, if you won, you lost.

Having got the complex rules for this game firmly in my head, I won the next round as well – just to show willing. One-browed David dropped out, clutching his heart in a mock heart-attack swoon. I smiled. Just Chris, Teddy and myself left in the running. I didn't want to push my luck, so I got my rock papered by Chris.

'Fuck it, Tim, you bastard,' he said. 'Right, Teddy, this is it. Whoever wins this, or should I say loses this hand, gets to take Lucy home. Okay? Ready? One, two, three.'

Teddy won. Lost. Whatever. And tried to look suitably disappointed. Of course I understood but carried on the dim Tim routine. 'I don't get it. How is taking Lucy home, losing?'

'Do I have to spell it out?' said Chris. 'It's losing, because... well, would you want something that's going begging. Literally, she's begging for it. Anyway, it'll be one of us next time, but she gives it out so readily, none of us likes sloppy seconds, so we play to lose. Get it?'

I laughed, my heart breaking at the cruelty of it. 'Yeah, I get it. Thanks for letting me know. Wouldn't want to take her home with me tonight knowing she puts it about so much.'

'Exactly,' said Chris. 'I don't normally turn down a shag, but sometimes, you know, you just have to. She's too... too obviously gagging for it. Too grateful to whichever man fucks her. When I had sex with her, she freaked me out. She was too clingy. Wanted a fag after and a hug. A hug – can you imagine? It was a bloody knee-trembler behind the pub, not a *relationship*, for God's sake.'

'She wanted a *hug*? How very dare she?' I said, and then, deciding that sounded a little too me-like, added, 'Next thing you know, she'll be wanting you to marry her.'

Danial butted in, having been listening. 'No chance of that. She's married to some sorry bastard. Don't envy him any.' He laughed and I was covered in beer spray and a bitter old-smelling puff of his nicotine breath. I wished I could use my wet wipes to cleanse myself of his bodily outpourings but didn't think it was something Tim would do.

Danial said, 'But then again, fuck knows what she might have, what you might pick up. I wouldn't touch her with a barge pole. Thank fuck I lost.' He laughed.

I joined in. 'What happens when you win?'

'Duh. What do you think? I get to fuck her again of course. I'm not stupid.'

Of course I'd known he'd touch her with a barge pole. Had indeed already done so in a past encounter. I should have known it was too good to be true: if there was a hole going begging, a female orifice – any would do – you could guarantee that there would always be a man willing to fill it. Whoever the owner of said hole. The revulsion I felt was visceral and their attitude to women, depraved.

But that aside, a jolly time was had by all.

I assumed Lucy would have been thrilled to see men playing a game in order, she'd think, to win her. Had she known the truth, I think even then that she'd have put her own twist on it, convinced herself that it was she who had the power. Would have misinterpreted it as evidence of how much she was desired.

I wondered how Teddy had treated her that night. The sad thing was, I'm sure Lucy would have been grateful however he'd treated her.

33

ME

'You understand what I'm saying, Lucy,' I said. 'That means whoever wins, is the loser. Winning is a bad thing in this context. They play to lose. That's how your male admirers played the game. They were playing to *not* take you home. And in case you're not understanding or are disbelieving, I reiterate, the aim of the game, for those young men, was to lose the opportunity of delighting in your company for the evening. And that's rather tragic, don't you agree?'

I sat and quietly watched Lucy crumple. She sort of collapsed in on herself, and with her head bowed, I could hear her whimper like a baby, grizzling for milk.

Throwing himself from his chair, Frank made a feeble attempt to hit me. Bearing in mind he was still about three feet from me when he fell to the floor, I wasn't overly concerned for my safety. I told him to sit back down.

'You bastard,' said Becky. 'That was completely uncalled for. Why did you tell her that? What was the point? What did you get from it?'

Shaking my head, I said, 'Not a lot, to be honest. I'm not an unkind man, and I genuinely try not to be cruel for the sheer spite of it. I didn't know how else to tell her the truth. She had to be told.'

'And why precisely is that, John?'

'Because secrets are intertwined and inextricably linked with lies. Truths and untruths. Get them confused, and life runs away with itself. One has to be aware of one's transgressions, otherwise one is bound to repeat them. And I can't allow badness to be repeated ad infinitum. I just can't. It's not right. People have to take responsibility for their actions. You must see that, Becky. Surely?'

Lucy jutted her face up and at me, bringing me back to her. 'You're lying. You must be. I know you're lying, you shit. Men sleep with me because they want to. Because I'm beautiful. Right, Frank?'

I thought it unkind to ask Frank if she was beautiful. Under the circumstances. But, true to form, he came to her aid, her knight in shining armour. Although, the weight of his much-needed armour was too heavy for him to endure; his shoulders bowed with the wearing. 'Of course you're beautiful, Luce.'

'Nothing more to say on the subject, Frank? You're not angry, perhaps more than a little peeved at Lucy's indiscretions?'

'Lucy is my wife. She's got her problems. And no, I'm not condoning what she's done to me, her infidelities, but I understand her. I want her to stop, and she will.' He turned to her. 'Won't you?' She nodded like a reprimanded tot, and Frank said, 'But she lacks confidence, despite the... despite how it looks. The sex with other men – it's a mistake. Obviously. But she thinks it will make her feel more desired, right, Lucy? That's why you do it, isn't it? It's just a way of making yourself feel better.' Back to me, all pleading and bleeding heart. 'She doesn't have a lot of self-esteem, no self-worth. I've told her again and again, she should be proud of herself. I love her.' He turned to

Lucy. 'You know how much I love you, don't you? I'd do anything for you.'

I said, 'Perhaps, Frank, therein, lies the problem. I rather think that deep down, you truly believe that you're punching above your weight. You can't believe your luck. Think you've got the golden girl, won first prize. But the fact of the matter is that you're both grubby little parasites, feeding off each other. You are truly made for one another. In my head, I see you both as a culinary metaphor. Picture a nice, lightly warmed crusty baguette, just out of the oven, with a melting knob of natural full-fat butter, oozing and dripping from it.

'Now imagine the opposite. Cheap sliced white bread. With margarine.

'You two are the cheap version of bread and butter. It's as simple as that. You've sullied and irreparably stained your union just by the very act of being yourselves, and you'll each end up destroying the other.

'Both of you are two sorry and pitiful young children who are frightened of the world. And having sex with random men is your way of taking control of your life. Am I right, Lucy, or am I not?'

She was past the mortification of my revelation, and intent only on disproving my words. 'I never saw you in the pub. Bet you've just heard some prick making up stories about me. Lots of people are jealous of me, you know.'

'I was there. I even played a round of rock, paper, scissors. With monobrow Dave, Danial, Teddy, Chris et al. You saw me. You just didn't *see* me. Looked right through me, but please don't feel bad on my account for that oversight. It's perfectly okay. I don't mind. Everyone does it. And it's helpful in my line of work, so believe me, I'm more than happy to play the invisible man. But I *am* speaking the truth. And I take absolutely no pleasure in doing so.

'I'm often embarrassed to be a member of the male species; a disgusting and revolting breed. And never more embarrassed than I am right now. The boys' behaviour was unforgivable. And unfortunately, I think you're right, Lucy. Ninety-nine per cent of the time, men will take sex if it's offered. And worse, even when it isn't.'

Becky said, 'Lucy, you stupid, stupid girl, why would you do that to yourself? You'll only feel worse in the long run, and these men sound like complete users. Not worth your time. Stop torturing yourself. You're better than that. Better than those men. I know I haven't exactly been a shining role model for you, but don't rely on anyone to make you feel good. Just believe that you *are* good.'

'Leave her alone,' said Frank. 'She'll stop. I'll help her. She just needs help. That's why I'm here.'

'Frank, you're the biggest drip I've ever had the misfortune to meet,' I said. 'We all know you're here, tied to Lucy by your heartstrings, but I want to know *why*, Lucy. Why degrade yourself like that?'

She shrugged, less embarrassed now that the knowledge of her sexual exploits was out there and being verbally dissected. I rather think she liked the attention. 'A girl's got to do what she has to in this world. I like being noticed. Simple.'

'There must be simpler ways. Less humiliating,' Becky said.

'It's because of Roger, isn't it?' I said.

Knowing that mention of her father would get the ball rolling, find the origin of the badness, the source of her pain, and ultimately get the truth out of her, I had mentioned Roger purely and solely to upset her. People speak when they're upset – catch them off guard, and they'll start talking. There was most definitely an as-yet unspoken and unadmitted secret about Lucy that I was missing. And I was curious to discover what it was.

'Dad's got nothing to do with it? Why would he?'

'I'd put money on it that he treated you like you were cheap white sliced bread, Lucy. Told you you were nothing but a tart. A slag. And those are his words, I suspect. They are certainly not mine.'

'He never said that. He didn't.'

Then Lucy burst into tears. Frank sat there, bent forward with his hands hanging over his overly large and knobbly knees – which looked bigger than his thighs in his ludicrously skin-tight jeans. Becky also craned forward, looking all extra Mummy-like.

I spoke softly. 'If there really is nothing that your father did or said to you, nothing that had any bearing on your life, then it's rather sad that your only secret is a complete non-starter; everyone apparently already knew of it or had guessed it. It turns out that your deviant sexual behaviour is very run-of-the-mill. Out of all the family, you are the only one with nothing to say, nothing to reveal other than a very tame and unoriginal story that's repeated by a million girls a million times over, every single minute of the day. All around the world. That's a very sobering and pathetic legacy, don't you think, Lucy? Is that how you want to be remembered? I don't think so.

'So that being the case, the only thing of any interest about you, is that you had a psychopath for a father. Anything unique and worthy about you, is because of him. How dull. Your secret is that you have no secret. You're nothing special.'

The glare Lucy gave me would have frightened most. She laughed. 'You don't even know what you're talking about, John. You know nothing. I do have a secret. I *am* special. You don't know my secret, so what would you know, you idiot?'

She had resorted to talking like a child having a tantrum. If she could have stamped her feet, she would have. Far too easy for me to manipulate her. Easy prey. I wasn't proud, but it had to be done. I carried on goading her. 'I don't believe you, Lucy.

As I say, you're nothing more than a Daddy's girl. A very bad Daddy's girl. What would he have thought of your antics, Lucy? What would your darling daddy have to say? I don't believe you even have a secret. You're lying.'

Shouting now, she said, 'I do have a secret. I do.'

'Prove it then.'

So she did.

34

LUCY

A s much as Lucy craved attention, she'd be the first to admit that *this* sort of attention wasn't quite what she had in mind. It was way, *way* too personal. But Mum had done it. So, she would. Solidarity and all that. She smiled at her mother, who smiled back encouragingly.

Mum looks frightened, wondering what my secret is. She should be worried. I don't want to hurt her.

'Right,' Lucy said, and then giggled self-consciously. Sweeping her hair from her face, she tried again. 'Here we go then. I was never close to Dad. Or Mum, come to that.' She stopped talking. Bit down on her lip. 'Sorry, Mum, but I didn't know what Dad had done to you, so sorry, but you have to admit, we were never cutesy close, mummy and daughter close, were we?'

Lucy watched with sadness as her mother gently shook her head. 'No, we weren't and I'm so sorry, Lucy. I did the best I could. But you're right: we were never *close*, close. I didn't show my love for you enough. But it was there. And that *is* my fault.'

Lucy flapped her hands at her mother, dismissing her apology. 'Don't be stupid, Mum. I'm not blaming you. I'm just trying to be honest. I definitely was *not* close to Dad. But you weren't *that* bad, Mum. Not really. I was probably being overly sensitive. Or being a bit harsh. It was just that you always seemed a bit distracted. You were there, but not really, if you see what I mean.

'You answered if I spoke to you, but you very rarely opened up any conversations for the sheer hell of it. Just for the fun of it. You were always too busy gazing out of the window or looking worried while doing nothing in particular. You didn't even say simple things, like "How are you? How you feeling? How's school? Are you pregnant?" No normal enquiries as to my health or welfare. Occasionally, we'd share a joke about something though. I do remember that. And we'd laugh. We'd laugh together and that was fun.'

God, her mother looked so grateful for that: Lucy pitied her. And hated herself. Felt wrong for being so truthful. But she couldn't tone down her story. It was impossible. Her mother hadn't sweetened up her story, so Lucy felt it fair enough that she kept up that same level of truth. As hard as it seemed. 'And we never really, *really* laughed. Not like fall-down hysterical giggles. Shame, really. Or maybe I expected too much. I don't know.

'Don't get me wrong. You were never cruel or anything. In fact, you were gentle and kind when I was like very little. Like when I was five or six-ish. I have strong and clear memories of you and me, playing in the park. The sun shone and we'd be together. I think it usually felt better when we weren't cooped up in the house. When we were outside, we were free and happy.

'I have fond memories of those times. It was just once I started to become a real child, older, with a real personality, that I became more demanding in my wishes, more vocal. Found it easier to ask for what I wanted. And then it seemed to me that you found it easier to not hear me. To not engage. Too wrapped up in your own world, I thought.'

'God, Lucy, I'm so sorry.'

Lucy watched as her mother wiped angrily at a tear, throwing it from her face.

'*Sorry*. What a stupid word that is. It doesn't even begin to explain how I feel, how I failed you. But what else can I say, other than sorry? Christ. Damn your father. And damn me, for not taking you and running away. I should have done better. It's my fault as well as your father's.'

'No. No, it definitely isn't, Mum. Maybe I asked for too much. Or maybe I was too difficult. Because, suddenly, I was older, because I could speak properly, I wanted things. So I asked for them. And that's when I lost you. I have no idea why – that's just how it felt. Perhaps I was wrong, but I constantly felt *in the way*. In *your* way. I sound like a bitch but I'm trying to be honest, Mum.'

'You're not a bitch, Lucy. Never that. Stop worrying about me and tell your story. I won't interrupt again. Selfish of me. Sorry. Dear God. There's that bloody *sorry* word again.'

Lucy and her mother exchanged a smile. Lucy realised then how much her mother had always loved her. And ditto, back at her. And Lucy felt the need to carry on. Be brutal. Tell it as it was. She slapped her hands down loudly onto her knees. 'Right, well, like I said, I felt in the way, although you never did anything to be in the way *of*. It wasn't like I was interrupting your exciting life because you didn't have one, as far as I could see anyway.

'It was like you were there, I was there, we were both there, except we weren't there together. We were sort of separate. I know that sounds really complicated but *I* know what I mean.'

Becky smiled an horrific smile. 'I know exactly what you mean as well. I'm sorry.'

'Stop apologising. *God*. You were *always* kind, don't get me wrong. Just in a sort of far-away type of way. I know you meant well, but you weren't like all my friends' mothers. Didn't bake cakes and organise picnics and jolly jaunts to the seaside. You were bloody hard work. But we were used to each other, were happily together in our very unconnected way. I don't think you were a great one for showing emotion. But you were all I knew, and for that reason, I did love you. I just didn't really know you that well. *Of course* I loved you.

'Dad, on the other hand, was aloof. Cold and totally separate from both you and me. He chose to be isolated from both of us. He ruled from afar. There wasn't even a hint of being together with him – not in the slightest. At least you and me were kind of a pair: an unmatched pair, but still a double act of sorts.

'If Dad was in the same room, he always ignored me. Made a point of doing so. Deliberately quiet. Then, when he felt like it, he instructed me to do things, gave me orders, made sure that I'd completed them in a satisfactory way. He called them "Roger's Rules", and I followed them.'

John said, 'And that, Lucy, was your first mistake. Never follow the rules of a madman.'

Lucy looked at John and his bland expression. Couldn't think of anything to say. Carried on speaking to her mother – the only one she cared about. When it came right down to it, there was only her and her mother. Frank and John had ceased to exist – at least for the telling of her story. Perhaps forever.

She said, 'But before I started being bad, I want to make it clear that there was never, and I mean *never*, any physical contact from Dad: no hugs, no holding hands, not even a goodnight peck on the cheek when I was small. Even you, Mum, could stretch to a hug at bedtime, a kiss goodnight, a cuddle to take away any tears. Dad couldn't or wouldn't. And definitely didn't.'

'God, forgive me, Lucy. I never realised how inept I was as a mother.'

'Mum, for God's sake, get over yourself.' Lucy smiled. 'You weren't inept. Neither of us was.'

Frank chipped in. 'No, just your bloody father. He was the inept one.'

Lucy gave her husband a cursory glance, thinking, knowing, perhaps for the very first time, that he was a complete fool. Saying only what he thought Lucy wanted to hear. Wanting her to love him for it. *Tosser.* He didn't understand the enormity of her father's sins, the crap she'd had to put up with, the abuse her mother had endured. Frank didn't get it at all.

Lucy felt her eyes glaze over as she blurred him out of her vision. 'Needless to say, as I grew both in age and size, I grew further away from my father. Psychologically. Made my hurried and long-awaited mental escape in a great, rushed, bloody sprint. So fast that it felt like I was flying. Couldn't get away fast enough. I'd given up the idea of trying to please him because it was an impossible task. And I didn't care anyway. Didn't care what the old fart thought. I'm lying. Of course I cared. I knew, deep down, that you loved me, Mum. Deep down I knew. You were strangely quiet and unemotional about it, but at least I *knew* you loved me. It just wasn't ever said a lot.'

Lucy stopped. Her mother had slumped in her seat. Hunched and bunched in sorrow. Lucy wanted to touch her, to hug her, to squeeze her, but she was too far away. 'It's all right, Mum. Really. Get a grip.'

She laughed and was relieved when her mother rolled her eyes. 'Right, grip got. Sorry.'

'Right, good. That was you. But Dad. Well, Dad was a different creature altogether. When I was teeny, I was a bit scared of him. Not scared that he'd hit me or anything like that. Scared because I got nothing back. Physical or emotional. He made me feel like a dirty great void. And a useless void at that.

'When adolescence took hold: the *fantastic* teen years so I'd been told, that's when home life really went tits up. When I was about thirteen, like most girls that age, I started to hate both you and Dad. Loudly. I think it's a natural rite of passage. Like a law. Like you're not really a teenager if you don't seriously dislike your parents and try to piss them off at every opportunity. All teenagers go through that phase. It *means* you're a teenager. I started ignoring *him*, just to irritate him at first. Because I could.

'It didn't work. He didn't even notice. He was so used to ignoring me, me ignoring him was a complete and total waste of time. Catch twenty-two and all that.

'I wasn't clever at school: never in the brainy group. I couldn't catch a ball, nor did I see the point in even trying, so the sporty group was out of the question. I found myself pretty much group-less. And when you're thirteen, it doesn't get much worse than that. It felt like the end of the world.

'Then I hit fourteen. And boys came into the equation. Fags and music and alcohol became a thing to do. *The* thing to do. I suddenly felt like I'd arrived. Felt like I belonged in this strange new body which was growing around me. I had to grow *into* my ever-increasing bust – my heaving bosom was much sought after by the boys at school, and hugely envied by the girls. I liked the instant popularity my breasts gave me, the power, the attention. I capitalised on them. Showed them off at every possible occasion.

'I became leader of my very own "Big Tits" group. Only double Ds need apply. And I was definitely queen of *that* gang.'

Frank laughed. 'That's my babe. Good for you.'

Becky scowled. 'It's not funny, Frank. Not even vaguely amusing. Just how insensitive are you?'

Lucy let the silence sit, proud of her mother's protection. 'Mum's right, Frank. You're not getting this. At all. But anyway, *Mum...*' She stressed the word, wanting to make it clear that she wasn't including Frank nor John in her words: 'I started wearing less on the top in order to show off my tits even more, to bring them to the fore every place I went. Shoved them into the face of every male person I met. Made damn sure that nobody could miss them. I loved them. I thought they were great. They were my saviour.

'And yes, I'm well aware that that makes me sound incredibly stupid. Shallow and uninteresting. Uninterested. But that's not true. There's nothing wrong with loving your assets. It would be a sin not to, and I didn't have many other assets to turn to.'

'Don't be stupid,' Frank said. 'You've got loads of assets. Millions. You just need to recognise them and stop putting yourself down.'

John made a show of crossing his legs. 'Shut up, Frank. Just shut up. You're offering nothing to this conversation. It's like having a needy child who wants attention and says all the wrong things. You're embarrassing yourself and me and everyone else in this room. Shut up.'

Lucy felt a strange, fleeting and inappropriate kinship with John. John was right. Frank needed to shut up. Until now, she really hadn't recognised how stupendously stupid Frank was. Every time he opened his mouth, complete rubbish came out, as if he wasn't used to being in adult company. Deleting him from her field of vision by simply turning completely towards her mother, Lucy said, 'Naturally I got invited to all the parties, the sleepovers, and just general stuff which meant plenty of excuses to escape my parents and the house. Mum was quite nice about it, as long as she knew who I was with, where I was going, how I was getting home, et cetera, et cetera.

'Dad, no surprises, wasn't as lenient. But as he was rarely home before half past seven, I just had to make sure that I was gone before he got home. You helped, Mum, on that score. Always. You had my back.'

Now Lucy was getting to the heart of her story, it was as if her body was shrinking, getting lighter, her voice quieter. Her facial expression more forced. She could feel herself getting less.

'The first time it happened, you know... the bad stuff, was when I was fourteen and all excited at going out. A young bloke I fancied, Pete, had asked me to go to the cinema with him – all perfectly innocent. More innocent than the shit I usually got involved with. That night, it felt like Mickey Mouse time to me doing such a normal, boy/girl date type of thing. No drugs or alcohol. Sex was a possibility. Sex was always a possibility. Since I'd learnt how to do it. On my thirteenth birthday. Needless to say, I was a natural at it.

'So, you can picture the scene. It was about seven o'clock, and Pete's father was picking me up in their family car and driving us to the cinema. Hence the tick of approval from Mum: an adult chaperone on wheels to and from the venue. I'd got ready, Mum had tut-tutted like a real mother would, at my choice of clothing. Or lack of. I had chosen the minimal look, for maximum affect. Pete's father hadn't seemed that impressed, but I couldn't help but notice Pete's expression as he'd swiftly cast his eyes over my heaving chest.

'His face went very pink. I made sure I swayed my breasts against him, by mistake on purpose, as I got in next to him, pretending to stumble. I stumbled my breasts right into his face as his father was busy waving a polite "goodbye" to my mother. Pete's eyes had gone stupidly cartoonish, and as I settled down beside him, I could see his erection already poking hard inside his trousers.

'You can imagine how the night went. Quick fumble in the

back seat of the cinema. Less than a fumble, more of a grope. A very quick one. But not actual sex. I think Pete got overexcited too quickly, so it never got that far. But it didn't matter. The film was quite good, so we watched that instead and held hands.

'The shit hit the fan when I got home. Pete's father dutifully dropped me off outside the house and waited to see that I got inside safely. I waved at him and glancing up, saw the silhouette of my father, outlined against his study window. I sighed theatrically, expecting a telling-off, pushed open the front door and entered the house. Just for a moment, pre the moment when I'd have to face Dad, I leant my back against the front door and smiled to myself. I'd had a good time. It had been refreshing doing something that would have been deemed acceptable by adults. I'd been age appropriate. No sex, just a grope. It had been sweet. It was nice to do something that respectable fourteen-year-old girls do, instead of taking it that one step too far, as was my usual habit.

'Dad came out of his study and shouted from upstairs. "Lucy. Up here. Now." His voice was tight with fury. Tighter than normal. I couldn't imagine what the great fuss was about, what rule I might have broken, what punishment might be doshed out by dear old Dad. I slipped a piece of chewing gum from my pocket and put it in my mouth. Started chewing. With attitude.

'Two flights up and I came face to face with him. He stood, like he'd been practising the stance of stern-father-about-to-reprimand-child: his hands were on his hips and he was actually wagging his head in apparent disbelief as he looked at me. I made a point, maybe too big a point, of mimicking his gaze, and giving myself the once-over, exaggerating the head movement as I body scanned myself with my eyes from top to toe. Because I knew how to annoy him and I was angry. I'd had a really nice evening, and *nice* wasn't even a word I would ever have used normally. Not in front of my friends. *Nice* was for geeks.

'And I knew that Dad was going to spoil it all now. Take all that niceness away. "Just what the hell do you think you're doing?" he said. "Nothing, Dad. I've just been to the cinema with a friend and now I'm going to bed."

'Of course I knew it wasn't going to be that easy. As I turned, hoping rather than actually believing that I could escape that easily, he stopped me with the words, "You are no better than a whore, do you know that? Are you aware of how you look? How you smell? Cheap. You look and smell cheap. Cover yourself up. I cannot believe that you are any child of mine. You resemble more a child of the night. An underage sex worker. Is that the look you were going for, or aren't you even trying? Perhaps it comes naturally, that cheapness? God, you're just like your mother."'

Lucy had to stop as she heard Becky's intake of breath, like she couldn't get enough oxygen. Lucy couldn't look at her. Thought she was betraying her mother by telling the story: highlighting Becky's betrayal. Not a betrayal at all, but simply a not-knowing. She really didn't blame her but knew she was sitting there and blaming herself. Lucy stared at her. 'Stop it, Mum. It was not your fault. You couldn't have known.'

'But I should have known. I should have.'

'No. Not,' Lucy said. 'Just let me tell it, Mum. Listen to what I'm saying. *It was all Dad.* All of it. When he spoke to me like that, I was shocked. I mean, really shocked. I was so unprepared for this barrage of insults, I was speechless, with a dawning horror that anything I said to him would be laughed at. For the first time in a long time, I felt my age. Out of my depth with such adult hatred being thrown at me.

'It felt like forever, but it could only have been seconds before the telltale hot flush of a deep red blush started at my neck and covered my face with shame. At least my voice returned. "What are you going on about, Dad? It's a top with shoulder straps. It's meant to look like this. And jeans. I'm wearing jeans."

'Maybe I'm a bit slow on the uptake, but I didn't think I looked cheap. Far from it. But as I glanced at Dad, I saw that his face was almost as red as mine. Except his was red with anger, as opposed to my red of shock. Humiliation had kicked in and settled in my head, refusing to leave.

"'I have no difficulty in seeing your mother in you," he said. "Cover yourself up. Now. Why is your body even on display like that?" He took off his jacket and threw it at me. I let it fall to the ground in a heap. "Cover yourself up, I said. You might as well be naked, you little tart. I'm amazed that you don't advertise in phone booths, or in the windows of newsagents, selling your wares. *Child prostitute for sale – Free sex if you say you love me.* Do you have a professional name like, Scarlet, or Honey, or fucking Pussy Galore? Or do you simply go by your birth name: *Lucy Twist – Cheap Child Whore.* Is *that* how you operate, Lucy? Is it?"'

'I would have killed your father if I'd been there,' said Frank.

'No. No, you wouldn't, Frank,' John said. 'You haven't got it in you. You have nothing worthy in you, so stop pretending you're someone you're not, and be quiet. I'm not telling you again.'

Mum said nothing.

Sighing, hating herself for having to carry on, Lucy said, 'After he said that, my cheeks flamed with shame. And, thankfully, the beginnings of anger. Just the embers: not any real fire yet. It was like I was reacting in slow motion. From having a nice evening five minutes earlier, my life had descended into a mortifying horror show. With me the more-than-reluctant star attraction. I stood there, head bowed, and I let the silence grow.

Heard my father make a tutting sound, like I was seriously eating up his time.

'And then, like a switch had been flipped, I was suddenly enraged. How dare Dad talk to me like that? How fucking *dare* he? I wasn't cheap, I wasn't a tart or a prostitute. I was just me. And I thought that was fine.

'I'd never been so angry. I swear to God, if I'd had a meat cleaver to hand, I could easily have plunged it into his stupid face, splitting his skull in two. I let myself enjoy that image for a moment.

'Instead of shouting at him, I turned, and without speaking, I left him standing outside his study and went to my room. Left his stupid jacket on the floor. My fists were clenched so hard that my nails dug into the palms of my hands. My teeth were clamped so tightly together, my jaw ached. My stomach cramped and I thought I might vomit and spew anger all over the cream carpet that was Daddy's pride and joy. Stiff with rage, rigid with a barely controlled desire to hit my father until he dropped to the floor, I silently went to the top floor and opened the door to my bedroom. I didn't slam the door, but very, very quietly closed it, making no sound at all.

'If I started making a noise, I thought I might start screaming and never stop.'

35

LUCY

Lucy took the time to look at John, Frank and her mother. John looked fascinated, bent forwards, as if frightened he'd miss something, Frank looked... well, he just looked like Frank with his blank face on. He was hiding his anger well. Lucy knew he'd be unhappy that she was sharing her secret with anyone else. Obviously he knew her secret. And thought he owned it. He was wrong. She'd never realised until now just quite how selfish he was.

And her mother. God, she looked sad. Lucy wanted to apologise to her, for what she was about to say, but couldn't see the point because she had no choice but to carry on. Her mother would understand that. Lucy said, 'Anyway, my bedroom's at the top of the house, on the third floor, and has its own en suite bathroom. And there I stood, in front of the big mirror above the basin. I wasn't in a hurry. Wasn't sure what I was going to do. Wasn't one hundred per cent sure if I was going to do anything at all. But of course, some part of me already knew that I was definitely going to do *some*thing. Just wasn't sure what exactly.

'The more I took in my reflection, the younger I looked. And the stupider I looked. My reflection showed me, in a brutally honest way, because that's what mirrors do – they reflect the truth – it showed me the real me. It was a picture of a child. A fourteen-year-old girl. Angry and vulnerable. With outrageously large tits. Disproportionately large. Verging on ridiculous. Almost freak-show material. My once wonderful breasts were now mirrored back at me, and they mocked me. For the first time since I'd got them, since they'd grown on me uninvited, they suddenly *did* look cheap.

'I watched, strangely outside myself, as tears started falling from my eyes. I just looked pathetic and even younger. And still cheap.

'Pressing my nose against the glass, I stared into my eyes. Checking that my life, my inner person, was reflected back at me and not missing. I looked pretty empty to me. I stood back and continued to survey my body. I'd always thought I had a great figure: slim but curvy, shapely legs, good hair. And a huge bosom.'

Predictably, Frank said, 'But you *have* got a great figure. Fan-bloody-tastic. You're–'

'Shut up, Frank. I don't need you now, telling me how much you love me. I don't *want* to hear it.'

She didn't bother looking at him, already knowing how he'd look: all crestfallen and withdrawn. Ignoring him, she said, 'Standing there in front of the mirror, I couldn't understand how a part of my body which had previously brought me such happiness and reward, could so unexpectedly and quickly take on such a different meaning. Were they grotesque, as my father had hinted at? Should they be covered up as he'd suggested, hidden away, and kept under lock and key? Was that where they belonged?

'Were they the reason that I was a cheap tart? Or was it something else entirely, buried inside me, that gave off whore-ish vibes?'

Mum said, 'Oh, Lucy.' Her voice sounded like it was breaking, the two words seriously and frighteningly full of total, raw grief. Perhaps she anticipated what was coming.

Lucy mouthed *sorry* at her and gave a little shrug. Tried out a smile but instead felt her chin wobble. Clamping her teeth together she sat for a minute. Quiet. Trying to get her shit together. Finally, she continued.

'Whether my bust made me cheap or not, I realised that the fury that filled me, was that I had been shattered so easily by Dad. How could he be so cruel? It wasn't the shock of the century – I'd always known he was a cold and cruel father, but this was too much. Who speaks to their daughter like that? I was only fourteen. Too young to process what he'd actually said and more importantly, too inexperienced to comprehend the enormity of his words. But I got enough of the meaning, believe me.

'And still I was left with the anger. I didn't know what to do with it. It felt like a live thing, moving and shifting around inside me. It wanted release. Without thinking, I punched the mirror hard. Glanced at my knuckles: grazed and cut, they now showed a glistening layer beneath my outer fleshy covering, and I could see naked red, raw, virgin skin beneath. All shiny and new. Body tissue nobody had ever seen before. A teeny blob of blood bubbled up. I wiped it on my jeans.'

Lucy involuntarily shuddered as she said the words; hearing, really *hearing* for the first time, the enormity of them. The sadness of them. *God, I'm a complete nutjob*, she thought. Suddenly desperate to get all the words out of her, she said, 'Sitting on the lavatory, I patiently waited for the rage to leave me. Leave me well alone. But it wouldn't go away. It just stayed there, and I hadn't even invited it. It had just turned up and I didn't know how to handle it. I bent forward and put my head on my knees, opened up my mouth and silently shouted into my knees. My fists joined in, pounding on my thighs. I spent ten minutes doing that.

'And yet, I still felt incomplete. Like I still had something to do. Something I must do to rid myself of the hatred that sat like a heavy block inside, weighing me down, making my breath come in short little gaspy, panicky hiccups.

'Back in front of the basin again, I scanned the area. Aimlessly picked up my toothbrush. No, not sharp enough. I picked up my red flannel. Again, no. What was I going to do, smother myself to death to stop the internal screaming, the inner shouting of the same words: over and over again: *I'm not good enough?*

'And then I saw it. I'd never used my razor – I'd bought it for myself for if and when I decided to start shaving my legs or under my arms. Neatly, with hands that didn't tremble now that they had found a real purpose, I slid out the razor blade. Held it flat against my fingers, enjoying the cool of the metal against the hot of my hands.'

Lucy screeched to a halting stop as she saw her mother cover her face with her hands.

'Please, Lucy. Don't tell me. I can't bear it.'

Lucy waited while her mother stayed, gently rocking in her chair and then watched as she saw her take a deep breath, and lowering her hands, her mother said, 'I'm so sorry, Lucy. Really, please forgive me. I had no right to say that. Carry on. I want to hear. I *need* to hear this. And remember, I love you so much it hurts.'

'Thanks, Mum.'

Lucy waited, sort of out of respect for her mother, and then said, 'Picking the razor blade up between my thumb and first finger, I held it. Clocked my movement in the reflection of me. That's how I felt anyway. A reflection of myself – not the real me. But just that taking of the razor into my hands, that simple action, had calmed me. I knew straight away that this sharp rectangle of metal would make it all go away. For the first time since leaning my back on the front door, when I'd still felt *nice*, I smiled again. But this time I knew the smile wasn't a nice one. It felt demonic. Possessed. Grinning, I sat back down on the loo seat and pulled off my jeans. Kept my knickers on though. I waited for a bit, unsure how to proceed.

'The first cut was a shock. It hurt. But not in a bad way. Just in a gentle parting of the flesh type of way: more fascinating than painful. I'd picked the top of my thighs as the starting point, and at first, the slashes were gentle, shallow. Not deep. Not *too* damaging.

'And then I really got into it. Was intrigued by the blood as it ran in scarlet streams down the inside of my legs. I opened my legs further, watching sort of hypnotically, as the blood dripped down and plopped into the lavatory. Each drop hit the water and then softened and blossomed into a bigger pinker non-shape. It morphed with the water and turned it a soft crimson colour.

'Some of the blood fell onto the inner side of the bowl, taking a detour before making a splash. It reminded me of the streaks of mascara that had run down my mate's face when she'd cried about something. Except these lines were a perfect and beautiful red.

'I didn't feel pain. My legs felt nicely warm – there's that word again: nice – and my body, my mind, relaxed as I sat there slicing away at the very meat of me.

'I stopped as suddenly as I'd started. Couldn't believe how I felt. All that rage seemed to have slipped out of me, with the blood. All my badness had been released. I was pure again and strangely exhilarated. In control.

'My head felt clearer and cleaning myself up, I realised I'd found something, something very, very secret, that I could do which made me feel better. It got rid of Dad's words, it made my tits feel good again. Made *me* feel good again.

'And I knew right then that I'd do it whenever I was filled with bad thoughts. And I'd never tell anyone. Not a soul. It was my very own secret and it belonged only to me.'

Lucy stopped and was surprised to find the palm of one hand covering the other, which lay on her inner thigh. Remembering where she'd cut. Absorbed by the reliving of that first-time cutting. She was aware that her voice had lowered in volume and she wondered if her last words, her description within which she'd become lost, had all come out in a whisper.

She smiled to show that she'd finished.

36

BECKY

No one spoke. Lucy's words landed into an explosion of silence. Guilt washed over Becky. Not a cleansing washing, but a washing sensation that made her feel dirty. Filthy. She was deeply and personally shamed by Lucy's secret and wished, in an internal admission to herself only, that she hadn't heard it. She'd lied. She hadn't needed to hear it. Becky licked her lips.

'Why didn't you tell me, Lucy? I never knew Roger treated you like that. Spoke to you like that. If I'd known... if I'd known, I really think I might have killed him. There and then. How can you ever forgive me?'

Becky watched her daughter's body slump into the armchair, as she brought her wrists together and attempted to cover her breasts. The cause, as Lucy seemed to think, of all her problems. 'It's not your fault,' Becky said. 'It's Roger's fault. You do know that, don't you? You've nothing to be ashamed about. Nothing at all. You're a beautiful girl. You're my beautiful girl.'

Lucy's body sagged and caved in on itself even further, trying to make herself invisible. Her magnificent bosom deflated and slumped in sympathy with Lucy's embarrassment.

Frank said, 'You shouldn't have told, Luce. That was your secret. Our secret. Now you've told them all.'

John made a big show of sighing and said to Frank, 'Why do you always make everything that is Lucy, everything that she has, about you? What's wrong, don't you feel special now? Now that you're no longer the sole keeper of her secret? Is that it?'

Becky watched Frank colour, heard him mumble something unintelligible, and then he rubbed his ankles. She joined John in sighing.

Everyone was waiting for Lucy to speak. Becky wanted to go and hold her hand, to give her comfort, but suspected she might be rebuffed. Wasn't sure how her daughter was, after her secret-telling.

'Did Dad *ever* love me?' she asked.

God, how to answer that one? Becky decided on the truth. After everything that had happened, if she sugar-coated her answer, Lucy would know she was lying. After what Roger had said to Lucy when she was fourteen, when she was *a child*, she'd know if Becky lied now, so she said, 'I don't honestly think Roger loved any of us. I don't think he was capable of loving anyone. Other than himself.'

'Was he pleased when you got pregnant? Before you gave birth to me, I mean. Before I proved to be such a disappointment?'

Becky shook her head violently. 'No, no. That wasn't how it was at all. You weren't a disappointment. Never. Certainly not to me. To me you were my saviour and I apologise now if I never made that clear. I loved you so very much.

'But Roger was angry when I told him I was pregnant. Told me in the hospital when I offered you up to him to hold, all wrapped up like a knitted pupa, that you were "not his domain". You were "my job". I was the mother and that was the job of a mother. To bring up baby. He never bothered defining his role.

One day you were there, all pink and scrunched up and so sweet I wanted to eat you, and Roger just accepted your presence in the house. Much like he'd accept a new fridge. Like any new item, one day you weren't there, and the next, you were. In his eyes, you were something that took up space.

'He never knew how to treat a baby, how to love a baby, any baby, not just you. I think he had something missing in his makeup. He viewed you as property: much the same way as he viewed me. He was a despicable man and I shall never forgive him for what he did to you.'

Lucy had paled and sat, defeated and upset. 'God. He really was a prize shit, wasn't he?'

Becky made herself smile although she felt more like expressing herself using violence. Preferably directed at John. He'd started this stupid secret-telling, and she'd kill him for that. If it turned out to be the last thing she did, then that was fine. It would be worth it. She'd kill him.

Frank said, 'You've only ever told me about that first time, when your father said that you were cheap. But I never knew the details. Awful.' He shook his head slowly, as if he couldn't understand Roger's behaviour.

At least he'd got that right, Becky thought.

Frank continued, 'So did it carry on? I've never asked because I know you don't like talking about it. But did your father talk to you like that again?'

Lucy's eyes travelled up and over him, full of disdain. Her face dripped with it. 'What do you think, Frank? That it was a one-off thing? He bloody *frequently* humiliated me, okay? Whenever he was bored. The more frequent the better for him. As it turns out, when he wasn't crushing me, he was playing weird and nasty mind-fuck games with Mum. It's apparently what he did – he humiliated women. For sport. Fucking shit.'

Frank, apparently realising that his question had been a

tactless one, averted his gaze from Lucy, and then eventually closed his eyes. Refusing to engage at all with anyone anymore.

John coughed into his closed fist and automatically took out a wet wipe. Becky gritted her teeth at his hysterical fear of germs. Or whatever ailed him. He was seriously annoying her, and he was as emotionally unattached to real life as Roger had been. John said, 'Tell me, Lucy, and I don't ask this to embarrass you, but your body, which by the way *is* beautiful, despite what your father tried to make you believe, but I want to know, where, if you've carried on over the years cutting yourself, *where* are the scars?'

Lucy looked flattered, thought Becky. Flattered that a maniac had complimented her. Told her that she had a beautiful body. That was so weak and self-destructive, that it reminded Becky of herself. And to add insult to injury, John had lied to her. Because Becky didn't think for one moment that John thought Lucy had a beautiful body. He didn't think like that, and she seriously doubted that he even looked at women as women, as things of beauty. Nor as sexual entities. Not even as people at all. John viewed all of mankind as beasts. Didn't realise that they were all sentient beings, with emotions. Of which, he was evidently severely lacking.

Lucy answered him. 'I've always cut in secret places on my body, on parts that won't be visible to anyone else. It's why I don't wear bikinis though. Ran out of space. Most of the cuts and scars are around my inner thighs, around my panty line, under my bra line, places that even men that I have sex with don't notice. Mind you, that's because they're not making love to me, are they? It's just a quickie fuck, so no caressing of my body comes into it. Only Frank knows where my scars are.'

'Do you still cut yourself?' Becky asked, although she already knew the answer. If she still had random sex with virtual strangers, it was almost a given that she still despised herself enough to continue to cut.

'Yeah. You know, if I'm upset. Feeling crap. You know. When I feel bad about myself.'

'Normally after you've been with one of your men, you cut,' said Frank. 'I can smell the men on you when you come in from the pub. Did you know that? I can smell them on you.'

His voice was raised and he was crying at the same time. Becky felt sorry for him. But more sorry for her daughter.

John said, 'Interesting though, isn't it? How everything always comes back to bad old Rog. What a corrupting influence he's been on you both. It's like the Roger effect: he left so many damaged aftershocks which rippled through his family, he warped you both with his unique brand of mindless psychopathy.'

'Like you?' Becky said.

'No, nothing like me. I'm all mind, and few, if any, feelings. Roger actively *enjoyed* hurting people. A sadist. I most certainly am not in that particular gang. He's better off dead. I, at least, am more than happy at his departure. I did you both a favour. I did women of the world a favour. I saved you both.'

Secretly, and guiltily, Becky agreed with him. Had now got over the shock of Roger's death and was actively pleased that he was dead. She certainly didn't plan on shedding any tears on Roger. Why waste them?

Ignoring John's comment, Lucy said, 'You'll all be happy to know that I'm back in love with my breasts now.'

She spoke brightly. Overly brightly. Brightly brittle, Becky thought. And she was clearly lying. Lucy was being so brave. Making such an effort. *Making an effort?* What a stupid thing to think; as if an old and unlikable relation had come to tea, and her daughter was making the effort to be polite. It was so much more than that. They were all making an effort. *Not to die.*

'Are you, Lucy?' said John. 'I don't think you're back in love with anything, but I would want to happily believe you if you say that it is true. But you must agree that your father, your mother's husband, has destroyed this family, has ruined you both. You and Becky *should* have been closer, ironically you should have been brought closer through your shared trauma of being connected to Roger. But both of you were incapable of reaching that state of bonding. *Because* of Roger. What a strange world it is.' John crossed and uncrossed his legs. 'But I think you'll both agree that this secret sharing session has now bonded you. Together you can unite, *because* of how Roger treated you. Because both of you have been completely honest, because of that, you are now closer than you've ever been. And that's a good thing.'

'You're mad,' said Frank. 'Why don't you just leave? Go. Go back to whatever place you came from. I don't want to talk to you. About anything. I have nothing to say. All you've done is upset Lucy, and that's enough.'

'And killed Roger. I did that as well,' John said.

Frank looked embarrassed that he needed reminding. Blushed again. Agitated, he looked to Becky and then to Lucy. Becky couldn't drum up a quick enough response for him, and Lucy simply didn't bother. His fear had intensified suddenly, Becky noticed.

He was very frightened. They were all frightened, but he more so. More than he had been all day. All evening. It was obvious why.

Frank was next.

What had Frank done?

What the hell had Frank done?

37

ME

I wasn't really being fair. I was asking a lot of the Twist family and their appendage, Frank. Forcing them to tell their secrets, and not really giving them any time, certainly not enough to digest the enormity of their personal stories. The impact on themselves and on each other, even I recognised, must be riven with a whole glut of useless but apparently strong emotion. And there I was, denying them hand-holding, weeping-on-shoulder, can-you-forgive-me time. We were fairly whipping through their lives. It really wasn't fair. Looking at my watch, I remarked, 'Twelve o'clock – dead. Feels like some sort of an omen, doesn't it?'

'Are you going to turn into a pumpkin and bugger off?' Lucy smiled broadly at me, and I reciprocated. She had brightened considerably after telling all and seemed almost euphoric now. Relaxed and accepting of whatever her fate might be. An enviable place to be. But ultimately a stupid place. For she thought herself safe.

Becky was quietly holding her own. She was busy thinking. Analysing the situation. Trying to think herself out of the trouble only she truly realised they were all in. But she wouldn't show fear. I knew, whether she cared to admit it or not, that fear would certainly be there, that it hadn't miraculously disappeared, but I knew that she wouldn't show it to me now. She'd made her decision to bury it. And that was that.

I wondered if I could be cruel enough to disinter that fear.

Maybe later. Maybe not.

Meantime, there was Frank to consider. He was unable to physically settle. His eyes had nowhere to rest, his limbs nowhere to relax, and his facial expression was a demented and frightening spectacle to behold. I wondered what he was so frightened of. Easy to find out. I asked him. 'So, Franky boy. How are you?'

'Fine. I'm fine.' His voice whispered out the words quickly, not sure if they were the right words or not. He was in full panic mode.

'Calm down. I'm not going to kill you.' I placed my hand on my chest. 'Honest, Injun.'

'I haven't got a secret. I swear to God I haven't. I've already admitted to knowing you, meeting you in the pub.' He turned to Becky. 'I just told him to burgle this house but there's nothing else. I promise you. I'm not hiding anything, John. I wish I was, just so I had something to tell you, to make you stop. But I don't. I haven't done anything. Nothing. I've done nothing at all.'

'Frank, *God*, just stop babbling, will you,' said Lucy. 'And what do you mean, you told John to *burgle* this house? What were you thinking? Are you completely mad?'

'I didn't mean it. I was joking. It was a joke. That's not why John's here, is it? He's not burgling the bloody house, is he? God. It was a joke, Rebecca. I didn't really tell John to rob you. He just took it that way. And I haven't got a secret. Why won't anyone believe me.'

'Stop talking, Frank,' I said, with as much kindness ladled into my voice as I could muster. Just to stop his infernal blubbering panic. 'And think. I want you to just sit there quietly and think.'

'What about?'

'You. Your life. Think about what you've done, what you've achieved. What you're proud of. Who loves you. Who you love. Anything. Tell me anything you like.'

His face was like an old-fashioned picture. If you appreciate still-life. It was as if my words hadn't sunk in, or that I had spoken in tongues. 'I don't understand,' he said. He was pitiful. His eyes beseeched mine, imploring, begging, pleading for enlightenment. I wasn't going to give him any help. Why should I?

I sat back and with interest, noted that the two women did the same. They unintentionally mirrored my actions. Perhaps I'd got them on side. Us against the useless Frank. I didn't really think so but it amused me. I waited. We all waited.

Finally, he got his breathing under control, decelerated his heartbeat. Inhaled through his mouth and out through his nose. He rubbed at his ankles and his fingers came away bloody. He looked to me. Perhaps he wanted a wet wipe. He'd carry on wanting.

Unable to handle the silence any longer, Frank said, 'Tell you about my life, you mean? That's all?'

'That'll do. For starters.'

He relaxed. Slightly. He thought this was going to be easier than he'd anticipated. He'd been frightened for nothing. Almost smiling he said, 'Well, that's quite a big question, isn't it?'

'It's as big or as little as you make it, Frank,' I said. God, it was like pulling teeth. Impacted ones.

'I don't really know where to start,' he said.

'Just start.' *Before we all die of boredom.*

'As you all know, I married Lucy a little while ago, so you could still call us "newly-weds" if you like.'

Dear God, I cannot bear this boy. 'No, I don't like, Frank. Not one little bit. You, with your formal introduction to your exceedingly dull life. We all know how in love with Lucy you are. How you allow her free rein to trample all over you. Which she does, with her great big boy-kicking boots on. And do you know why she does, Frank? Simply because you allow it. She wouldn't even take your surname when you married her. Kept her own name – Twist. You must have found that a bit insulting, surely?'

'No, I'm a modern man. It was fine by me. In fact I applauded her decision. It's old fashioned her taking my name. I don't own her. She's her own woman.'

'But I'm not sure she is *your* woman. Not entirely. It makes no odds for whatever Lucy does is fine by you. Tell me something that isn't fine by you.'

'How do you mean? I'm happy. I'm not complaining.'

'Maybe you should be complaining, Franky boy.'

'Stop calling me that. I'm not your boy. Why try to belittle and patronise everyone? It's unkind.'

'Would you really like to know what's unkind, *Franky boy*? Would you? I could tell you a tale that would make your hair curl. Do you want to hear it? Go, on, say "yes."'

His head shook, violently. 'No. Don't tell me anything. No. Whatever you say isn't worth hearing. You enjoy terrifying us all. Why? What's the point? Stop it. I'm not listening.' He cupped his chin with his handcuffed hands and managed to plug both his ears with the index finger of each hand. Like a three-year-old. I sighed at his petulance and carried on regardless.

'I'm not stopping. I'm just starting. And I'll tell you the point. I'll tell you a story which I think even you couldn't fail but see the importance of. Ready? Well, ready or not, I'm going to tell you.'

38

ME

I obviously knew all about Frank's parents. I'm nothing if not thorough. Mr and Mrs Bauld: pronounced 'Bold'. Sydney and Rita. Two fine and upstanding members of the community: he a general practitioner, and she a nurse. A marriage made with an automatic ease of access to bandages and antiseptic if and when required, while traversing their way through their sacred union.

And as they discovered many years ago, they'd needed all the dressings and gauze available to patch up the damage that had ripped through their coupling.

A sticking plaster hadn't really done the trick. But I'm sure they tried one anyway. In case miracles really did come true.

But I'm getting ahead of myself. Consider it a given that the couple have been comprehensively researched, and I know all.

Now I just had to meet them. Face to face.

Particularly Rita. The weak link in the pair.

I knew their routine. Everybody has one. People seem to enjoy repeating patterns: they think that it keeps them safe. They assume that knowledge and repetition and especially *familiarity* is key for their own protection. How wrong they are. Routine is the very opposite of that which they seek.

I was aware that Rita and Sydney met every Monday night for a 'special night'. More generally known as a piss-up, if I were to use the common vernacular. A night when they sat together, held hands and talked and drank too much. Rita always got there one hour and fifteen minutes early. To get as many drinks as she could down her neck before her husband with his messy curls arrived. I rather thought he knew of this little habit of hers, but for reasons which I couldn't care less about, decided to let her run with it.

Rita was already on her third martini – extra dry, straight up, with a twist – and seemed only slightly inebriated. I had forty-five minutes before Sydney turned up. Which would give me plenty of time to engage thoroughly with the middle-aged, and deeply sad looking woman as she sipped her drink. Pretending that she didn't want to knock it back in one.

Her face was still etched with pain that made her look prematurely older than her years. *Still.* Still the pain showed. The marionette lines that ran from her nostrils to the edges of her lips were deep grooves full-to-brimming with sorrow. The channels grooved out in her skin looked as if they operated her jaw, making her speak. They ran deep. Ingrained in her face: there for eternity.

Shame, because she was otherwise a rather attractive woman with dimples in her cheeks, neatly dressed, hair immaculate, and nails perfectly manicured.

I had yet to make initial contact. But I was confident. I was good at this sort of thing. Had been practising all my life for this very type of occasion. I had yet to fail.

Grasping my glass of white wine by the stem, I wandered past her table. A subtle pratfall was easy enough to pull off, and I stumbled convincingly, deliberately spilling the contents of my house wine over her table and knocking her glass over in the process. Imagine my mortification.

'I'm so sorry,' I said. 'Entirely my fault. Let me buy you another. I insist.' I beamed at her and she politely reciprocated. Because that's what women do. They follow the rules of social interaction. I'd learnt them well so was au fait with the ritual.

As close as I was to her now, I could see that her eyes were blurred only minimally by the effects of the alcohol. She waved her hand through the air. 'There's no need. My husband will be here soon. He'll get me another.'

'But you can't sit there with an empty glass on my account. I spilled it, so it's only fair that I refill it for you. What is it? Martini?'

'Okay, if you really want to. You don't have to, but if you insist, it's a vodka martini, please.'

'From the remnants of your glass, I see you like it the same way I do – the only way to drink a martini. None of this olive nonsense. I'll just be a tick.'

Delivering the drink, I placed it in front of her with a little bow and made as if to carry on to the next table. She stopped me. As I knew she would. It's what lonely women do and I knew for a fact that loneliness was who she was. She was suffocating in it. And here I was, conveniently there on tap for her to unload on. As again, I knew she would. As she did every Monday night, to anyone who'd listen.

'That was very kind of you. You really shouldn't have.' She pointed to the seat opposite her. 'Why don't you join me? I could do with a little company.'

I asked her if she was sure, and finally accepting her offer, I sat down. For this particular meeting, I had had to 'age' myself. I was thirty-five but now, with a little grey tint to my hair, and a small unassuming goatee and wire-rimmed spectacles, I could now pass for a late middle-aged man. Perhaps fifty –

maximum. I rather liked the look, as it made me feel completely un-me.

I also knew my physical change made me look soft, verging on the benevolent, so I gently and slowly turned the stem of my glass in my big fingers, my head angled to the side as if in contemplative thought. She watched the glass revolve, the movement calming her. I was welcoming her into my world. Softly does it. There. Easy.

'So.' I took a sip from my glass. Holding out my hand I said, 'My name's Oliver Trentwell. Very nice to meet you.'

'I'm Rita Bauld. The pleasure's mine. And thanks.' She held her drink up in a toast. 'Cheers.'

We clinked glasses and both sat back. I let the silence settle in a familiar, cosy way, as if we were old friends. And she was easy to sit with. A sad bundle of a woman. But eager, I guessed, to talk of that sadness that had her so crippled. Aware of the time, I decided to initiate the conversation. 'I'm so glad you asked me to join you, Mrs Bauld. I–'

'Rita. Call me Rita. That's my name. I might as well not waste it.'

I laughed. 'In that case, I'm Oliver.' We each took a sip, hers rather larger than was strictly necessary. 'I was saying how glad I was that you asked me to join you. It was kind. Very kind. Especially today, of all days.' I waited for her to ask 'why?', as she surely would, because she was playing the polite game.

'Why?' she obligingly asked. Adopting an am-I-being-too-forward type hesitation, she prompted me. 'Go on. Tell me. What's so special about today?'

I sighed and put on a downcast expression. 'It's the same, every year. Today is my son's birthday. Well, I say it's his birthday. I say it every year. I should say it *was* his birthday. Because he's no longer with us. He died. Twenty years ago. But I still celebrate every year. Without fail.' I offered up a soft embarrassed smile. 'Probably because I'm a silly sentimental old sod.'

She sucked in a strangely vigorous inhalation of breath, more of a shocked gasp really, and her hand automatically went to her heart. The well-manicured coral-varnished nails of the other hand found my outstretched forearm and she said, 'I'm so sorry. How dreadful. It must be an awful day for you. All those memories.'

'Exactly that. So many memories. And all of them happy. He was called Ben. He died in a car accident, along with my wife. But I try not to dwell on it, not to be too maudlin about it. I know people have far worse things in life to contend with, but I always fail miserably.' I laughed at my own soppy stupidity. 'Usually end up in a bar, drowning my sorrows. Will I never learn?'

'Have you any photographs of him? I'd love to see them.'

I felt bad. Truly I did. She was a genuinely nice woman, open to listening to the woes of a stranger and offering any help and comfort that she could. But my job can be a cruel one, and this was one of those times. I reached into my hip pocket and took out a weathered wallet. Flipped it open to reveal a file of little plastic sleeves, each containing a photograph of a happy smiling boy. Some with his mother. Rita took it from me and held the wallet gently, as she turned the photographs, really looking at each of them in turn. Not pretending. Not in the slightest. She showed real, honest-to-God interest. I thought that was very sweet of her.

'Why, he was a beautiful boy. How old was he when he died?'

I did my sad face again, adding a hint of a chin wobble. 'Three. Just three years old.'

Again she gasped but this time her hand clutched her throat. Not wanting to let out her own personal scream that I knew was lurking there, eager for escape. 'Oh my God, I'm so, so sorry. How awful for you. So young. That's simply too dreadful.' She moved her hand down my forearm and whispered her fingers over my hand. Gave it a soft reassuring squeeze. 'How truly awful for you.' She glanced again at one of the photographs. 'And such a handsome little man.'

'He was, wasn't he? I miss him every day.'

'I can imagine.'

She went to drink from her glass again and seemed surprised to find it empty.

'One more?' I said.

'Let me. It's my turn.'

I was already on my feet. 'Too late. Back in a jiffy.'

And I was.

We naturally got back into our respective sipping regimens, although I was only wetting my lips – very little alcohol was actually going down my throat. One glass was more than enough for me. 'Sorry,' I said. 'Didn't mean to be depressing. It was rude of me. Let's talk about the other love of my life. The child I *do* have. Still have. Would you like to see a picture of *him*?'

Personally, I thought I was hogging the conversation, but I had to steer her in the right direction. I had to make sure that we were in sync for when she told her story. As she would. As she so desperately needed to. I knew because I'd studied her and watched her and could see that she was grief-stricken. And her grief was real. Still very real to her.

She smiled and nodded and said that of course she'd love to see the pictures of my Tommy. We duly went through the tedium of looking at photographs of a boy – a complete stranger to me obviously, and as a private joke at my own expense, I'd picked out a singularly plain child. Nevertheless, she ooh-ed and ahh-ed in all the right places. Exclaimed over his beauty. Said how he took after me. I almost blushed.

'He is exactly the same age as Ben would be now, actually.'

Rita's eyes, definitely glassy from one martini too many, furrowed in confusion. 'How can that be?' Then she slapped her hand to her forehead as if she were a fool. 'Silly me,' she said. 'They must be twins. Right? That would make sense.' She laughed, sounding a bit drunk.

'No, not twins. After my wife and son died in the car crash, it took what seemed to me to be forever to get over it. Well, that's a stupid thing to say, isn't it? It's not something that you ever get over, is it? But I made a herculean effort to move on. And finally found my current wife. Sally. A lovely woman whom I love to pieces.

'She couldn't have children and I still missed Ben. So we adopted. It took years to get approved. The hoops we had to jump through, let me tell you. You'd never believe it. A couple wanting to adopt who'd only been married for three years. Not ideal for the powers that be. And then I had an idea. Why not adopt a child, a boy, who would be Ben's age *then*. A ten-year old. Far fewer parents want to take on a child that age, and so decision made, from there it was a relatively quick checking and vetting process. And the adoption services were so happy to off-load a ten-year-old. Everyone wants babies and toddlers: someone they can mould and pretend is truly theirs.

'We chose him *because* he was exactly the same age as Ben would have been. My wife was more than happy to do that to make *me* happy. And of course, Tommy.' I laughed in embarrassment. 'Obviously that wasn't the only reason we picked him. He's a great boy, always has been, ever since we were lucky enough to find him. Or he found us. And of course his being the right age as far as I was concerned wasn't the prime reason for choosing him. Certainly not. But it ticked a nice box for me. It felt right. Do you know what I mean, Rita?'

I watched as slow tears fell down Rita's face, running down her marionette lines and off her chin. I carried on, hammering in the final nails on my fictitious child's coffin.

'It's just that every time someone said, "Oh, look, Tommy's got your eyes, your smile, your mannerisms," I knew they were lying. For how could he? He wasn't part of me. He has none of my genes, so as far as well-meaning compliments from kind people went, their words only ever felt like an awful reminder that he wasn't Ben. He wasn't really mine at all. Not in the real physiological sense anyway. He wasn't Ben and never will be. However hard he tries.'

I shook my head in shame. Bluffed my face into a mortified expression and avoided making eye contact with Rita – my demeanour screamed *I'm not good enough to even look at.* 'Please forgive me. I should never have said that. He's grown up now and is a wonderful young man and I love him dearly.'

'Oh, you don't have to apologise to me. I know exactly what you mean, Oliver. You have no idea. I understand *exactly* what you're talking about.'

39

ME

R ita sat back and closed her eyes. Opened them. Wiped the tears from her face and then *she* apologised. 'You must think I'm mad,' she said. 'Crying at your story. But you don't understand. Listening to you speak, was like listening to myself. Do you understand?'

Yes, I have a pretty good idea. But I shook my head in the negative, putting on a confused expression. Slightly, but not overly, bemused. It was a pity that we had to go through all this, or, rather more to the point, that *she* had to go through all this, as I thought her an extremely nice woman. With values and heart. I waited quietly for her story. She was having difficulties in knowing where to start. Then plunged right in.

'I can't believe it really. How alike our lives have been. We've been living in parallel worlds and we've never even met. How strange that is.'

'What do you mean?' My face was the picture of innocence. With empathy clamouring for a look-in. I allowed it to slide onto my face as I sat, ready and waiting.

'I had a son, you know. William. Or Billy, as we always called him. He was a dream child. Perfect.'

'Have you any pictures I can see?'

She scrabbled about in the depths of her expensive handbag and took out her mobile. Swiped and swiped until she swiped her son into view. She passed the phone to me. 'Here he is. Beautiful, isn't he?'

And he was. He really was a beautiful boy, with white curls and dimples. He was almost cartoonishly beautiful. Created with an almost-exaggerated perfection. I said so, making my eyes water as if in wonderment and awe. She said, 'Like your son, Billy died. When he was three. Of cancer. He stood no chance at all.' Gently she rested her forehead on the palm of her hand and spoke to the table. 'How could something like that happen? That you get the gift of a child and then he is taken so cruelly away from you. I used to think that it wasn't fair, but of course it's fair. Children die every day. Why not my child? But of course it didn't feel like that. It killed me. Really. I honestly felt I died on the same day as he. I sank into months and months of despair, grief, depression. Months became years. I couldn't live without him, it was as simple as that.'

I murmured my deepest felt condolences and sympathies and she nodded; her eyes glazed in memory and vodka.

'Let me guess,' I said. 'You adopted. Like me. Hence our living in parallel worlds?'

'No. I mean, yes, but that's not the only similarity between us. My husband, Sydney, and I, also adopted a boy. And he was the same age as Billy. My husband wasn't too keen on the idea at first. Felt it was like *replacing* Billy. But he came around. Eventually.'

I smiled encouragingly at her. 'And what's your new boy like?'

'I love him. Really I do. Always have.' She was drunk and her words, whilst not actually slurred, were joining together as if she were unable to separate them. Guilt made her talk faster.

'He's a fine boy. Grown into a polite, hard-working young man. It's just that...' She shrugged.

'I think I know precisely what you're going to say, Rita. It's just not the same as the real thing. Your little boy, Billy, is way above and beyond anything your adopted son could ever be. I know because I feel the same.'

The relief that washed over her was like a tidal wave: it rocked her back in her seat. 'Thank God you understand. I've never said it out loud before. To anyone. Not even my husband. It's just I remember Billy's eyes, *my* eyes – the same shape and colour – looking up at me. He was part of me. He *was* me. A very real and physical part of me that, I discovered after many years of pretending, my adopted son could never be. I know that makes me a dreadful person, but you do understand, don't you? There will never be any child that even comes close to the real boy I gave birth to. Never.'

I felt something akin to what I presumed was guilt. Such a nice woman and there I was, planting an evil seed and watching it grow, out of control, with little extra prompting needed from me. I didn't believe she *really* meant what she said anyway. She was drunk and too open to suggestion. She had simply allowed herself to get caught up in the nostalgia and love and loss that her first son had engendered. All washed down with far too much vodka.

'You don't have to explain it to me,' I said. 'I think my wife's guessed that I'm not as loving to Tommy as she feels I should be. I love him, don't get me wrong, but I'm not *in* love with him, like I was with my real son, Ben.'

Rita pushed her glass away and smiled at me: a person who truly understood her. 'That's it. That's it *exactly*. I was *in love* with my son. As soon as I saw him, I fell as deeply in love with him as is possible. Every breath he took, his first words, his first stumbling steps, they were magical. I can still hear his laughter.

His tears. His screams of delight when he found something funny. The smell of him. God, that smell. He had a very special smell that was all Billy. How could my adopted son ever compete with that?'

'He can't, Rita. He never will. But that doesn't matter, not really. I love Tommy, I really do, but I haven't got that very unique bond that was a natural thing. Like you had with Ben. As you say, that biological parent/child bond that is like no other. You can't manufacture it, can you? You can't replicate it and hey presto, there it is. Another beautiful boy, as perfect as the first. It doesn't work like that.' I grimaced. 'Unfortunately.'

'Are we very awful people? Do all adoptive parents feel like this?'

'If they do, they certainly don't have the courage to admit it, do they?'

'No. I have no one to talk to about it, and just feel so guilty all the time. Especially when I visit Billy's grave. I still go. My husband says it's not healthy, but I don't care. I go because I loved Billy and now I've lost him. Forever.'

I'd watched her often, sitting alone, hands clasped in her lap, at her child's grave. I didn't think it unhealthy. I thought it a good thing. The right thing to do.

She continued. 'I've tried, and like you say, I do love my adoptive son. Of course I do. But how I still feel about Billy, well, it's not my new son's fault, is it? He can't help *not* being Billy. Of course he can't. I *do* love him, but I'm not his mother. Not his real mother. And I never will be.'

'But you'll go on pretending, surely? You can't give up being his adoptive mother. That's a wonderful gift to give to any child.'

'It's not a question of *pretending*. I'm not pretending. As I say, *I do love him.* Just not as much. I talk constantly about him to anyone who'll listen. Maybe I'm just trying to convince myself. Overcompensating. Who knows? It doesn't really matter. I do love him and how I feel about Billy...' She shrugged. 'That's my fault. When we adopted, I'd stupidly examined his features, for any physical evidence that this new toddler looked a bit like me. Ridiculous, I know, but I couldn't stop myself. And every time I studied him, I realised that he looked less and less like me. The more he grew up, the less I could believe he was mine. I pretended, at the beginning, that he had my eyes. But of course he didn't. He didn't even have dimples.'

She tutted and pinched the bridge of her nose. 'It's pathetic, isn't it? The things wanna-be-mothers, or *fathers*, do,' she added quickly for my benefit. 'It's so sad what we'll try to convince ourselves of, what we'll pretend to see when it's not there *to* see. It doesn't exist. If my adoptive son knew, it would break his heart. He really is like a son to me. Of course he is. But *like* is the operative word here. Because he can never truly be my son. Simply because he isn't.'

I leant forward and took her hands in mine. Squeezed them. 'Don't feel bad. You've done nothing wrong. You're just being a mother. A real one. And you do love your new son. You said so. And you always will. As I will always love Tommy.' I leant in even closer and whispered, 'But let's not tell anyone else about our discussion and our admissions of... Is it shame? Perhaps we're both lacking something, but the important thing is that we both know *how* to love and we're both doing the best we can. Can't ask for much more than that, can we?'

She squeezed my hands back. 'You're a kind man, Oliver. And yes, this discussion never happened. And how *did* you get me to admit all of that to you, you wicked man? We've never even met. And *if* we were to ever meet again and you ratted me out, I might have to kill you.' And then she laughed and her face transformed into what it used to be when she was genuinely happy. A genuinely happy mother. A real one.

Looking up, she said, 'Here's my husband, Sydney. You must stay and meet him. You've been so kind, and...' She waved in greeting to a messy, blond curly haired man who raised his own hand back. Smiling as he approached.

Rita turned her back on him, putting her mobile back into her bag and whispered fiercely, 'And don't say anything to Sydney, please don't.'

She'd suddenly lost her nerve and realising that she'd just told her deepest and darkest secret to a complete stranger, she worried now that I'd repeat it and embarrass her. Worse than embarrass, I would harm her by telling her secret.

'I won't tell, don't worry, Rita. It was great meeting you and even greater talking to you. I feel better for it and I hope you do too.'

Rita nodded quickly with a brief but final smile. She wanted me gone.

I stood to shake the hand of Sydney Bauld, who appeared unfazed that his wife was drinking with a man he'd never met. He said, 'Hello. See you've met my wife, Rita. I'm Sydney. And you are?'

A very bad man.

'I'm Oliver.'

'Hope my wife hasn't been bending your ear about our marvellous son, Frank, has she? She talks about nothing else.'

'No, not at all,' I said, putting on my coat to Rita's visible relief. 'She hardly told me anything about herself. I did all the talking. Bored her rigid, I'm sure. Anyway, nice meeting you both.' I looked at my watch. 'Must dash. I have a prior engagement. Enjoy your evening. Bye.'

At the door I turned and Rita wiggled her fingers in the air at me in farewell as she simultaneously dipped her head in a thank-you gesture. I dipped mine back.

I'd got what I came for.

My mobile had recorded the conversation. In case I needed to prove it, which seemed unlikely.

If I did feelings, I suppose that I would be feeling bad for having misled Rita, for leading her up the garden path and watching her as she'd rushed down it, real truths coming from her like shots from a rifle. All I'd done was give her a little push. Given her the opportunity to speak openly and honestly. And she'd run into and welcomed that opportunity with open arms.

But as it was, I didn't really feel much of anything. Perhaps a headache from my one glass of martini, but that was all.

Mad, bad me.

40

BECKY

'But we all know Frank's adopted,' Lucy said. 'That's not even a secret.'

Frank shook his head. 'No, that wasn't the secret, Luce. The fact that my mother, my adoptive mother, doesn't love me – that's the secret, isn't it, John?'

'It's certainly *a* secret, yes. You can't deny that.'

Becky was chilled. John chilled her. There was an underlying menace to him that was truly frightening. And he was becoming ever more menacing, in his very quiet and superficially polite way, and that concerned her greatly. It terrified her. It also made her angry.

Her voice when she spoke was as cold and as unforgiving as a block of ice. 'Why would you say something like that to Frank? He loves his mother and she loves him. According to you, she even said so. She's still grieving for her dead biological son, so big deal. That does not take away her feelings for Frank. *She said she loved him.* Anything else she said was because you manipulated her, John. You tricked her into confiding her grief over the death of her son. *Of course* she's still bloody grieving. She lost a child. And you toyed with her. Made her speak of it.

Why would you do that to her? And why would you now tell Frank? You're grotesque. Sick.'

'No, I'm not sick. Not sick at all. Just getting to the heart of things.'

'Yes, by teasing Frank's mother, by pretending you'd suffered a similar loss. How dare you?'

'But she felt better. She thanked me. Which means I did the right thing. She wanted to talk of her dead child. I helped her do that. How can that be wrong?'

'Because *you're* wrong. Something inside you is so broken you don't even realise how wrong and damaged you really are. And now you're trying your damnedest to rip the heart out of Frank. You're nothing but a cheap animal. I can't bear to be in the same room as you.'

'But you have no choice in the matter, do you? What precisely, are you going to do, Becky? I know you are just dying to kill me, but pray tell, how do you propose to carry out that feat?'

'This isn't about me and you, John. This is about Frank now. You've made it about Frank. I want to know the reason for your careless destruction of him. There must be a point. You always have one, or at least you tell yourself you have one. So, come on. What was the point of that story of you meeting his adoptive mother? Where has that got you and what has it proved?'

'It's proved a lot to me, but you shall have to wait and see what that is. For the moment, you're right, this is about Frank. Not about you and me. Us.'

Becky snorted. '*Us?* There is no *us*. There is you and there is this family. Now without Roger, but still a family. Who by the way, love each other very much, which I rather think confuses you. You don't understand that particular emotion, do you? It's beyond you. You can't fake that one.'

'How do you know?'

She tossed her head back, refusing to be drawn. 'This isn't about anyone other than Frank.' She turned to him and softened her voice. 'How are you feeling, Frank? Frank?'

He didn't answer. He sat in his chair, with his eyes wide open, his gaze unfocused. And then he shut them. Opened them again. Shell-shocked. The flesh on his face looked as if it didn't belong there; had been trowelled on like wallpaper paste. There was no recognisable colour in his cheeks, as if emotion had sucked all the skin tone from him – leaving him bleached.

'Frank,' Becky said again. 'Breathe. In and out. Slowly. You can cry if you want. Ignore what John's said. It's completely untrue. And even if there is a grain of truth in what he told you, that your mother never got over the death of her first son, so what? Boohoo. I was apparently derelict in my duties as a mother to Lucy. She professes that I didn't show her enough love. Maybe I didn't. But I tried. Like your mother tried.

'Being a mother doesn't come with a bloody rule book, with notes and instructions on the rights and wrongs of what life might throw at you. Get over it, Frank. It's meaningless nonsense. She loved you. Accept it and move on. Have a little faith in yourself for once. Grow up. Be a man. Stop behaving like a bloody baby, for God's sake. You're not two years old. You're twenty-two. Act like it.'

She stopped. Christ, that was harsh. Had she gone too far and made him feel worse? That hadn't been her intention, but her words had had an effect. Frank had sat up. As stiff as a corpse but at least his shoulders had straightened and his head was up. Admittedly, his expression was also rigid, but thankfully he'd lost some of that pallor, and his eyes were alive again.

And then she heard laughter. It sounded like the false laughter you heard on televised comedies. Because it came from John, and he hadn't quite learnt the art of laughing in a convincing way. Having spent an eternity of hours with the man, she'd realised that his personality, his whole character, was as shallow as a puddle; a one-dimensional man. Any real depth or understanding of basic human behaviour eluded him. She wondered if this contributed to his lunacy, or if his lunacy was the cause of his lack of being.

But his words struck home. 'Well, well, finally let us all welcome Becky Bee to the party. I wondered when you'd come out to play.'

Had her former self really resurrected itself? She did feel stronger, there was no doubting that, but she'd never been *harsh*. Never. Not once. Becky Bee would *never* have spoken to Frank like that, in such a cavalier manner, uncaring of his fragile state. She'd have been sensitive, caring. She'd have been gentle to him, cradled him, kissed him and made everything all better. Because that's precisely what Frank needed.

What he didn't need was to be told he was behaving like a toddler.

This other side of her, buried for so long, seemed to have evolved into something lacking that special light that she'd naturally had. Becky Bee, the real Becky Bee, Queen Bee, had been as naturally joyful as it was possible to be. Without even trying. She'd been full of happiness and kindness and fun. She had radiated her enjoyment of simply being – had revelled in it. She'd gone through life laughing. At everything. *This* Becky Bee was darker. Wouldn't know what laughter was if it belted her around the face.

Becky wasn't sure she wanted her younger self back if she was capable of being that unkind. She was ashamed at the words she'd said to Frank. She wanted to apologise, but the damage was done. He looked at her, with a child-like hurt. Before turning away, she whispered, 'I'm sorry.' Wasn't sure he'd heard. Was too humiliated to look.

What was wrong with her? Why this anger? It coursed

through her body as if alive, filling her veins with venom. And hate. So much hate. She'd repressed all of herself for so many years, that now John was getting a lifetime of stored-up fury. Directed solely at him. And she couldn't think of a better candidate for it. He deserved everything she could throw at him. He'd inveigled his way into their home and forced them to openly reveal their innermost selves. And for that she couldn't and wouldn't forgive him. She was bloody *livid*.

But she had nothing that could hurt him.

She wasn't stupid though. Was well aware of the origin of her anger. It was fear. Pure and simple. She was very, very frightened.

Lucy and Frank had fallen into the trap of overinvesting themselves in the secret-telling game that John had created. And consequently they had forgotten the very current and immediate threat from their uninvited guest. Had forgotten the danger that John posed. Had always posed. They'd allowed themselves to become accustomed to his presence in the house. They needed to remember that he was mad. Very mad and very bad.

And now the inevitable was here. After the unenlightening revelation that Frank's mother might not actually love him as much as she perhaps should, there were no more secrets to be told.

Which begged the question, *what would happen next?*

Becky could only see one ending to the day.

John would have to murder them all.

41

LUCY

'Jesus, Mum. Don't speak to Frank like that. That was mean. It's the sort of shite Dad would have come out with.'

Lucy glared at her mother and then at John as he audibly sucked in air through his teeth. 'Low blow, Lucy,' he said. 'Don't speak to your mother like that. That was uncalled for.'

'She shouldn't have spoken to Frank like that then, should she?'

'Stop,' said Frank. 'Enough. *God.* Will you all shut up. None of you need say anything to me. As Rebecca has kindly pointed out, I'm not a spoilt brat, wanting my Mummy. I can speak for myself.'

'But, Frank,' said John, 'that's precisely what you want. Your mummy. You want and need her love. Hence your dripping tears and trembling lips and wobbling chin. Would you like me to get you a bottle? Would that make you feel all better?'

Becky's voice suddenly screamed into the room, frighteningly loud. The unexpected volume made Lucy jolt in her seat. 'Stop it, John. Shut up for once. And Lucy, Frank. Both of you. Stop squabbling like bloody children. This is what John wants. Don't you see? You're playing into his hands. Everything's descending into chaos. We're destroying ourselves. We're losing control. So just stop it. Both of you. Be quiet. Stop reacting to John. He's not worth it. It's all some stupid game. Stop playing it.'

Jeez, where did that come from? Her mother had lost the plot. Lucy wasn't about to follow her lead. Start screaming her head off. *She* hadn't lost control: her mother had.

'This is most certainly not a game,' John said. 'A game is for fun. There is no fun in this.'

Lucy looked at the strange man calmly sitting there in their living room. So at home. But his words now, the tone he'd used, scared her. He was right. Nothing was fun about this day.

But in order to carry on living this day, she had to comfort Frank. It was the least she could do. Glancing over at her husband, the very faint irregular heartbeat in her chest risked promoting itself to palpitations. She bent double for a minute, knowing how to stop the rising panic. This was when she liked to cut. It took away the panic, the pain, the guilt, the anger. The sadness.

The slicing and dicing option wasn't there for her now though. No handy razors secreted about her person. But she most certainly recognised the emotion she was so desperate not to feel. It was her old and familiar ally. Guilt. Guilt was bad. Intellectually, she knew that guilt was a totally negative thing; all it did was eat away at you until you wondered what the point of it all was. It eroded and destroyed everything. Made you question why you bothered carrying on breathing. She didn't like guilt. So she bit down on her lip and blocked it out.

Now was most definitely *not* the time to allow herself to acknowledge the hurt she knew she'd caused Frank. *Fuck off guilt.* She wouldn't allow the emotion houseroom. She also refused to admit that Frank had every right to hate her. Because that admission would make her a real bitch, and she didn't want to give guilt a way in.

All points of entry closed to guilt: No through road here. Please make a detour.

It was all about self-preservation. Lucy mentally beefed herself up; her heart hardened itself against feeling pity for her husband. Pity for herself.

But Frank seemed so very alone sitting there, his eyes still moist. He was completely defeated and she was surprised to find that she didn't have to force herself to accept how badly she'd treated him. The admission came quite naturally just looking at him.

She needed to empathise with what he'd been told by John. In order to connect with him and help him. She owed him that much. Guilt nestled uncomfortably in her gut because of her acceptance of her own behaviour. What had she been thinking? Nodding internally, giving herself a mental consoling rub of her shoulders, she also admitted that were she being honest, and frankly, that appeared to be the agenda of the day, he wasn't the best catch in the world. He *was* weak and he *was* pathetic. But was that enough to treat him so cruelly? With such open disdain. She'd treat a dog better. God, what a complete cow she'd been.

She slid off her chair and buttock-rolled, thigh-pulled and elbow-walked over to him. He needed her now. This minute. It wouldn't kill her to support him. And she did love him. She *did*.

Even to her own ears, it sounded untrue.

Sitting on the carpet at his feet, she held up her hands and he gratefully took them, cupping them with his palms. They were as good as cuffed together. His hands were sweaty and she resisted the urge to disentangle her fingers. *God.* Did she love him? Is that why she'd married him? Or was it simply because he'd been the only man to ask her?

No, that wasn't it. She'd married him because she knew *he* loved *her*, that was the reason. He really loved her. Loved and adored her way too much. But that was what she needed, wasn't it? He'd wanted her for keeps. Unlike all the other men she'd slept with. The dicks she wasted her time with. That's all they were. Dicks. Dicks with dicks.

Or perhaps marrying him had been an easy and quick escape from her father's cruelties, and her mother's aloofness; although now she understood and forgave her mother for that. Maybe that's why she'd chosen Frank – purely because he was everything that was opposite and alien to her father.

She squeezed Frank's hands, wanting to convey her love to him, but not enjoying the public nature of the situation. It wasn't the right time to declare her undying love for him. Or was it? Was it the decent thing to do? Even if it was a bit of a teeny-weeny lie. She told herself she wanted to make him feel better. Wanted to kiss him and take away his pain, take away his rejection by his adoptive mother. Lucy had always liked Rita.

She decided to play it safe. 'Frank, I know your mother loves you. Mum's right. Don't listen to John. He's just playing games. Rita does love you. And you know it. Of course you do. You're getting upset over nothing. Really, babe. Don't cry.'

She swung her knees around and managed to kneel on them. Held her face up to his. He bent his to hers, his lips pursing, ready, too ready for a saving kiss from his wife. At the last minute she turned her face, and he ended up pecking her awkwardly on the cheek. She felt snot from his nose wet the side of her mouth and she had to hide her shudder of disgust and physically stop herself from wiping it off.

God, I really am a bitch.

I don't love Frank.

Simple as.

42

FRANK

When John had finished his tale of the shaming of Frank's mother, hearing the trickery he'd used, the cruelty of the lies that John had reeled her in with, Frank had almost not heard the punchline. The fact that his mother professed to not loving him as much as Billy. Frank had looked at John. His eyes hadn't been able to blink – they'd stretched wide open, staring. And then they'd started to sting and his lids had closed. Feeling a tear fall from his eye, he'd blinked, trying to stem the flow. Unable to, he'd hung his head and stared at the floor. Unseeing. Blinded by the unexpectedness of it all.

And then it had hit him. What his mother had said – *He can never truly be my son*. Unbelievable. He didn't know what was worse: the lack of love from her or the way John had used her.

He hadn't been able to speak for some time. Had listened to Rebecca going bonkers, John being frightening, and had watched Lucy, his whole reason for being, as she'd bravely shuffled over to him. He'd bent to kiss her, eager for her, *needing* the physical contact with someone he truly loved. It was just what he had needed. It had given him strength. He didn't want to let her go, but she'd unclasped her hands, saying, 'Sorry, cramp.' And now she was back in her chair, keeping her gaze down and rubbing her cheek. Not engaging with anyone. Most definitely not with him.

A relative calm returned. If you could ever call being a hostage calm, and he broke it, saying, 'I know my mother loves me. I've always known I was adopted; she made no secret of it. Why would she? She wasn't ashamed of me. And she loved me. Loves me. And I love her. So whatever you say, John, it doesn't matter. It really doesn't.'

He wiped his dripping nose with the cuff of his sleeve and sniffed loudly. And then he closed his eyes and gave himself time to really remember his childhood. His parents. His adoptive parents. They'd told him that he was adopted as soon as he was old enough. Had explained that it made him extra special because they'd actually chosen him. He knew that was a cliché, a thing all adoptive parents said, but he'd happily accepted it at face value. Had no reason not to. Because he'd always felt loved by both of them. And he'd loved them back. He'd *adored* them.

He also knew his parents went out every Monday evening. Had done for years. It had been their routine for as long as he could remember. As it turned out, according to John, it was their wallowing-in-grief night for the son that they'd lost. For his mother it certainly was, anyway. Frank could understand that. But was it really a wallowing-in-disappointment for the son they'd got as a replacement as well?

Was that why they'd always come back totally slaughtered and laughing and crying and falling about? Was that what Mondays was all about? A weekly vigil for their dead son. Their real son. And a quick cheers-in-passing to pathetic and useless Frank. *Bless him, he does try so.*

No, bollocks. That wasn't how it was. He would have known if they were that disappointed in him that it was a date in their calendar to raise a glass in misery to him. Rubbish. That wasn't true.

He'd also always known about Billy, and his mother's frequent visits to his grave, so felt her pain. Sympathised with it. Thought it would have been weird if she'd never spoken of her biological son. Frank wasn't jealous, for Christ's sake. Was that what John was getting at? Surely not.

He was startled out of his remembering by John's voice. 'How's it feel, Frank, to be a replacement? It's not dissimilar to when a kitten dies in some horrific accident, don't you think? It doesn't matter, not really. Because, guess what? You can tell yourself *never mind*, and just go out and buy another one. They all look the same anyway. Where's the harm? That's what you are. You're a stand-in pet to the Baulds, that's all you are, Frank. How's that feel? Tell me, I'm interested.'

And just like that, out of nowhere, Frank felt John's words bouncing off him, not landing, not hitting their mark. Missing by a bloody mile. He smiled at John. Shook his head. 'No, John. I know they love me. I can tell. You might not be able to recognise love, but I can and I do, and they brought me up so I should know. Don't you think I'd have known if secretly my mother hadn't loved me. I understand completely her ongoing grief at the loss of Billy, but that doesn't lessen who I am. It never will. So don't even try going there, John. Because it won't work. You can shove it up your arse.'

And then he laughed. Really laughed; a full bodied, hearty, relaxed laugh that released him from the secret-telling game. If that was the secret, it was bloody pathetic. It wasn't a secret because it wasn't true. His mother loved him for him, for who he was. He wasn't Billy, and he didn't want to be Billy. He was Frank. And for that, for now, at this very minute, he was proud to be Frank.

John didn't join him in his laughter but stared at Frank as if he were missing the point. He said, 'But, Frank, you were, well, not actually *purchased*, but you might as well have been. You were acquired as a sort of like-for-like deal, or worse, it was a swapsies gone horribly wrong. And that's not something to be proud of. If you're trying to sit there and convince yourself that the lovely Rita Bauld loves you, I'm telling you that you're either a misguided fool, so wide of the mark that you're positively delusional, or you are attempting to ignore what is staring you in the face. You are nothing but a substitute and you've failed at even that. A failed substitute. A double negative. You sit and stew on that fact. Then tell me you feel loved and wanted, Frank. Go on, tell me and say it like you mean it.'

Frank's newly found confidence wavered. It was that fragile. He could feel it falter and threaten to fade away to nothing. As easily as that. Destroyed in the space of time it took to click your fingers. He had been so sure of himself a second ago, and now, one second later, he doubted himself again. He gritted his teeth and pictured his mother and father; the joy they'd shown when he'd passed his exams, got a job, got a girlfriend, had married Lucy. They'd been so proud. His mother had cried with joy when he'd told her he was marrying Lucy.

He said that to John who replied, 'If that's why you think she was crying, Frank, you carry on telling yourself that. Has it not occurred to you that the lovely Rita Bauld might have been crying with happiness that you were finally moving out of her house and she could rid herself of you, whilst passing you onto another woman? A woman, who would in turn, only pretend to love you. That maybe Rita was crying because she was so disappointed in you? As always. You and your silly little car mechanic job. Do you really believe she's proud of *that*? *Honestly*? Has none of that crossed your mind? Ever? What have you ever achieved in your life with your great upbringing with your great parents living in your great house? How have you repaid your parents for the life they gave you?'

Inhaling deeply, trying to get some of that pride back in himself, he said, 'I've loved them. That's my biggest gift to them. As they love me. And that's it. You've got nothing else on me, so fuck off and leave me alone. You've had your fun. Now move on.'

Frank had surprised himself with his answer. Had actually believed the words as they'd come, naturally, from his mouth. He hadn't had to think about them, because they were true, and the truth was always easy to speak. He smiled at John. Smiled at his wife. Smiled at Rebecca. He'd survived the secret-telling. Had fared better than the others in fact. Had come out whole the other side and still sat there, alive and breathing.

And smiling.

John smiled back.

43

BECKY

Becky's anger had lessened. Still there, but its presence was weaker. In its place, there was the deep heavy, leaden weight of dread which sat heavily in her chest. She had definitely felt something shift in John's mood. Maybe it was John's malicious teasing of Frank that had highlighted the change. It was probably her imagination, but it was as if the atmosphere in the room had darkened, and the temperature dropped.

She told herself she was being fanciful. But the fear that had been sitting in her gut since John had entered the house had unaccountably ratcheted up and felt like it was strangling her. She couldn't rid herself of the notion of a new and as yet unidentified danger. Very real and very close. Her heart thumped wildly for no apparent reason.

There was too much smiling going on. It was creepy and surreal. A horribly misplaced grin of triumph from Frank. A strangely muted smile from Lucy. A teasing, smirk from John.

Something was very wrong. She'd been right when she'd challenged John. He *always* had a point to make with the secrets that he was forcing them to tell. He knew them already and there was *always* a reason for their telling. *Always*.

So Frank's secret couldn't possibly be as mundane as the apparent lack of love from his mother. There had to be more. She met John's gaze and they stared at each other, she careful not to lower her eyes. Now was not the time to show how truly terrified she was. 'You know,' said John. 'Don't you?'

Stupidly frightened, Becky didn't want to play. Didn't like what was coming because it had been so carefully and spitefully orchestrated by John. He'd gone to a lot of trouble to let Frank believe that his secret was told and finished, that he was off the hook. It was unnecessarily cruel and she couldn't bear to watch. And listen. To what*ever* John was about to reveal. Shaking her head, she said, 'No, John. I don't know anything.'

'Yes, you do. Don't start lying now. I expect more from you. You haven't disappointed all day, Becky. Far from it. So don't start now.'

She nodded. 'Okay, yes, I know you haven't finished. That you've methodically worked us and the day, for this very moment – now. You want to finish on this next secret. The ultimate unveiling. It shows in your controlled but mocking taunts of Frank. Which isn't really like you – to be cruel just for the hell of it. You always have a reason and there is no reason to be that spiteful to Frank. Which means there must be more to it. You can't contain your excitement. Is it excitement?'

'Possibly it is. I'm not highly skilled at identifying my moods, but overall, I'd say you're probably right. Very good.' He rubbed his hands together. 'Onwards then to the next secret.'

'What next secret?' said Lucy. 'Frank's done his. Leave him alone.'

'Yeah, who's next, John?' Frank asked. 'I'm done, so move on, mate.'

Becky winced at his naivete and ridiculous showboating.

It was glaringly obvious that John hadn't even started with Frank. Why couldn't the stupid boy see that for himself? It was also glaringly obvious that John wasn't stupid. The question of how much Frank's mother did or didn't love him wasn't a secret, it didn't even rate as trivial chit-chat. It didn't compare to the terrible secrets of the three Twists. Murder, blackmail, self-harm and promiscuity.

More importantly, John had *deliberately* left Frank's secret until last. John wouldn't go out with the enforced telling of a whimperingly weak secret. John had saved this one for maximum effect.

It was going to be bad, Becky knew.

She thought it would change everything. Was pivotal to why John was here.

Why else leave Frank, harmless and weak Frank, why leave him until last?

Unless it was really worth it.

Worth it for John.

And there sat Frank, totally oblivious, knees relaxed out in machismo style, his ankles stretched against the cable ties, still smiling, still not getting it. He was cock-a-hoop, thinking he was in the home stretch, had got off lightly, had *won*.

The poor boy had had no idea until today quite what a dysfunctional family he'd married into, but he didn't appear to care. Because he thought he had the love of Lucy. For him, that was the only thing worth having. And he didn't even have that, Becky thought sadly. She wasn't a fool. Her daughter's distaste for her husband was written all over her face, however hard she tried to conceal it. Becky didn't know how to warn Frank that it wasn't over. She feared it would never be over for him. It was only just beginning.

John smiled at her, more openly than he had thus far, as if he was actually connecting with the facial expression for once.

Because for the first time, he was actually *genuinely* enjoying the moment. But God, he was elongating every minute to get as much fun as was possible from each and every second.

Lucy said, 'What? What's going on? Why the mood change? Who's died?'

Her daughter's smile faded on her lips as she took in the silence. Her eyes squinted and she frowned. 'Mum? The fuck's going on?'

Becky found herself holding her breath. Tried to count her heartbeat as it boomed in her ears. Whatever John was going to say, she didn't want to hear it. And she was damn sure Frank wouldn't want to hear it either. Whatever the secret, it was big. It was big and it was bad.

Eventually, John turned to Frank, his movement slow and measured. Relishing the power that was horribly more real than it had ever been before. 'How do you feel, little Franky boy, now that your wet and weedy secret is out? Relieved? Happy that you think you've got one over on big bad John? Think you've beaten me, don't you?'

Frank squirmed, not quite so sure of himself. 'I *have* beaten you. What you told me had no effect on me. You've done your worst.'

John let the silence draw out. Frank got more unnerved and uncertain, fluttering his fingers on his knee as if desperately playing a frenzied piano concerto. He was so nervous, that against his better judgement, Frank said, 'What? What is it?'

Don't ask, Becky thought. *You do* not *want to know.*

'I want to talk about your secret, Frank.'

'But we've talked about it already. It's done and dusted, right?'

Becky watched with an awful fascination as John turned to his rucksack. Took out his knife. Took out his gun. He held them each by their respective handles, one in each hand. He showed them to Frank. 'Just in case,' John said. 'Can't be too careful. Not too sure how you'll take the news.'

'Just in case of what? What news?' said Frank.

Becky almost had to lip-read him, as his voice carried no volume. He'd huffed out the words on puffs of breath that evaporated into the air.

And then Becky guessed the real secret. She closed her eyes briefly and felt like weeping.

John sprang up from the sofa and strode across the room.

Frank immediately cowered, held his hands up in front of his face, but couldn't tear his eyes away from John, so peeped through his splayed fingers.

John softly pushed the short barrel of the gun in between Frank's hands, and let it rest on his forehead. John pushed harder, forcing Frank's head back. Frank froze. Becky froze. Lucy froze. All eyes were on the gun on Frank's head.

Before she could stop herself, Becky said, 'No, don't. Please don't, John.'

John turned to her. 'Don't what, Becky? Kill my own baby brother? Just what sort of person do you think I am?'

44

ME

I stood there with the gun to Frank's head and didn't move. Nobody else moved so I let the moment linger. It felt good to have finally told him. To let Frank know precisely who he was. Ironically, Frank, the weakest of them all, was the reason I was here. It was all about him. Had always been about him. Pity he didn't seem overexcited by his starring role. He certainly didn't deserve it.

I'd known, as soon as I'd met him, that this would not end well. That he would never be good enough, that he was one of those people that always lost at whatever they did. But stupidly, I'd hoped. I'd shown a little optimism for the first time in my life. And now I knew why optimism was such a ridiculous honey-glazed and doomed-to-fail concept. Much better to be a pessimist – it meant one was never disappointed. But I'd *hoped* that Frank might come into his own, that he might surprise me. But he hadn't. He was just another familiarly depressing waste of space. No different than other people. If anything, even weaker than most.

I squatted down in front of him. 'Don't worry, I'm not going to shoot you. I just wanted your full attention for my announcement. I wanted it to be a very special moment for you that you wouldn't forget. You won't forget how you first heard the news, will you, Frank?'

His eyes, yet again, teared up. Good God, it was difficult for me to accept that this sorry specimen of a boy was in any way related to me. The idea that we were genetically connected, that we shared DNA, that the blood that flowed through our respective veins, came from the same source, made me despair.

I almost felt cheated. He was *such* a disappointment, and his very frailty, his complete inability to do or be anything worthy, made for a very unhappy ending.

Unhappy for all.

My mother would be very upset.

Our mother would be very upset.

I took the gun away and noted with satisfaction that it had left a near perfect reddened circle on his brow. Like a warped and perversely misplaced version of the stigmata. Sitting back on the sofa, gun and knife neatly aligned next to me, side by side, I said, 'Wouldn't you like to know what your real name is, Frank?'

Frank didn't answer. Struck dumb. He was understandably shocked. I could understand that. I couldn't and wouldn't berate him for that. A faint sheen of sweat speckled his cheeks and his mouth hung slightly open making him look gormless. I dropped my own lower jaw and with my index finger, propped it shut again. 'Flies, Frank. You'll catch flies like that. Close your mouth. It makes you look like a moron.'

'What? Wait. Wait a minute,' said Lucy. 'I can't believe it. You're Frank's brother? God, tell me you're joking.'

'No, no joke, I'm afraid. It's true.'

I had known how this would play out before I'd even stepped into this house, but I'd persevered, for Hermione's sake, and prayed that it would turn out differently. But as God is not real, the quick and wholly plea from me to Him, had not been answered. No great surprise there.

My mother deserved to at least meet her second baby boy again. It had been such a long time for her. And yet Frank was nothing short of an embarrassment, better that he never be seen. He was certainly not fit for purpose.

I said, 'Becky, could you advise? I'm only thirteen years older than Frank and Lucy and yet, by comparison, I feel like an old man. I'd like your input: adult to adult. Talking to these two, well, let's just say we're not of a similar mind. Their combined life experience doesn't even register with me. Their innocence of life leaves me speechless. I have no point of reference. I can't connect with them. But with you I can. Come on, Becky, what do you think?'

'If you don't know how to finish this yourself, what do you expect me to say? I cannot believe that you have the temerity to ask for my help. *You* explain to us what it's all about. I'm not holding your hand while you do it. You started it. You finish it.'

'I'm not asking for your help. I was asking for your view on the state of play as it now stands. But is that how it feels for you, Becky? The end?'

'Look me in the face and tell me it isn't.'

'It isn't. Not necessarily. I tried to give Frank every opportunity to prove himself. To rise to the occasion. But he's failed miserably. You have to agree with me on that one.'

'I don't have to do anything I don't want to. Not anything. If you're going to kill me, I won't make it easy for you. Believe that.'

I admired her. I really did. If not for the tremor in her voice, I might actually have believed her. But she couldn't hide her fear. Very few people could.

I could hardly blame Becky for trying so hard to be brave. I nodded politely at her, showing her that I understood her viewpoint. I said to Frank, 'Surely *you* must have something to say.'

Shaking his head, he remained mute. But he couldn't tear his eyes away from me – he studied me, drinking in every physical aspect that was me and, I suspect, he compared us. Our differences. And there were many. I hadn't as yet discovered any similarity between us that might suggest that we were related.

I sighed. 'Would you all like to hear *my* secret? I believe in reciprocity. Give and take. As Candi said, "Fair dos." If I reveal all, would that make you all feel that it's fairer? If I tell you exactly why I'm here?'

Lucy said, 'Yeah, why not. Fire away. It's not like I've got anything better to do. Go for it. And don't come out with some sob story that you think will excuse what you've put us all through. Nothing will make me feel sorry for you. So, tell away. I'm all ears.'

'Why would you think I'd want your pity? I couldn't care less what you think of me. I couldn't care less what *anyone* thinks of me. I'm not here to make friends. And I'm sorry if I've upset you, but I had to show you how miserable your existence was, so that you could better it. Better yourself. Stop doing the wrong thing. Tell me you don't feel released after telling your story? As does Becky. I've brought you two together. You should be thanking me, not being rude.'

'You're absolutely right. If you hadn't come today, God knows what a dreadful day it would have been. And now I find that I've never felt better, and it's all thanks to you,' said Lucy, her voice weighted down with sarcasm. 'Send me the bill for the counselling service you've provided us all with today. Better still, leave it on the table next to the front door when you go.

When I next need a therapy session, I'll be sure to give you a bell.'

Ignoring her, I started talking.

45

ME

'You're an odd one, aren't you?' said Greg. He was also known as Bones. His job was selling heroin and crack and apparently you had to have a nonsensical street name to have any real kudos. Plain old 'Greg' just wouldn't cut it out there on the mean city streets.

He also sold my mother. When he felt like it. My mother never felt like it but had no say in the matter. She did it for the drugs. And because she thought she loved Greg.

Punching me not that lightly on my bicep, Greg said, 'Hey. Talking to you, mate. I *said*, you're an odd one, aren't you?'

'If you say so. Greg.'

He punched my arm harder. 'Stop calling me Greg. How many times do I have to tell you?'

I didn't answer. What was there to say? But he was obviously in the mood for talking. He was rarely a fascinating conversationalist at the best of times. And this wasn't the best of times. It never was. Maybe he was bored.

'You're like some weird little old man hidden inside a child's body, do you know that? Seriously weird. It's like you live in no-man's land. You're not a child and you're not an adult. You loiter about in the middle somewhere. Loitering with intent.' He laughed at his own joke. I didn't – no surprise. 'You're more than a bit spooky, mate. All you do is go to school, and that's fine – good for you...' He was doing his in-loco-parentis thing now: pretending that he cared. '... But then you come home, wash yourself, put on clothes you've ironed, clean the house, put on a pinny and start cooking. Why do you do it? You're thirteen, for Christ's sake. You should be doing normal boy stuff. Like girls and shit.'

I said nothing. He punched me again. My arm went dead and I put down the cheese grater. I didn't want my cheese sauce to ruin, so I took it off the heat as I waited for the feeling to return to my arm. 'So?' he said. 'Why do you do it?'

'If I didn't do it, who would?'

He snorted, which was better than his conversation but then he went and spoilt the beautiful silence. 'Like I said, you're odd. Spooky, that's what you are. Bit touched in the head.' He tapped his own temple to demonstrate what he meant, in case I wasn't keeping up with the sophistication of his language skills.

I waited patiently for him to finish his substitute father lecture. He continued to stare at me, up and down. I was bigger than him already. A quick grower. Huge for my age. Seriously tall. Intimidatingly tall. Greg rubbed my arm all better. 'And now your mother is pregnant, you'll probably be helping out there as well? When she has it, I mean.'

'Probably.' I rolled my shoulders slowly. 'You know she's on a script now, don't you? On Methadone? To help the baby? Your baby.'

'Yeah, right. That won't last. She'll always go for the gear instead of the Methadone. You know that. And the baby will be fine. No worries there. Good genes.' He preened stupidly. 'And you'll still be changing nappies, washing all those little romper things baby's wear, feeding it. Getting up in the middle of the night when it's crying and your mother's too stoned to pick it up. You're happy with that, are you? And in case you're not, you just remember, I'm the baby's father, so you make sure you look after Hermione. And the baby. It's *my* baby.'

'It's also hers. And Hermione has had a baby before, you know. Me. If she needs help, I'm sure she'll ask for it.'

'Yeah, and you're still a baby, aren't you? Doing whatever your mummy wants.'

'You just said I'm like an old man. Now I'm a baby. Which is it?'

He raised his eyebrows and I watched his teeth clench. Greg was no fun. He was old, at least thirty, and here we were, in a war of words. And I was winning the verbal exchange. It was too easy. Boring. 'Just watch yourself, you fucking nutjob,' he said. 'I'm warning you.'

'No problem. *Greg.*'

He stepped into my space, touched noses with me, even though that required him to stand on his tiptoes. 'I'm warning you, mate. Don't push it with me. Or I'll beat the shit out of you.'

Standing there, his nose actually made contact with mine and I reared back. *We were sharing air.* Christ. How revolting was that? I turned my face and sucked in fresh air. Greedily inhaled the fresh-air fresh smell of the clean clothes that I'd brought in from the washing line in the garden, now in neatly stacked piles ready to distribute to their respective places.

Giving him my dead-eyed stare, (which I'd practised in the mirror, although it has to be said, it took little practice – it came naturally to me), and it had its desired effect. Like the students at school, he took a step back and looked, there was no other word for it, *frightened.* Good. I was pleased.

Taking a step back myself to further distance his filthy smell from my own recently soaped cleanliness, not wanting the two aromas to co-mingle, I said, 'Greg, if you ever even think about "beating the shit out of me" I'll kill you. Okay? Are we clear? Now, are you staying for dinner? Tell me now because it will make a difference to how much sauce I make.'

Greg/Bones made a feeble attempt at a laugh. He was actually worried that I might in fact kill him. And I might. He walked backwards out of the kitchen, twirling his index finger at the side of his head. Made a cuckoo noise and still pretend-laughing, he retreated out of the house.

I heard Hermione shout my name from upstairs. Tutting, because I'd just put the cheese sauce back on the heat and was cooking out the flour before adding the milk – a crucial point – I reluctantly turned off the gas and went up to my mother's room.

Knocking on the door, I waited for her to answer. Her voice shrilled out, 'Come in, come in. What are you waiting for, permission to enter? For the butler to open the door for you?'

'Thought I was the butler.'

'Very funny. Did Bones leave me something?'

'Yes.'

'Do it for me, would you, Sweetie? Be a dear. I'm sick. Too sick to cook it up. Do it for me. Please.'

To give her credit, she did look sick. Her hair was greasy, but that's because she hadn't washed it, it wasn't a withdrawal symptom. The shivers were though, and I could see her arms covered in goose pimples. Exactly like the proverbial cold turkey. But I still tried to get out of it.

'You're on a script now, Hermione. Why haven't you taken your Methadone?'

'Because Bones said he'd sort me out, today. Come on. Do your old mother a favour.'

'What about the baby? That's why we got you a script. So you could get your life a bit more organised. Look after the baby when he or she comes. Anyway, I'm cooking dinner, Hermione. I can't do two things at once.'

'Yes, you can. You're very good at precisely that. Now go on. Do it. For me.' She smiled and pleaded all in one. I couldn't help but notice, as I did every time she smiled, that she really should go to the dentist. The gap where her front tooth had been knocked out wasn't a pretty sight. Did her no favours. But instead of reminding her to get it fixed I nodded that I'd do her drugs and down the stairs I went. Up and down every morning, evening, and all day on the weekends. My mother's personal valet. But I didn't mind. She was my mother and that's what sons did. They looked after their mothers.

Quickly assembling the required paraphernalia, I took the wrap Greg had given me and inspected it. Checking the quantity. It was a brownish harmless-looking powder. Funny, don't you think? Because it isn't harmless. Everyone knows that. I often thought when I was younger, that heroin, instead of being brown, should have been red. Red for danger. Red for warning. Red for bad.

The amount looked good enough, perhaps a bit short, but so was Greg so it wasn't entirely unexpected. I tipped half of it into a spoon which had a bent handle. All the better to pick it up and not spill the precious powder that would turn an ugly brown liquid when heated. Getting a cigarette from the drawer, I used my front teeth to take out the filter and tore off a small piece. Adding a little pinch of citric acid, from its very orange little tub, I then took a new 10ml syringe from its packet and drew up water from a clean glass. Squirted it onto the powder and held the flame of a lighter underneath the bowl of the spoon. Until the heroin browned and bubbled. Bit like real cooking. But I preferred cooking food. It was more nutritious.

Finally I drew up a decent but not overly large amount of

the now liquid heroin into the syringe and took it up to Hermione. Didn't want her overdosing. 'Here you are,' I said.

'Stay,' she said. 'In case I can't get a vein.'

Tutting again and realising that I was doing a lot of tutting recently, I sat on the end of her bed. Watched as she got the tourniquet around her mid forearm and started the desperate search for that all elusive vein just above her wrist. Even a capillary would do. A thread vein if necessary. Anything would do, as long as it didn't collapse as soon as she stabbed it with a needle. All the big, fat, juicy veins had gone long ago.

Her teeth held the tourniquet tight, and her puffy hand went a dark red as the blood supply was cut off from it. 'Fuck, fuck, fuck,' she said, on the verge of desperation tears. 'Can't find a bloody vein. They're all buggered.'

'What about the one in your ankle?'

'I can never get that one. It always blows.' She retched and I moved away. Withdrawal from heroin made you gag, amongst other things; too much heroin made you vomit. It was an emetophobic's idea of hell. And yet here I was.

After watching her pull up the right leg of her jeans, listening to her swear and sob and swear and scream in frustration, I said, 'I'll do it. Calm down.'

The initial insertion of the needle brought no joy, but with the second, success. I pushed down on the plunger gently, not wanting the vein to fail from the assault of the needle, and then halfway through, I drew it back, both of us watching the brown liquid mixing with the red of her blood as I flushed it in and out. The change in her was instant. The transformation was extraordinary. Like a magic elixir delivered and received with thanks.

Her head slowly nodded downwards, where it stayed on her chest, her eyes closed and her whole body sagged with relief.

She looked utterly and wholly serene and so very deeply relaxed – a stark contrast to her awake state.

Eventually, after checking that her breathing wasn't compromised, I left because dinner wouldn't cook itself. I rarely let my mother cook. She was a liability in the kitchen. Either too sick or too stoned. It was common sense that she be kept from the proximity of open flames and boiling hot water. The treatment of scalds and burns was not a skill that I wanted to add to my childhood curriculum vitae.

I left her on the bed happily stoned off her face and went down to finish my cheese sauce. I was doing a cauliflower cheese with sugar snap peas and new potatoes. Nothing fancy, but I'm not a fancy type of child. I'm actually very ordinary.

Ish.

46

FRANK

Frank kept quiet. He had so many questions, he wasn't sure where to start. He'd been shocked by John's story. A child giving his mother a fix. But it was also the story of his own beginning. And he wasn't as shocked by this as he might have been. Which surprised him. He actually felt like it was all a bit of an anticlimax. Was he trying to persuade himself that he was okay with this news? No, he didn't think so – he simply wasn't connecting to it on a personal level. Was totally disassociated from it.

He was the son of a woman called Hermione and a man called Greg. So what? A drug dealer father and a junkie mother. All this time when he'd so desperately wanted to be 'bad' and a 'criminal', it seemed he'd been naturally born into it. Had been created by those that he had so desperately striven to be. He'd become his very own pastiche. Was genetically a baddie as it turned out. He didn't know whether to laugh or cry.

Instead he just kept quiet. Couldn't think of anything appropriate to say. John, *his brother*, said, 'Haven't you ever wondered who your biological parents were? Purely as a matter of interest, if nothing else?'

'No.' Frank shook his head. 'I never wanted to know. It didn't seem important. I had my new parents and they loved me. That's always been enough. Nothing else mattered.'

'And that's the first time you've surprised me. Also, the only thing that you've said which sounds even vaguely like me. You couldn't give a hoot as to the identity of your biological parentage. Good for you.'

'Don't compare us,' Frank said. 'We're nothing alike. Just because we share the same parents, it doesn't mean I share anything else with you.'

'You only share my mother with me. Greg isn't my father. Couldn't tell you who my father is, but as you say, it doesn't really matter does it? I feel the same as you. I had my mother and she loved me. What else matters?'

Lucy made her *pfft* sound. 'Doesn't sound like your mother gave a rat's arse about you. You were her minder, or carer – whatever. What did she do for you?'

John touched his hand to his chest, his eyebrows raised in surprise. 'Me, a *carer*? That's laughable. All of you insisting that I'm incapable of love, and now you're saying that I "cared" for my mother. It's a contradiction in terms. For I'm the man who cares for no one. Not even myself. Not in any real sense. I looked after her. It was my duty. An apparently impossible difficult concept for you to grasp, I'll grant you. But a carer? Don't be ridiculous.'

Lucy persisted. 'Your mother did nothing for you. Nothing at all. Can't you see that? She just cared about herself and where her next hit was coming from. What did she actually do for you, personally? Her son? You? What did she *do* for you?'

Frank watched as John's face took on an insulted expression. No, that wasn't quite right. He was more bewildered. 'What do you mean, what did she do for me? She did everything. She gave birth to me, looked after me, sent me to school, fed me. Loved me. What more do you expect from her? I genuinely want to know what you mean. I'm confused as to your reasoning. She didn't abort me, throw me out, beat me, sell me. She did her best. Again, what more could she have done?'

'Not given birth to you at all,' said Lucy. 'Would have done us all a favour.'

Before John could respond, Lucy smacked her forehead, as she made a connection. She said, 'And that's the reason you were so kind to Candi, wasn't it? Because your mother could so easily have been her? You *do* have a heart after all. A self-serving one.'

'No, I was kind to Candi because she needed my help. How could I not help her? It was the right and only thing to do. Don't try to find things where there is nothing to find. Candi had been violated by your father. I helped. The end.'

Quickly, wanting to stop Lucy antagonising John any further, Frank said, 'So what's my real name?'

He didn't want to give John time to react to Lucy's comment, but then he realised John didn't seem fazed at all. Wasn't even angry. Frank couldn't get a hold on what set him off into one of his rages, and what didn't. John, his half-brother, had a very, very skewed version of life, of the world. Of people. It was like he existed on another plane altogether – separated by his madness from mainstream life. He was just John. All-alone John. He didn't want or need anyone. Not even his mother. He didn't love her. He didn't know how. Because he was a complete bloody psychopath.

Who had a gun. And a knife. *Don't forget that, Frank. Remember that. It's important.*

'Hermione called you Anthony,' John said. 'Ant for short. Our surname is Mann. She kept her maiden name. Which makes your name, when written, "A. Mann." Funny, don't you think? Bearing in mind that you bear no resemblance to one at all. You're a disgrace to the species. Hermione would be so disappointed. I'm going to have to go back and tell her all about you. She won't be happy. No, not at all.'

'What's she do when she's not happy?' Rebecca asked. 'Is she violent?'

This time, Frank saw John's face cloud in utter and total incomprehension. John said, 'What *is* the matter with you, Becky? Or are you just angling for a row? What would ever possess you to think that my mother is violent? Because she's a junkie? Surely you are not that stupid nor naïve? Indeed, I know you're not, so why say it?'

'Because I can.'

'But, John, you're so...' Frank said, then faltered.

'I'm so what, *bro*?'

Frank coloured slightly. 'You're so articulate, you sound so well brought up. I don't understand.'

'And there we have it, Becky. Proof positive of the idiocy of youth. Now listen up, Frank. Are you really saying that you think criminality is the domain of only the poor, that the working class own the rights to addiction problems? What a juvenile stereotyping you use. So infantile. Where have you been existing? Yes, we were middle class. And yes, Frank, or should I say, little Ant, middle-class people are also troubled sometimes and use and abuse drugs and suffer the consequences. That particular market is open to all, irrespective of race, gender, religious denomination or social standing. All and sundry are most welcome. Not dissimilar to church, I think you'll find.'

Frank nodded, smiled at the dig at his naivete but was still confused. His reaction to learning that John was his half-brother seemed not to trouble him. In fact, it didn't affect him at all. He was directly related by blood to John: *Could be worse*, he reasoned to himself, and found himself drifting away from

that line of thinking. Not thinking it worth any fu...
exploration.

He felt no attachment nor feeling for this female stranger
who'd given birth to him. Found to his surprise that he wasn't
even curious about her. Had no more interest in Hermione
Mann than he would in any other stranger he passed in the
street. He felt nothing. And that gave him the advantage.
Because he thought he'd surprised John with his easy
acceptance of his heritage. It genuinely changed nothing
for him.

'You know what, John,' said Frank. 'I couldn't care less.
Really, I couldn't. So what? This news, this fact that you've told
me, means nothing to me. There is no point to it. Which means
I win, and you, by definition, lose. You're finished, but you
haven't finished me off.'

To Frank's surprise, instead of John looking crestfallen and
beaten, he laughed. One of his proper laughs. 'That must be a
joke. Tell me it is. It is, isn't it? If it isn't, it should be. Is that
what you really think? That I've *finished*? Think again, you
imbecilic boy. There's more. Much, much more to come.'

Frank shut up immediately. Clammed up. He shouldn't
have said anything. *Shit.* What did John mean? What more
could there possibly be?

'And what's *your* real name, John?' asked Rebecca.

'Joseph.'

'Okay. And where does this startling revelation of your
deprived and tortured background bring us, John? Frank and
you share a mother. And yet, here we still are, talking and not
achieving anything. What does it all mean? What do you want
to happen next?'

'I have a job to do. A task to carry out. And I've done my
best with not a lot to work with.'

'What does that mean?' Rebecca said.

aven't decided yet.'

don't believe you – not for one minute. Of
ecided. I think you'd decided the outcome of this
:fore you even walked through our door. I don't
in your story. I don't care about it one way or
another. Neither, thankfully, does Frank.

'I do, however, care about how it affects us and why you felt
the need to share it. Because I for one couldn't care less about
you. Or indeed your mother. May she rot in hell for bringing
you into this world and leaving you to fend for yourself. She's
neatly and most decisively created a monster of a son, with her
negligence and her complete lack of maternal love. All this
nature and nurture rubbish. It's pie in the sky rhetoric. No baby
is born bad. It's impossible. They are incorruptible *because* they
are a baby. They are pure.

'You, however, are most assuredly *not* pure. In fact you
personify everything that is impure in this world. You, John, are
seriously flawed. And you want to know why? Because of your
nurture. Lucy's right. Your mother didn't give a rat's arse about
you. She created a madman from an innocent child. She should
be ashamed of herself. Better still, she should be locked up.'

Frank wanted to applaud Rebecca but didn't quite dare. He
saw Lucy's mouth turn up at the sides, trying to hide her smile.
For the first time since this ordeal had begun, he thought that
they seemed to have the upper hand over John. Had collectively
bonded to form a stronger team. Frank hadn't given him the
interest in his biological parentage that John had clearly
expected, and Rebecca had told him what a criminally negligent
mother he had.

Newly heartened and emboldened by Rebecca's speech,
Frank felt a flicker of hope that this could mean they could
somehow get out of this alive. He wasn't sure how, but it was
now at least a possibility.

Ant turned and smiled at his brother, Joseph. With confidence restored by Rebecca's words, and the faith and belief in him shown by Lucy, little Ant now said, 'Whatever the more to come is, I'm sure I can handle it. Do your worst, Joseph. I'm ready.'

47

ME

W ith the advent of Ant, my life became harder. The fact
that my mother even had the wherewithal to conceive,
bearing in mind her chronic drug misuse, was exceptional, and
the added bonus that he was born 'normal' – with all his fingers
and toes in all the right places – was considered extremely
fortunate. Not surprisingly, Ant, the one-day-old baby, was born
addicted to opiates, and had to be nursed and detoxed; his little
hand held as he was treated with the love and expertise of the
medical team. That's just life. Little Ant's start to life, anyway.

Suddenly Hermione was given a female social worker. Like
an unexpected gift from an unlucky dip. From the off, it was an
unfair contest. Clare, the social worker, was a plain woman with
thick ankles, lank hair and a permanent simpering look. As if
she really understood and really cared. She had a singularly
unattractive habit of angling her head to one side and crinkling
and crumpling up her face, adopting a tearful expression in an
oh-so sincere pseudo empathy.

My mother went directly and seamlessly into her woman-
who-lunches routine; using her majestic language skills and
wardrobe like a weapon against the unprepared and

unsophisticated Clare. A blur of class. My mother in lethal mode. She charmed Clare, who found her simpering self in the unlikely position of *liking* and being impressed by Hermione.

Obviously, the Methadone made it all possible: 40ml in the morning made Hermione 'normal'. Not stoned, just normal. It would have killed me, but the tragedy was, it just made my mother *normal*.

But all well and good.

Cursory checks were made by Clare as to the suitability of Hermione's fitness as a mother, but the house was spotless and there was food forever on the oven, bubbling and simmering away if anyone came to visit. Because I had things under control.

And on the surface, so did Hermione. On the medical side, on the Anthony side of life, the midwife always came, by appointment only, to find my mother clean, beautifully dressed, everything running smoothly on the domestic front. My mother did her charming, middle-class welcoming bit. The midwife was very pleased. Reported and liaised with Clare, with Hermione's consent, and both felt that all was as it should be. The baby was as he should be.

Hermione took her medicine like a good girl but preferred to stockpile her Methadone – for a rainy day, a just-in-case ready-to-hand secret stash. And obviously continued to inject her heroin as well. But on the days when either the midwife or Clare came to us, or Hermione went to either them or the child health centre to get Ant weighed and checked, she swigged back 40ml of Methadone and looked as good as new. You would never have guessed that she wasn't the perfect mother. A little on the thin side perhaps, but nothing that well-chosen clothes and artfully applied make-up couldn't disguise. And of course, that beautiful, well-educated accent fooled many.

Both mother and child passed that first critical six months

with flying colours. Occasionally, a random urine test would be given to my mother, just to make sure that she wasn't using on top of the Methadone. And that eventuality was always expected by Hermione and accordingly covered.

Any old junkie worth their salt knows the trick of urinating into a small bottle with a screw top lid – ironically usually an empty Methadone bottle – it being the right size apparently, and peeing pre-heroin, inserting it into the female cavity to keep it at body temperature and then, when and if required, squatting over the loo and releasing it by simply unscrewing the top. Hey-presto, no illicit drugs were ever found. It was all child's play to Hermione. And she knew how to play the game.

Social Services had no option but to allow my mother to keep her second son, checks completed, although Ant was put on the 'at risk' register and regular spot checks were made. Spot checks that became less frequent, and eventually stopped after about a year. Hermione had passed and it was felt that there was no need to carry on monitoring what appeared to be a fully functioning example of middle-class family life.

As long as you didn't look too, *too* closely.

And they never did. Because it's hardly a secret that social workers have huge caseloads, are overworked and under resourced. It was unanimously agreed that it would bear little if any fruit to waste further time on a picture-perfect family who'd conquered their demons. In their eyes, my mother had been '*through the mill*' – a social worker term of phrase, and had emerged triumphant, baby on hip, on the other side. Hermione was a good news story. One of the successful ones. They patted themselves on the back for all their hard work and a job well done.

I was never considered at risk, for on their rare unannounced visits, there I was, scrubbed and polished and gleaming, in regular attendance at school, getting above-average grades: an outwardly happy, polite and well-adjusted boy. I was the miracle child who had grown up unscathed amidst potential chaos. Praise be, I imagined them intoning. Hail, the clean boy with a junkie mother. What an unprecedented outcome; toasts all round.

Naturally, the novelty of the baby wore off pretty rapidly as far as my mother was concerned.

Being a heroin addict is a full-time profession. It's not a part-time casual affair, but a full-on, hands-on, twenty-four-hour-a-day grind. Add a wailing baby into that mix and disaster will ensue. Something had to give. Sooner rather than later.

Greg/Bones had done a bunk when Ant was about one. On to pastures new. No great surprise there, but it only further depressed my already depressed mother. She had no way of earning money for drugs other than with her tired and track-marked body, which she refused to do. Remortgaging of the house saw us through the lean years. Of course she could have survived on her prescription medicine, but for her, where was the fun in that?

Anthony became my charge. I was in control of the Ant. Had been really, ever since he came home. I actually enjoyed it on some weird level. I think it was the order that was required to efficiently and effectively run a house and bring up a baby and go to school, and succeed at all of them, *that* was what really appealed. I was good at organising. At being methodical. At keeping things sanitised and clean. Clean and controlled – the perfect combination.

Having lived my first three or four years in complete squalor, which fact I remembered more than vividly, I had acquired the need for the complete opposite. I hated filth: the copious vomiting that accompanied fixing crack, or indulging in too much heroin, the piles of forever-dirty clothes that were left and stank of God-knew-what, the mounds of unwashed plates in the kitchen sink that were stacked high – I loathed it all. It revolted me. But in amongst the chaos, I discovered that I loved cooking; that became my true passion.

But then, when I was sixteen, I became acutely ill. Some virus or something. Was laid up for weeks. Perhaps a month. Never did get to see a doctor, so sweated it out in my bed, keeping up my fluid intake and not much else.

Without receiving any medical intervention, and therefore, unable to carry out my usual and daily administrations, the state of the house, and the state of the Ant deteriorated quickly and shockingly. One day, the Ant escaped. Hermione, it later transpired, was off her face and hadn't missed her son as he'd toddled out of the house and off down the street. He was found by a neighbour some hours later, crying and lost and dirty, and life went pear-shaped. The neighbour informed Social Services. Clare made a visit, made several visits and I couldn't help, struck down as I was, with an undiagnosed sickness. I could control nothing as I lay supine on my bed, unable to move. Eventually, inevitably, the Ant was taken into care at the tender age of three.

I had to rejig my routine after he left, but soon things returned to normal: the house controlled and smoothly run once again.

After a show of grief, hard-hitting and genuine, but lost in the haze of now even more chaotic drug use to blur her loss, my mother never spoke of Ant again. I recovered my health and we carried on as before. Just the two of us.

Over the years, things for me, and therefore, for my mother, improved with my increased wealth as an adult with a more than decent income. I looked after Hermione as best I could, making sure that she had enough money to spend on food: I organised and acquired a cleaner, (a professional one who was decidedly an under-performer by *my* exacting standards, but who was good enough), and I provided a private doctor who supplied a constant-but-sensible supply of drugs to my mother. Both were on the payroll. I kept Hermione safe. Kept her clean. Kept her fed. Kept her functioning.

Kept her alive.

Kept her stoned, but not at risk of overdose. This responsibility fell predominantly to the doctor, who was particularly skilled in his trade. Especially skilled and attentive to Hermione considering the wage he received from me. It was all a delicate and fine balance to maintain, but possible with enough preparation and organisation. Anything is possible if you just make that extra effort required.

It was approximately a year ago that she texted me to come down to her kitchen. We'd moved to a bigger house so that I could live with Hermione, but still had my own private wing. I liked to be alone. I was happy enough though to meet with and speak to Hermione when summoned.

'Joseph, how are you? You look tired,' Hermione said. She placed her hand on my cheek and left it there. I wasn't too sure how to respond. We'd never been especially tactile. I made a quick visual assessment of how stoned she was. Not *stoned* stoned, but enough to keep her ticking along with an outwardly normal veneer which fooled most. To the outsider you'd never know she was anything other than a nicely groomed middle-aged woman; you'd never suspect drug use. Her façade of respectability had definitely been improved now that I'd paid for her to get her teeth fixed, and she wore designer clothes which suited her and hung naturally on her slender frame. And of course, the chaos and risk had been taken away by the good doctor.

I made sure that her life was as easy as it could be. Under the circumstances. It was my job after all.

'No, I'm not tired,' I said. 'How can I help you, Hermione?'

'We need to talk.'

That was new. We chatted, but we rarely *talked*. She hesitated, clearly unsure as to the best way to proceed. I waited politely. Gazing into my eyes, she took my hands in hers and held them. Silence. Not knowing what was expected of me, I quietly allowed her the physical contact.

She said, 'You're a strange man, Joseph. And you were a strange child. Always. A bit more than strange.'

I remained quiet. There was no answer needed. It was a true statement. I acknowledged my own strangeness as a fact. Not even a particularly interesting observation, but merely a statement of truth.

'Let's talk about that, Joseph. Your strangeness. Let's talk about you. And me.' She smiled in encouragement. I smiled back, forever mirroring, even with my own mother.

'Let's not,' I said. Hermione broadened her smile, so I relented. 'Well, if we must. What do you want to say?'

Still with our hands locked together, swapping sweat, she blinked slowly, as is one of the gentler side effects of heroin, and stared at me. As if trying to find me. The real me. A bit late, I thought, considering we'd known each other for thirty-five years. If she didn't know me by this point, what was the likelihood of her finding me now?

'I wanted to tell you that I know and appreciate how good you've been to me over the years. How you've looked after me. Always.'

I nodded.

'But I want to talk specifically about you. How you are, as a person. Okay?'

I nodded.

'Are you going to do anything other than nod?'

'If you'd like me to. I've nodded thus far because what you say is true, so what else can I do but nod?'

'For Christ's sake, Joseph. You've told me how in your work you have to use different disguises, different personas. Do me a favour, would you? Put on your loving son mask and play the bloody game. It's like talking into a black hole. I'm expecting to hear an echo any minute.'

Smiling, I squeezed her hand. 'Mother, your wish is my command. How about a tipple, to get the conversation going? White wine do you?'

'Thank you, yes. I assume you won't be drinking?'

'You assume correctly, Mum. You know me and alcohol – a dreadful mix. I'm the world's cheapest date.' I grinned again and she just looked at me.

'See, you're pretending so well. Playing the son role. And that's my point. You can only play at it.' She accepted her wine and carried on her observation of me, eventually saying, 'I've always known you were different. Not quite normal. Not quite like other children. You were always such a fastidious little boy. Do you remember when you asked me what my name was and I said, "Mummy," and you said, "No, I mean your real name." So I told you, and you said, "Then I shall call you Hermione, because that's your name. You don't call me "son" so why should I call you "Mummy"? A fair point I thought at the time. But odd, for a six-year-old. Unique.'

'But I was right. Your name *is* Hermione. Hence my use of it.'

She took a sip from her glass whilst I toyed with my own glass of water. 'So, Mum, what is it you really want to know? I shall, as always, be as honest as I can be with you and have no fear that you'll upset me. I don't get upset.'

Sighing, she upended her glass and held it out to be refilled. 'And that's rather my point. Your inability to behave like other people. Or conversely, your incredible ability to act like other people. But you've never had the ability to be yourself. Do you know who you are, or are you just a copy of others? A composite of people you've seen and met over the years?'

'Does it matter? I am who I am, and I can't change nor improve it. I just am.' I grinned roguishly and waggled my eyebrows for comedic value. Although I didn't think I'd said anything even remotely amusing. But I was making the effort to connect so she couldn't say I wasn't trying. Frankly, my heart wasn't in it. I shouldn't have to pretend in my own house. It was tiring keeping up the pretence. Especially with Hermione.

She leaned back in her chair and gazed up at the ceiling as if admiring the cornices. But I could see her instead forming a memory into words which for some reason she felt compelled to share with me. I was sure her point would be made soon enough. She was nothing if not blunt. Had never shied away from the truth. And the truth is always right, however distasteful. That's why I like it. She said, 'You were always such a clever boy. But always alone. You didn't make friends at school – forever by yourself; completely solitary. By choice. You didn't mind it at all. Seemed to prefer your own company.

'Of course you were never bullied – partly because of your size, but mostly because you frightened people. With your oddness. Your dead empty eyes – they scared people and your peers gave you a wide berth.'

I was truly fascinated as to where Hermione was going with this and was equally enjoying listening to her dissection of me. I didn't deem it as harsh, although was aware that some might think it so. She was simply speaking the truth, as she'd always done. I was more interested in the timing of her telling, and the *why* of it. I wondered what her message might be and what her intent was. I do love a mystery so was content enough to sit it out and wait to be enlightened.

I brushed some crumbs together on the table and scooped

them into the palm of my hand and standing, dropped them into the kitchen bin. Wet wiped my hands before sitting again.

Hermione said, 'You were smart. As you got older, it didn't take you long to work out that in order to pass as normal, to not stand out as different and thus draw unwanted attention to yourself, you safeguarded your privacy by learning how to fit in. I'd stand at the school gates, watching you play. This was before my drug use became chaotic and I, at that point, was still managing to keep some semblance of a normal family life together.

'You didn't see me and I didn't see my strange son, Joseph: instead I saw an array of different characters – all played by you – as you interacted with the other children. You were whoever you needed to be to fit in with whoever you were with.'

She, thankfully, released her one hand that had gripped mine again as I'd sat down, and leant across the table and kissed me on the cheek. I didn't do anything as I wasn't in 'son' character properly and was unsure what a son would do in this situation. I was faking my own fakery, so I had to think about it. Oh, yes. *Smile.* So I did.

Smiling vaguely back at me but not really connecting with it either, she said, 'You've been masquerading as someone else ever since you realised you had to, in order to survive. To pass as 'normal'. I cried the first time I saw you do it. But I understood your predicament and understood why you had to. You didn't do it to make friends: I think you're incapable of making friends because you neither wanted nor needed them. You did it so that no one would notice you. It meant you were constantly and forever changing personalities, always evolving, shifting, morphing into someone different. I never knew who you were. Not really. You were always my son, but who *was* my son?'

'Me. I'm your son. The man sitting here is your son. Has always been your son. Was it not enough?'

'It was enough for me. I got used to your funny little ways. Your *quirks* as I liked to think of them. But you lacked the capacity to be yourself. You never worked out the recipe that would give you your very own personal character traits. Whatever it was that would make you uniquely *you*. You remained someone else. Always someone, *anyone* else. Sad, really, don't you think?'

I didn't think so, no. 'Yes,' I lied, politely.

'When I knew beyond a doubt that you would always be a fake, that's when I thought, *So what's that make me?* I gave birth to you. I gave birth to an empty child. Did that make me an empty fake as well? Or horribly lacking in myself? Or perhaps terribly unlucky?'

Just being me, because frankly it was easier not to have to pretend with my mother, I said, 'You're not lacking, Hermione. If you're blaming yourself for who I'm not, then don't. I've always done right by you. I learnt the importance of truth when I saw you being on the receiving end of everything that is wrong. I quickly realised that most people didn't know the meaning of doing right. Nor of telling the truth.

'Growing up in an environment with criminals, drug dealers and thieves, I saw the fallout of cheating and lying. Saw the effect it had on you when some other junkie stole your drugs or your money. Why did they do that? I thought it unnecessarily cruel. I refused to live by that code. Because it was wrong. Being right was how I coped with the carnage and it became the mantra by which I lived. I was guided by the truth. Formed by it.'

'And you did a marvellous job of it. Sticking to the truth, because the truth, although often messy, is simply that – the truth. I know why you were so entranced with things being *right*. Being *true*. You liked the simplicity of it. The undeniable fact of truth. Anything wrong confused you. You observed life and people living it, had a keen and natural gift for gleaning the truth from those around you, created your own value system which was, I have to admit, a very good and noble one.'

She ran her fingers through her recently cut hair and rearranged the scarf at her throat. 'You hated, and I mean *really* hated mess. Not literal, physical mess – but that too, my little neat freak.' She laughed and bent forward. Tousled my hair as if I were still a child. 'But you hated even more any and all *emotional* mess, because you couldn't comprehend it. It baffled you. You had no clue. Instead, you controlled everything, and that way, you ensured that you stayed intact. Whole. As whole as you could be. But you worried me. You still worry me. Because no one can sustain that control forever. It's not possible. Not even for you. You're like a tarnished button, hanging on to life by a thread. A button that might one day fall off and get lost.'

She finished her wine. 'Has that happened yet, Joseph? Are you lost?'

I patted myself down with my hands, gave myself a quick frisk search. 'No, all here and accounted for. Definitely not lost. Don't worry about me. I don't, so you mustn't. I'm here. All present and correct.'

Hermione looked sceptical, as if she wanted to say, *But are you* really *here?*

I said, 'What is it, Hermione? What are you trying to say? What do you want? Is there something I can do? Something you need? You're being too cryptic, even for me. I can't read minds.'

'I worry about what will happen to you when I'm gone.'

'Where were you thinking of going?'

'I'm dying. I was diagnosed with terminal cancer. Recently. I didn't tell you because it wasn't necessary that you knew. But I'm telling you now. The doctors have given me perhaps two years to live. Possibly even three, or four more years. It's impossible to know. It rather depends on how I respond to treatment. I thought now was the time to tell you. I'm starting chemo next week.'

'Yes, that's something I should definitely know. I'm sorry. I really am. Are you frightened?'

'No, not especially. I have to die of something – isn't that what people say? And it's true, so that in itself should appeal to you. It was me all along who lacked the ability to really care about myself. Hence my attraction to drugs. Such a self-destructive thing to do. Maybe I infected you with my nonchalance about myself, my negligence of life itself.' She laughed and I nodded. It was a theory, but one which was essentially rubbish. *I* had made me. I alone was responsible for me.

I was also responsible for Hermione. Always had been. 'Why are you telling me now? What do you need?'

'I need to see my son again. My second boy, Ant. Little Ant. You could find him for me, couldn't you? Bring him to me. I want to see if I infected him as well as you, with my cavalier attitude to life. I wonder if he is like me: perhaps he has problems with addiction, or perhaps he's just odd, like you, or *maybe*, he has weathered life more easily than us. I want to see him to say "goodbye".

'A stupid reason, you'll think. But that's what I want. I want and need to see who I gave up. The boy I lost. To say "hello" again and then "goodbye". Spend a bit of time with him. Get to know him. That's what you could do for me. Find him and bring him to me. Will you?'

'Of course. Whatever you want. I'll bring him to you.'

'Thank you, Son.'

'Thank you, Mother.'

48

BECKY

Put on your loving son mask? How could a mother encourage her son in such a perverse and warped manner? She'd *encouraged* him to be someone else to make it easier to deal with him. Lazy bitch. Becky thought Hermione Mann an outrageously evil woman.

Refusing to show any sympathy towards John, Becky said, 'God, and I thought *this* family was dysfunctional. Your mother sounds seriously damaged herself.'

John looked quizzically at her as if she'd failed some sort of test. Had failed to understand why he'd told them this particular anecdote. 'I don't think Hermione's request an unreasonable one. Do you?'

Becky sighed. 'As you like the truth so much, I shall be truthful with you. No, I don't think it an unreasonable request. But I doubt very much that her wish will be fulfilled.'

'I agree. There's no chance of Frank fulfilling his duties. None at all. I am under no illusion as to his reaction. He is too selfish.' He turned to Frank. 'What say you, Frank?'

'I say no fucking way. Not a cat's chance in hell. Why would I want to see her? She means nothing to me. I owe her nothing. And what you've just told us hasn't changed my mind. I repeat, no way. One hundred per cent, no.'

'And therein lies your innate idiocy. Unfortunately for you, you lack the brains to realise what Becky already knows: you are making a fatal mistake. Has that not occurred to you? What do you think it will mean to disobey our mother's request? What do you think the repercussions of that decision will mean for you in the long run? Go on. Have a guess.'

Becky watched as Frank turned forlornly to Lucy, lost in the complexities of the situation. Desperately in need of her help, his face strained and pale, he couldn't find the words to ask for assistance. He just stared at Lucy, unable to save himself and unable to ask.

It came as no surprise to Becky when Lucy averted her eyes, avoided Frank's silent pleas, and pretended that she wasn't involved in this. Apparently, rescue was not on the horizon. Help would not be coming from Lucy, Becky knew.

Her daughter squirmed with embarrassment, and finally lost her temper with her husband, saying, 'Don't look at me like that. With that melancholy big doe-eyed expression that you've honed to just the right level of neediness. I'm not throwing you a rubber ring. Start swimming, Frank. Start swimming now because you're drowning and there's no one to save you, only yourself. You're going to pull us all down with you. God, you're selfish. Selfish and stupid.'

Becky barely listened to Lucy. She thought only, *Dear God, it really is all about Frank. Had always been all about him. The rest of us are merely collateral damage. All this came down to hapless Frank and his desire to be a tough guy.*

It sounded as if the stupid boy had behaved in a particularly juvenile fashion when he'd first met John in the pub. If he had not so willingly and happily fallen under the spell of John and agreed to burgle the house, betraying Lucy and this entire family with such ease and lack of consideration, then none of this would be happening. He had not only been misguided, which might, on its own, have been easy to forgive, but he had also shown a malicious streak, and for that, she couldn't forgive him.

Four people's lives would now be snuffed out for such a ridiculous reason, compounded by Frank's inability to show any sensitivity and maturity after hearing the tale of his mother. His dying biological mother. Even after hearing John's story, Frank had failed to grasp the importance of his response to it. All he'd had to do was pretend some empathy, feign an interest in seeing his mother. Say 'yes' to meeting her.

But Becky knew that even if he now back-pedalled furiously and recanted his dismissing of Hermione, it was too late. Had been too late from the moment that he'd met his half-brother. He couldn't undo that mistake and she didn't think he realised that even now.

For a moment, she was tempted to scream and shout at him, to verbally accuse him of bringing a madman to her door. Because, but for his actions, that was precisely what he had done. If not for his selfish and self-serving behaviour in the pub, it was clear that John would not be here. He wouldn't have needed to be. He could have taken Frank to see Hermione. Had Frank shown any maturity, John would have had only to deal with him. Need not have involved this family at all. If Frank hadn't been such an obvious disappointment. To everyone. Even to Lucy.

Becky accepted the situation as it now was. Had no choice but to accept it. But surely one's impending death should have some sort of gravitas to it? One should die for something worthy, not for a young man's dismal failings and weaknesses.

Don't blame him. He didn't know what he was doing. He

doesn't know what he has done. Still. He sits there oblivious to the situation he's created. But he's only a child. ⁣

No, he's not. He should know what he has done. He's twenty-two, for God's sake. That should be old enough to understand the consequences of his actions.

Becky didn't scream at him. She'd gain nothing from berating him. For blaming him.

Why make his last minutes on earth shameful ones?

John stood, bringing her back. For a big man his movement was extraordinarily quick, deceptively light on the balls of his feet he again went to stand in front of the unfortunate Frank. 'What is wrong with you, little Ant?'

'Nothing is wrong with me.'

'I beg to differ. If Hermione could see you now. You know what she'd see and think? That she was right, that she really is a raging infection and looking at you, she'd assume that she'd infected you with the same weakness of spirit with which she herself has been burdened with. The weakness that made her turn to heroin. Perhaps you actually *do* take after Hermione, for you have that very same weakness. But with none of her courage. Shame on you, young man. You should be truly ashamed of yourself.'

Becky zoned out. She'd heard enough. She knew what it all meant. What it had always meant. The ending of this entire thing had never really been in any doubt. Frank had just sealed the deal.

She wondered how she'd face death.

Could she cheat it?

She'd try.

Or die trying.

49

LUCY

Lucy wasn't sure how she felt. Apart from being seriously pissed off with Frank. Her mother's reaction to the new situation also worried her. She seemed to have accepted their fate. She obviously knew what was coming. As did Lucy. The only person who remained in blissful ignorance was her stupid husband.

Frank was a fool. It had been the worst decision she'd ever made, marrying him, and now she was going to die for it.

It didn't matter that Hermione sounded as mad as John. Frank still should have understood the lay of the land, understood what was required to quiet the lunatic John. Frank should have known and given the correct reaction, responded with some show of sympathy. Anything. Instead he'd shown what he presumably thought was bravery. How misplaced and stupid that was.

And now they were all going to pay for him being the same old fool he'd always been.

Lucy was also aware that throughout the day and on into the now of the early morning, she'd sort of forgotten that John was a killer. Even though Dead Daddy remained sitting opposite her. She'd somehow grown accustomed to the lump that was her father and she'd simply stopped seeing it as a corpse. As a dead parent. She no longer really *saw* him. As he now was. A murder victim.

How could she have forgotten that John could kill them all? She had always known that he could, had even asked him earlier when he was going to kill them. But after she had revealed her self-harming, the reason for her telling had been forgotten. She'd convinced herself that she'd wanted to tell and had fooled herself into thinking that it had been a voluntary confession.

But of course it never had been. She'd been given no choice.

Instead, and she supposed it was self-preservation kicking in, she'd blanked out the possibility of being murdered, whether by gun or by knife, because how else could she have carried on sitting there? Talking and listening.

And for the first time in his pathetic life, it turned out that something really was all about Frank. This was all his fault. She couldn't get over that fact and supposed that on some level, it being his fault, also made it hers as well. For marrying him. For being with him. For allowing him to carry on being such a loser.

I am responsible.

No, that wasn't right. Didn't feel right. She wasn't responsible. Frank was. And for that she hated him. Realised that perhaps she'd always hated him, just a little, but had been happy to pretend. To get through.

And then an even worse thought.

I should have cut deeper. Made it a permanent cutting.

But if she were being honest, the simple truth was that she'd never wanted to kill herself. Hadn't even done it for the attention, for she'd told no one of it. It was only from sheer physical proximity with him that Frank knew. Her scars had been impossible to hide from him, although she hadn't wanted to share her secret with him. But she'd had to.

No, she'd never been suicidal, so wishing that she'd cut herself deeper, fatally, was a stupid thought. She couldn't even begin to convince herself that it had ever been an option. Because it never had.

At the same time, now, as she sat and watched John transport himself effortlessly from sofa to standing over Frank, she wondered if maybe suicide would have been better than what was to come. At least there would have been a sort of dignity in her choosing to end her own life. Instead of it being taken from her.

Now she'd never know.

50

FRANK

Frank felt very alone. Both Rebecca and Lucy had abandoned him. He could feel himself stranded, in a misery of his own making. Too late he knew that he shouldn't have so lightly refused to see John's mother. *His* mother. She was dying and wanted to see him: her son. It wasn't much to ask, and he'd denied her.

He hadn't thought. Just reacted. And that was always his problem. He opened his mouth and out flew shit. It was slowly dawning on him that all of this went back to that first meeting with John in the pub. But how could Frank be blamed? He'd been drunk. John had made him drunk, and as easily as a silly teenage girl, he'd allowed himself to be plied with drinks and then had laid himself bare and was consequently taken advantage of.

But it wasn't fair. How was he to know that John was a complete nutter? He'd seemed so nice.

Because I'm an adult and shouldn't have been so easily taken in, manipulated, influenced and flattered. I should have known better. And worse, I carried on the relationship. Saw him several times. Saw him loads of times. And that had been a big mistake.

Frank said, addressing his words to the very big man standing over him, 'That's what you do, isn't it? You go around manipulating people and making them do things that they wouldn't otherwise do. *Say* things that they wouldn't otherwise say. Is that your job? Is that what you do for a living?'

'Yes, that's precisely what I do. I, for want of a better word, am a cleaner. A cleaner-up of mess made by stupid people.'

'And by cleaning up, you mean killing?' Becky said.

'Not always, no, but certainly often. People hire me to do their dirty work. I work for... I suppose you'd call it an organisation of sorts. I'm sure Frank here would call it a "Firm." Mafioso style. But it's not that at all. It's a well-run, highly efficient organisation with a large staff. There's a person for every occasion: the watcher, the researcher, the organiser, the finder, the computer hacker, the financier, the alibi-maker, et cetera et cetera, the list goes on.'

'And you're the cleaner,' Lucy said. 'Sounds a lowly position in your hierarchy of nutters.'

'Would you prefer the term "the deleter"?'

'I'd prefer the truth, as you're so keen on it,' said Lucy. 'You're the killer.'

'If you must then; yes. Correct. I kill people who deserve to die. The cleaner, the term I prefer, is key. For without me, nothing would ever change.'

'And who makes that decision? The decision as to who is to die?' said Becky. 'You? Who made you God?'

'No, not me. I get paid to carry out the wishes of others. If they pay me and want someone to die, they are allowed to state their preference as to how they'd like the killing to be carried out. For example, do they want their targets to suffer? Or do they want a quick in-and-out job, done and dusted in minutes? A clean kill. The choice is theirs.'

'So who asked you to kill us?' Frank asked.

Frank watched John throw his hands in the air and roll his eyes. 'Good God, you still haven't quite grasped it yet, have you, little Ant. Little Ant, who shall never have the privilege of seeing his real mother. Little Ant whose fault this all is. This isn't a job. Not a professional one, certainly. *It's purely personal.* A first for me. A personal job for my mother.'

'Who's paying you?' Frank insisted.

'Which bit of this are you not keeping up with? *No one* is paying me. It's free and gratis, as they say. I was doing it for Hermione. I *am* doing it for Hermione. But as the day has worn on, I find myself doing it for myself as well. I discovered Roger's secret and punished him for it. I killed him purely because he was a truly bad man who committed truly bad acts against women. I did the right thing. I righted the wrong that was Roger by taking his life from him. That particular act had nothing to do with Frank. That one was just for me. And of course for those women who Roger would have gone on to kill in the future.'

'And there I was thinking you were one-dimensional,' Becky said. 'And yet here you are, a man who hates men who hate women. You've brought a whole new meaning to the word "misogyny". Congratulations.'

'Thank you. I'm glad at least one of you understands,' John said. 'I *did* hate Roger. For everything that he stood for.' John stopped speaking and Frank watched him bow his head as if suddenly weary of it all. Lifting his head slowly, John said, 'But I've discovered throughout this strange day, surprisingly, that it's true what people say. One really shouldn't mix business with pleasure because I am not enjoying this. It is not fun. Not in the slightest. It is giving me no pleasure. I am not looking forward to the finale. I dread it, in fact.' John rubbed the bridge of his nose. 'Apart from killing you, Ant, apart from that delight, I dread the rest of it.'

'Then don't do it,' said Frank. 'You can stop now, John. Just leave. We won't say anything, will we?' He turned to Rebecca and Lucy who looked back at him only vaguely, their expressions blank, unreadable. But he did pick up *accusatory*. He could see it in their body language, their stiff and rigid postures, their slightly angled-away faces. In their subtle physical distancing from him, they silently blamed him.

'Please don't kill me, John. Please don't,' he said, desperate in his aloneness.

John squatted so that he was at eye level with him. 'Don't beg. And Frank, it's not going to be that easy. It's more complicated than that. Because I absolutely do not want neither Becky nor Lucy to suffer. Only *you* must suffer.'

Frank watched John straighten up and return to his spot on the sofa.

And started to cry.

51

ME

'I knew immediately from my first encounters with Frank in the pub that he was a lost cause. He would forever disappoint. Disappoint everyone. If for even a moment he'd shown any backbone, any courage, I need only have dealt with him. It should have been an easily resolved issue between him and me. But I saw very quickly that I couldn't present him to Hermione as he was. The disappointment of what little Ant had become would have killed her. She is still ill and frail. But she is surviving and will continue surviving as she is, against the odds, responding to treatment. Because she is strong.

'You, however, won't be surviving, Frank. Had you been a strong, dependable, *good* man, a person who could offer my mother some comfort in the time she has left, then I would have had no need to come to this house.' I turned away from him and addressed Becky and Lucy. 'Having wasted enough time on Frank, I knew very quickly that I'd have to meet the family in order to get the job done properly.'

I was met with blank uncomprehending stares. I broke it down for them. Speaking slowly, I said, 'The only way to get through to Frank, to make him fully suffer and understand his betrayal of Hermione, was to hurt those whom *he* loved the most in the whole wide world.' I smiled at my childish expression, but no one else joined in. I carried on regardless.

'Frank's weak point? Well, we all know who that is. The beautiful and tragic Lucy. And unfortunately, that meant that you were all involved. Frank denied his mother her final dying wish, and for that I sentence him to as similar and fitting a punishment as is fair. To repeat, I have to kill all those *he* loves the most. Thus he will suffer the same loss as my mother. And so it is very simple. Frank loves Lucy and Lucy loves her mother, and I shall make Frank watch me kill them both first. To make sure that he really *does* suffer the very worst of it. He will see Lucy's pain as she watches her own mother die. He shall see Lucy die and that alone will destroy him. And he will know that Lucy will die, *hating* him. Isn't that great? Couldn't be more appropriate.'

'Why warn us of what you're going to do?' Lucy asked. 'Why not shut up and kill us now? Get it over with instead of torturing us.'

'Because I want *Frank* to know what's coming, that's why. I want him terrified.'

'But why make us tell secrets?' Lucy said. 'What was the point of that? More torture and humiliation just for the fun of it? Was that the only reason?'

'Don't be ridiculous. I always have a reason for everything that I do. I'm not a "for-the-fun-of-it" type of guy. You should know that by now. As I've said, having met the inimitable and very disappointing Frank, I found myself in the position of having to move on and to research *all* of you. Find out all about you. Normally a job that would be carried out by a colleague trained in researching the backgrounds and lives of people – were this a proper job.

'But this time I had to do it myself. Imagine my surprise

when I found such a veritable hoard of secrets that you were all so desperately trying to conceal.' I smiled at Becky and Lucy, giving them what I hoped was a genuinely sympathetic gaze. 'But I wasn't overly surprised at the discovery of such a cache, because most families, behind their happy façades that they present to the world, hide varying shades of darkness, keeping hidden truths, both big and small. Always, there is more than meets the eye to any family unit. *Always*. I don't believe there is such a thing as a functional family. If there is, I've yet to meet one. They all have their secrets.

'I didn't want them to go to waste and realised I could use them. Use them to free both you and your mother. Seeing you as a family at Roger's Christmas party, one would have had to have been blind not to recognise a wife who was the recipient of spousal abuse. And like mother, like daughter.'

'So this is your idea of an intervention?' said Becky.

'You can put it that way, if you wish. I knew I had the power to reunite you both, by your inevitable bonding that would ensue after your secret-telling. It was inevitable. And, as it turned out, heartening. A job well done.'

They listened attentively, interested in my reasons for the secret-telling. More than happy to delay the inevitable but fast approaching finale. I crossed one ankle over my knee and re-tied my shoelaces.

'As the dismissal of the dismal Frank was expedited fairly rapidly, I was given little option but to start on Roger. And you know what I found out about him. Disgusting little man. Like so many before him, he used and abused women. Even murdered one of them – Candi. And his crimes were compounded further by his treatment of his wife and child.

'I knew then that he, personally and very specifically, had to be punished in the real sense of the word, and by that I mean I had to kill him. Nothing else but death would match the enormity of his crimes. And it's what I do. I rectify wrongs. It is my day job after all. It's a bonus if I can punish wrongs committed by men who treat women so abhorrently.'

'Hermione made you that person,' said Becky. 'You appear to specifically hate men who are unkind to women, who treat them badly – like those louts in the pub playing for who'd get to take Lucy home at the end of the night. Unoriginally, you are a product of your upbringing. Your mother made you.'

I considered this. Thought it immaterial to the actual question asked by Lucy, but answered all the same, because common courtesy dictated that I did so. 'Consider me a sponge. Like a sponge cannot but soak up water when immersed in it, I could not help but be affected by the men that surrounded Hermione. Having witnessed many a betrayal and much physical and sexual violence against her, I'll concede that my view of men has been irreparably stained.

'To get back to Lucy's question, the point of making you tell your secrets was a way for you all to fully understand what real life is about. To learn the badness that people are capable of when backed into a corner, or how they react in order to survive. Here you each were, pretending a cosy family life, when in reality you were all living your own private hells.

'It was my duty, on a *personal* level, to mete out punishment. Firstly to Roger, to right the wrong that he committed to Candi, to you, Becky, and to you, Lucy. Killing Roger was most assuredly the right thing to do. Do any of you disagree with that?'

'No,' said Becky. 'He deserved to die. You were right to kill him. But it seems a contradiction in terms to now kill *all of us*.'

'Had it been a professional job, I would have simply walked in here, killed Roger for his crime, and made Frank watch me kill you both, before killing him. But again I stress, this is personal. I made it more so. I got to know you and all your secrets. By making you tell your secrets, you got to know yourselves and each other better. I bonded mother and daughter. *Frank* got to know his wife better. Saw the real Lucy.

'Therefore, the punishment for Frank will be worse, having heard things that he didn't know before about you both, most particularly his wife. The full depth of Lucy's despair, I hope against hope, really affected him. He needed to hear it. To fully understand the woman he is about to lose forever.

'And the piece de resistance will be Frank's dying knowledge that Lucy thoroughly despises him. That will be his last thought.' I smiled, nestling in the thought of the well-orchestrated conclusion of my idiot baby brother's imminent demise.

'It was also imperative for me to give you the opportunity to realise the lies you'd all been living, the secrets you'd been hiding and to release you from them. If you could see the truth of your lives, it would make you happy. However transitory that happiness proves to be.'

Becky laughed out a hard cracking sound. 'You wanted to make us happy? *Really?* And then you plan on taking that new-found "happiness" away by killing us. That doesn't make sense.'

'But it does. Even if that happiness is fleeting, at least I gave you the chance to realise that neither of you has done wrong. It was important to me that you both understood and accepted that undeniable truth: you were victims of men, victims of Roger, specifically. I wanted you to fully feel who you could have been. Without Roger, you would have been two happy strong women, who would have enjoyed their lives. You would have lived freely and with happiness. Surely that knowledge helps you?'

Becky laughed a bleak empty laugh. 'You're kidding

yourself. You're killing us to save yourself. For your own self-preservation. Looking out for number one. Where have your high and mighty morals gone now? You have no excuse for murdering us, other than to save yourself. And that's not *right* or just, is it?'

'Of course it's right. It's more than right. Because it's also justice being meted out. Frank is responsible for what he did to Hermione, and you're all attached to Frank. And your secrets, well, at least I've released you from them. Ladies, I believe you should be thanking me, for knowing and acknowledging your bad secrets allows you to become better people. Don't you understand. I really have *helped* you. However temporary the experience is for you, I've changed your lives in a positive way.'

Becky laughed. 'Thanks for the five minutes I'll have to enjoy my new-found self. Much appreciated. Perhaps it would have been better had this been a job that you weren't personally involved with. It would have been better to have been killed immediately and not know anything about it.'

'Yeah, Mum's right.' Lucy shook her head, as if not knowing what else to say. She sat, knowing that she was going to die, and I was sorry to be the one to kill her. But it's what I do.

'I know that I come from a good place.' I put my hand on my heart, indicating that I really did believe I was doing what I could to help others, and to punish those who deserved it. In this particular case, it was a pleasure to torture Frank. 'I not only right wrongs that have been carried out, but in this very exceptional and personal situation, I have been a saviour to both of you – Becky and Lucy. And I really am genuinely sorry that you both have to die, on account of stupid boy Frank. Doesn't seem fair, does it?'

'So, this is payback?' Becky said.

'This is purely and simply making a young man aware that the world does not in fact revolve around him alone. There are others, people like his mother, who needed him, had asked only to see him. Hardly a monumental request. Nor a difficult one. She didn't even ask for help. Just an opportunity to *see* him. And he didn't care.'

'It's punishment then?' Becky said.

'We all have to be punished if we do wrong.'

'Who's going to punish *you*?'

'I haven't done anything wrong. The contrary is true. I always strive to do right, and I cannot be faulted for always attempting to do that. I've helped both you and your daughter. I stopped Roger from killing another woman, which I am confident he would have. I offered Frank a chance to be a better man and he might as well have laughed in my face. I can only do my best. Frank didn't even try. He couldn't try, he *wouldn't* try. I am not the bad man here. He is.'

'But I'm not a bad man,' Frank said. 'Really, I'm not. Please believe me, I'm not bad. I'm sorry about your mother. Our mother. I really am. I'll come and see her. Talk to her. Be with her. Please don't kill me. Give me another chance.'

'Puh-lease, Frank,' I said. 'Too little, too late. And far too obviously a lie. You can't even lie with any degree of skill or imagination. You're an embarrassment.'

I made a final check of my shoelaces. All tied and secure.

I put my rucksack on my knee.

And watched their faces pale.

There was no delight here in a job well done. Especially as I'd made a mistake. A big one. I'd allowed myself, perhaps for the first time, to actually *like* someone. A rarity indeed. In fact, I wasn't sure it had ever happened before. But I'm lying to myself. I *knew* it had never happened before.

Becky didn't realise it yet, but she and I were actually very alike. She'd now never have the opportunity to embrace that fact.

She had changed position and was sitting forward on her chair, adopting a challenging posture. I was relieved to see the fight still there. Good. Her fists were clenched, and her face thrust forward. She was ready to do battle.

It was sad to see her like this, so brave as she stared certain death in the face. I felt a genuine regret that I'd have to kill her. Such a waste of a good and decent woman. She'd never got the life she'd deserved from Roger, and here I was, about to take the life that I'd given back to her and destroying any hope of her ever rediscovering and reconnecting fully with the full potential of her former Becky Bee status. Guilt, I thought it guilt – we'd never met before – made my stomach turn.

I averted my gaze from hers.

From paralysis, Frank's body had gone into overdrive. He was suddenly all over the place, like a crack addict on a bungee rope. He tried to pull apart his handcuffs – to no avail. Tried to break the cords that bound his ankles. Failed miserably. Disgusted at his cowardice and the whimpering that escaped his mouth, I looked instead at Lucy.

She sat as immobile and as fixed as a porcelain doll. Neither would actually try to stop me for they knew that whatever they did would be futile. And ultimately, any action they took, would change nothing. They wouldn't even try. Frank definitely wouldn't. He'd just sit and be killed.

Perhaps, at a push, Lucy would fight back. But only as a knee-jerk reaction. She'd be unable to mount any form of a sustained and organised attack. I had nothing to fear from either of them and they both knew it.

I knew I had to move fast. I didn't want Becky to suffer unnecessarily and see me coming. I actually didn't want her to suffer at all. But I'd left myself no choice.

No choice at all.

Taking my knife from my rucksack, I tucked it into a sheath

inside my jacket. The gun I placed on the sofa. Picked it up. Pointed it at Frank. Said, 'Bang.' Put it back into the rucksack. Finally, I got up and approached Becky.

Quickly.

So she wouldn't know what hit her.

52

BECKY

Becky felt his hands on her neck. Felt his fingers big and heavy around her throat. Squeezing. Suffocating her. Stopping her breathing. Black spots danced behind her closed lids. So many little black dots. *Like a murmuration of starlings,* she thought. Swooping, swirling en masse, blackening her vision. Until all she saw was black.

From far away, she could hear the screams of her daughter. 'Mum, Mum. Stop it, John. *Mum.*' Lucy's voice continued to sound further and further away, as if it were slowly disappearing down a long and empty tunnel. Until it faded completely and Becky heard nothing.

And then she stopped seeing the blackness altogether. But she felt it envelop her, like huge wings. Warm and comforting.

Coherent thought stopped as the birds took her.

53

LUCY

Before she realised what was happening, John was on her mother. His hands around her neck. The shock paralysed her momentarily. Then Lucy screamed. Heard her own voice as if it belonged to someone else. 'Mum, Mum. Stop it, John. *Mum.*'

And then she stopped screaming, never taking her eyes from John's hands as they encircled her mother's neck. She slipped as far as she could to the edge of her chair and extended her legs as much as possible. Resting on her bent elbows and bending at her knees, she crouched down on her haunches, pushed off from the heavy chair and dived forward. Wished she was travelling through water as her flight stuttered mid-air and she crashed to the floor.

Only inches away.

If she could just get to the knife inside his jacket.

Please, God, help me.

Too late she saw John turn and smile. Saw him throw her mother to the side, face down on the carpet, where she flopped, and stayed. Lifeless.

Lucy wailed as she saw the knife come towards her. She closed her eyes.

54

FRANK

Frank couldn't breathe. He'd watched blankly as John strangled Rebecca.

He'd then watched in horror as Lucy had screamed and thrown herself at John. Lucy, watching her own mother killed. He'd briefly closed his eyes. Couldn't bear to watch the situation he had inadvertently created. Couldn't bear Lucy's fear and her grief. Couldn't bear his shame.

And then he'd watched Lucy die. Had only been able to watch in horror as an arc of blood had spurted from her throat. Like a firework of red, it had shot out of her, high into the air. The sudden and shocking explosion of wet colour travelled with an alarming and unexpected velocity as arterial spray rained down around him.

He was in a shower of Lucy's blood. The torrent of crimson fell down on him in a fine but heavy, violent, mist. It covered him. Covered John. Covered the room.

Frank was covered in the red of Lucy's hate for him.

Big red John turned slowly towards him, the whiteness of his perfect teeth now even whiter as they shone from his crimson-coloured, smeared and bloodied face. John's face, covered in Lucy's blood. Lucy's blood, everywhere. Frank was drowning in it. He was unaware of anything other than the blood of the woman he loved like no other. Her blood. Lucy's blood. Everywhere.

Not caring, he stood, prepared to take his killing like a man.

He fell over, his legs unable to hold him up. They wouldn't stop shaking.

They didn't shake for long.

55

ME

People blather on about love, but I thank God that I am not afflicted by it. Love is not good. Love is bad. It destroys and it kills. You can keep it. I've never felt it and I never will and I am eternally grateful for that.

I'd collected my second rucksack from its hiding place behind the bush by the front door and proceeded to get down to the very satisfying job of cleaning up after myself. I quickly became absorbed in my work, whistling as I went from room to room. Eradicating any trace of myself: my DNA, fibres, all trace evidence, errant hairs that might have fallen from my head – it all had to be found and destroyed. Eliminated, as if I had never been here. It was what I did best.

Apart from cooking.

And I was extremely thorough. Not once, at least not to my knowledge, have I ever left a whisper of myself at a crime scene. It came from years of practice. Brought up with a solid cleaning ethos: it was in my bones. Clean, clean, clean. Until not a speck of me was left.

From experience, I knew my forensic knowledge was impressive. I had never been caught by the police, had never even been suspected of a crime, so I allowed myself to relax into the cleansing ritual which involved copious amounts of equipment: liquids – both toxic and not, lotions, potions and various things that go bump in the night. I smiled happily, at one with my hand-held vacuum.

It took some time to clean the rooms in which I'd been, but I had a very good visual memory and had no problems in remembering every item touched, every surface brushed, every piece of material sat upon. I left nothing to chance. It would be foolish to do so, and anyway, there was no particular hurry. Glancing at my watch, I noted it was half past two on Monday morning.

Of course, I'd made no attempt to clean up the blood because there was no point. I was leaving four dead bodies behind. Hardly a fact that I could conceal and I didn't need to. Being more than aware that I shared a filial DNA match with Frank, I had an unbreakable alibi already established. I had absolutely nothing to concern myself with.

I'd never be suspected of such a heinous crime.

Even if they looked, and they wouldn't, the police wouldn't bother looking twice at me. There was nothing that showed in my nature, my background, nor in my life as a fine upstanding member of the community that would suggest that I had such a propensity for violence. I looked like a good man with a good honest job which would stand up to the most stringent of scrutiny, with neither a shadow nor hint of who I really was. I was home and dry.

I had already showered and changed into clean clothes, with the added protection of a forensic crime scene pair of overalls. I was now cleaning the drains of hair and possible human skin I had most likely shed from my body. It was rewarding work and I relished it.

The deep cleaning kept me from thinking too much about

Becky. I had already conceded that I liked her. I really liked her. For the first time, I felt a bond between myself and someone else. She reminded me of me. Which meant I could feel... Well, it meant I could *feel*. And that was a real first. I was primarily *relieved* that I could indeed feel anything, but there was something else – an emotion that I couldn't put a name to. I wasn't entirely sure as to why she'd had this effect on me; perhaps it was the similarity between us that I recognised in her. It felt welcoming.

Does that sound deluded? After all, I'd only been physically and verbally interacting with the woman for a day. A very long day admittedly, but she'd managed to nurture and bring out in me a gentler side. I respected her strength and her guts and her ability to understand the concept of right and wrong. She'd genuinely seemed at one with my viewpoint but could hardly admit to it in front of her family.

That was our little secret.

Maybe she could have become a friend. Perhaps something more. But I would never know because I had killed her. Self-preservation is a strong motivator and needs must.

Giving myself a last glance in the mirror to see that I looked as normal as was possible, I snapped my latex gloves for luck and prepared for departure. It had been a long day and I now had the unpleasant task of informing Hermione that little Ant would not be coming round for tea and cake. There would be no happy mother/son reunion.

But she was strong. I could only pray that she wouldn't take the news too badly. I didn't relish being the one informing her that she wouldn't be getting the happy ending she deserved.

Whistling again, I realised I was ready.

All done here.

On to the next.

And I'd make sure that the next time would be back to what I knew and loved: the righting of wrongs of *strangers*. Making them face their truths and making them accept their punishments with as much dignity as they could muster.

56

BECKY

S he had to give him credit. As John walked back into the
sitting room to find Becky facing him, he barely missed a
beat. She watched as his eyebrows raised in an arc of surprise.
'Well, well. What have we here?' he said. 'You're meant to be
dead.'

'Sorry to disappoint.' She could hardly contain the anger
that ripped through her body. The gun wavered in her hand,
feeling heavier than it really was. 'You shouldn't have left your
gun in your rucksack. Stupid of you,' she said; attempting to
keep her tone even. *I can do this*, she told herself. 'You killed my
baby.'

'I thought I killed *you*. Most unlike me to make that mistake.
Never leave them breathing, is the rather obvious rule here.
What did you do? Play possum?'

'Yes. I played dead. But you were otherwise engaged I
assume, in the killing of my daughter?'

'You'd have been proud of her. She really went for me.
Disturbed me. I took my eye off the ball. I have never, and I do
mean *never* left a person breathing when my intent was murder.
I suppose, if I were being completely truthful, and you know my

298

feelings on that subject, that the reason that I failed so miserably to kill you, was because I didn't really *want* to kill you. Silly old me. Are you going to shoot me now?'

'Damn right.'

They stood facing one another, perhaps ten feet apart.

'But what if I turn round. Surely you wouldn't shoot a man in the back? How would you explain that to the police?'

'I think they'd understand. You've slaughtered my entire family.'

He held his hand up, as if in reproach. 'But, Becky, if you shoot me in the back, that would be deemed unlawful, using excessive force when your life was no longer in actual danger. If my back is to you and you fire a bullet through me from behind, that means I'm walking away from you. Not towards you, and therefore, not about to attack you. Your life would not be under threat in that scenario, would it? And that would be an act of vigilantism. And that's illegal.'

He smiled and she smiled back.

'Are you such a coward that you'd actually turn your back to me? Not give me the chance to do what's right and kill you, as is *my* right. An eye for an eye. I thought you were all about the rights and wrongs, the truths and lies, the justice and the injustices of this world.'

John angled his head to the side. 'Fair point.'

Becky jumped as he swept both of his hands out to the side, leaving his chest a target. Then as she watched, fascinated, he brought in his left arm and with his index finger, pointed to a spot on his chest. 'Right here, Becky. That's where you need to aim. Straight through the heart. Have you checked the safety catch is off?'

'I'm not a fool. Of course I've checked it. And it's ready to go. You don't need to have a degree in quantum mechanics to work it out.'

She *had* checked it but didn't know what she was looking for. Wouldn't have recognised a safety-catch unless it was labelled so. She could only go for the bluff. Hoping, *praying*, that because she couldn't find it, it wasn't there to find.

There was only one way to really know.

'But you like me, Becky. You heard my story. I killed your husband for you. For that, at least, you must be grateful.'

'Are you *completely* mad? I'm shocked you shot Roger. It was wrong – but yes, I'm pleased that he's dead. I can't lie. And why the bloody hell should I pretend grief over his death? I'll get over the shock of being covered with his blood and brains, and my world won't stop turning because of his absence. The opposite is true. My world will start turning again. Yes, I'm overjoyed you killed that bastard. At least now I can sleep at night. But you made the fatal mistake of killing my daughter.'

She inhaled, the gun heavier and heavier in her sweaty hands. Her body trembled with fury. 'You murdered my baby. And for that, I cannot allow you to just walk away. It was an unforgivable thing to do. You are unforgivable. How can I live without Lucy? How can I let you live having killed her? Everything you've done here, it's too much. You have to pay.' She steadied the gun, pointing it at his chest. This time it didn't waver.

'Look, I'm sorry about Lucy. I really am. But it had to be done. You must understand that.'

'No!' she shouted. 'I don't understand that. I shall never understand that. I hate you. *You killed Lucy*. You cannot imagine how much I detest you and how much I'm going to enjoy shooting you.'

'No, you don't detest me, Becky, you like me. I know you do. You'll come to accept Lucy's death because you're strong. You will live again. You've heard my story. You know why I did what I did. I had no choice. Come on.' He held his hands out. Not begging or imploring. Instead, he was trying to appeal to her better nature, she realised with shock. As if she'd forgotten that they were friends. 'You *do* understand me, Becky. I know you do.'

She *couldn't* comprehend his meaningless words, his complete lack of appropriate emotion at the horror which he had perpetrated. His story. Fuck his story. Her heart wasn't anywhere near bleeding.

Without taking her eyes from his, she could see that she was covered in blood. She was saturated from head to foot with it. Awash with the life force of her daughter. Lucy's blood that had coursed around her veins, kept her face rosy and her body alive. Becky's clothes were soaked red, where she'd cradled her baby in her arms. Finding Lucy lying on the floor, Becky had instinctively bent and raised Lucy's shoulders into an embrace. Her daughter's head had been nearly decapitated and had lolled back, leaving a gaping chasm, slit from ear to ear as she had been.

Becky had continued to hug and rock her baby, listening to the sound of John whistling as he cleaned the kitchen.

'I hate you,' Becky said again. 'You have to die. For Lucy. For everyone who you've come into contact with. For the filth and madness that you've spread. I'm going to kill you, and believe me, I won't lose any sleep over it.'

'Go on then. I dare you. Give it a shot.' He laughed. 'Excuse the pun. Really, go on. Give it a try.'

'You don't think I'll shoot, do you? Don't think I have it in me?'

He closed his eyes briefly, perhaps to contemplate her question. Then he opened them and smiled. 'No, I think you'll do it. You have the strength. You'll do it. It's all right. I don't mind.'

'Aren't you frightened?'

'Not really, no. Why should I be? I've lived my life and now you're going to end it. That seems fair enough.'

Becky was disappointed. And angry. *Furious.* She wanted him to be truly frightened, as she had been, as Lucy had been. But other than pointing a gun at him, how could she terrify him further?

So she pulled the trigger.

She was surprised when the gun went off, the sound again deafening.

John lay flat on his back, his eyes gazing upward: open and staring and unseeing. Becky couldn't help but notice that one of his shoelaces was undone. Smiling to herself, she thought, *lucky he hadn't tripped.*

And then she rang the police.

57

BECKY

It was eighteen long months since John had invited himself into her house and stayed. Stayed until he'd tortured and killed all of her family. He'd taken so much from her that Becky still had difficulty in thinking about him without being almost felled by a rage like no other that she'd experienced. It totally consumed her. Her anger frightened her.

Instead of burying her anger, she nurtured it. Encouraged it. Until the anger was as much a part of her as Lucy had been.

The strength of it still frightened her.

Until she learnt to fully accept it and then, and only then, did she fear it no longer.

Finally, she could relish the anger, welcome it and prepare herself to use it.

Not yet though.

She got herself through the aftermath of her family's slaughter, *Lucy's* slaughter, by consoling herself with the knowledge that soon it would be payback time.

There had been no trial. There was no one to charge with anything. The judicial system, which she believed normally ground on interminably, had inexplicably kicked quickly into gear. The wheels that drove it had been oiled by the high-profile nature of the case, and so unclogged the progress that usually so hampered those caught up in the machinations of the law.

For Becky, all the legalities had been dealt with in comparatively speedy fashion. There had never been any question that she'd be charged: manslaughter was certainly never even considered. It was pure and simple self-defence, and she had no case to answer.

In fact there'd been an air of muted congratulations surrounding her like a fluffy cloud; she'd been hailed as a heroine who had fought back and killed the man who had massacred her family. The public face she portrayed was one of grief. She couldn't hide *that*. Every breath she took, almost crippled her. Other than that, she gave nothing away. Kept herself, her real self, neatly buttoned up and concealed.

She'd shied away from the lights and the clamour as much as was possible, the pleading and demanding offers of exclusive interviews that she was showered with. They wanted her story. They wanted her.

She didn't want them. So she'd hid. Until she was ready.

Unused to and not liking being in the public eye, she'd scuttled back into her house where she waited patiently for the furore to die down. And eventually it did.

It had been a hard eighteen months though. Nothing had been easy. She quietly went through the motions until the time was right.

In a moment of weakness, she had made a show of conforming with a well-intentioned attempt to do what was expected of her. She joined a bereavement group. It wasn't her sort of thing at all. But she met people. Other people who had lost family and loved ones to unlawful killings.

Becky thought of it as 'the murder group'.

She even made a friend. A nice woman whose daughter had

been stalked and killed by her crazed ex-boyfriend. They'd been out for coffee a couple of times, but after a while, Becky realised that she and Mary had little if anything in common other than they both had dead daughters. Their liaison seemed ridiculous to Becky, and after that realisation, she'd quickly but politely severed all ties with the woman. She didn't want to wallow in a stranger's misery and grief. She didn't have the time. There was work to be done and pretending to care about the death of a girl unknown to her was too much. She was too full of her own anguish. Full to bursting.

But eventually, it did all come to an end. The story died and she began to live again. Quietly and always on her own, she ventured out of the house, each time going just that little bit further. Because she could. It took some time getting used to it, feeling able to be her own person again. Not used to not having to answer to Roger, to explain her whereabouts, her movements, her normal everyday comings and goings.

She'd expected it to prove to be an alien task so unused to it was she, but she found that she adapted quickly and more easily than she'd anticipated. Fuelled by her new ally – anger. She had to remind herself that she was no longer the wife of an abusive man, a man who'd destroyed her: a killer.

Slowly, day by day, she found and rediscovered more of herself. Her real self. She started to believe that she was again Becky Bee. An at-the-moment, watered down Becky Bee. But she was coming back to life. Becky could feel the re-emergence of her inner Bee.

She started to almost enjoy her outings, her trips to nowhere. It made her feel alive again.

Almost normal again.

John had set her free.

But he had made the mistake, the fatal mistake, of killing her child.

Lucy remained gone. Gone for ever.

And Becky couldn't and wouldn't let that fact go.

The funerals were held, the crowds gathered again, but Becky remained alone, lost in her grief. She'd gone to Candi's funeral: a sad and forlorn event. Her parents, bent with sorrow, accompanied by a scant smattering of family had come to mourn her. Becky had stood at the back, concealed behind a black veil.

The flowers that Becky left for Candi were a useless apology for her death. It was Becky who had married an evil man and so she reluctantly held some of the responsibility for Candi's death. The girl who didn't know what asparagus was.

There was nothing more personal that Becky could think to do.

Well, there was of course at least *one* thing that she could do, that might make the death of Candi not so utterly futile.

Happily, Becky's anger stayed. If anything, her anger grew. It grew exponentially as the months went by. But Becky knew what to do with it now, knew how and where to channel it.

She knuckled down and started to put her plans into action.

58

BECKY

Becky left her daughterless life in the house she hated and that only reminded her of that Sunday. That secret-telling Sunday.

She'd made her decision. Had almost, but not quite, formulated and finessed her plan. There was no point in rushing things.

Becky Bee had been dormant until its brief appearance with John. It was still drowsy but most definitely there, bumbling and buzzing about inside of her head. The bee was eager to be set free again. The old Becky agreed that in order to move on, to carry out her plans to the letter, she had to fully release the bee that was trapped, buzzing angrily, inside a house and banging its body futilely against the windows, desperate for escape. And sunlight. And air. Fresh, fresh air.

And revenge.

Old, battered, bruised and grief-stricken Becky eventually set the bee free and breathed a sigh of relief as her chest expanded and she allowed herself to be who she really was. What had Lucy called John? A fuckwit, a knobhead, an arsewipe? He had been all of those things. But they weren't words that Becky used. Until now. And why not? She was a different woman, after all.

John, if you're looking down on me, you fuckwit, knobhead, look what I'm going to do. Look and weep, you arsewipe.

Life could begin again, because she'd pressed *go*.

She had money.

Becky Bee escaped the English country and went on holiday. It was time.

59

BECKY

S he turned her face to the heat, enjoying the sting of the sun as it hit her near-naked body. It was a glorious feeling and she basked in it, happily cooking her flesh.

The villa she'd hired on a Greek island was beautiful. Simply breathtaking. The view from the balcony was stunning: miles and miles of olive groves lay beneath her, and to the left she could see the sea. Every morning she'd take her coffee and sit at a small table and inhale the view. Sucked up the good feeling. The good feeling that she needed to get in touch with. And stay in touch with.

She'd also taken up smoking again. Becky Bee had smoked and it was a nice habit and now she couldn't remember why she'd ever stopped. That was a lie. Of course she remembered. It had been an order from Roger. He hadn't liked the smell of smoke on her and had confiscated her cigarettes and banned her from ever smoking another one.

Her arsehole husband.

Now, if she felt like it, she'd go down to one of the local tavernas for lunch or dinner or whatever took her fancy. She'd wanted to escape England, feeling trapped in her country house. And she'd needed to go somewhere where people didn't know her, wouldn't recognise her. Who wouldn't simper with insincere condolences, really only avid for the blood and guts of her story.

People on the island greeted her as if she were an old friend, instead of a middle-aged woman who'd arrived only two weeks earlier. After eating, she'd be asked to join groups of people for a drink. Becky Bee was back and enjoying the attention. Knocking back ouzo, she'd laughed and told jokes and one night, she'd lifted up her skirt to her knees and danced on the table. Laughing and laughing.

But inside, crying and crying and quietly dying with grief.

Deep in the very core of her, the loss of Lucy was a hole. An open wound, festering, rotting her insides, spreading like bacteria.

There was only one way to treat and cure this hurt.

And because of that, she decided to stay on an extra month.

She needed more time to think. Wanted to make absolutely sure, one hundred per cent sure, that she was doing the right thing.

Now was not the time to be making rash decisions and making a mistake. She had to get it *right*.

Lying on a sun lounger, she finished her drink and rang the little bell that sat on the table next to her. She'd never dream of clapping her hands for service. It reminded her too much of Roger. He'd even taken away the simple joy of clapping from her. All she heard when hands were slapped together in fun, was that forever-echo ringing in her ears that had been the start of that terrible evening with the three piggies.

She watched the figure of a young man, wearing tight shorts and nothing else, approach, holding a tray with a bucket of ice. He stood respectfully at the end of her lounger. 'Yes, madam?'

Becky held up her glass. 'Another one of these.' The man bowed and turned to leave. The muscles in his back rippled, the sinews in his calves tweaked, the sweat dripped from him in rivulets. He really was a fine specimen of a man. Her own, personal and very real, live Adonis. She waited until he had reached the far side of the pool before she rang the bell again. He returned to her side. 'Yes, madam?'

'You forgot the olives.'

He bowed again: 'I'm very sorry. My mistake. I'll bring you some now.'

She lay down again, her mind whirring, plotting, scheming. Thoughts of actions as yet unfulfilled made her heart beat irregularly in excitement. Running her lips around her mouth, she realised that for the first time since *that Sunday*, she was beginning to feel real hope. It was all coming together in her mind. And it bolstered her.

The young man, Andreas, appeared again, tray in hand. His sudden presence startled her into sitting. Lowering the tray for her, he presented her with a choice of black olives, green olives, humous, tzatziki, and pitta bread.

'No,' she said. 'I've changed my mind. Not hungry.' She closed her eyes and embraced the heat from the sun. Embraced the thoughts in her head that she allowed to run wild. The possibilities were endless. But not really. She knew what she had to do. Had known for a long time.

Sitting up, she saw Andreas about to enter the villa via the French windows. Ringing the bell, she waited impatiently for him.

'Yes, madam.'

'Change the sheets on the bed and then get in it. Don't shower. I like sweat. I like it dirty. I'll join you in a minute.'

'Yes, madam.' He smiled.

She frowned. 'Did I say you could smile? Did I?'

'No, madam. I apologise.'

An hour later she sauntered into her room and got into bed. They had sex – nothing earth-shattering but it was nice to enjoy a man's body again. A *young* man's body. It felt good to be desired again, instead of fearful of physical intimacy – a left-over gift, courtesy of Roger. Now she relished it. Satisfied and feeling languid and relaxed, she told Andreas to piss off. She'd met him on the flight over, had chatted him up, had captured him like a butterfly in a net. Just because she wanted someone to practice on. Harsh but true. It was all about the truth. And knowing how to control it.

John might have been on to something with this control thing. She found it an empowering and exhilarating thing. But she made it a rule not to bully nor frighten. That wouldn't be fair. That would be too like Roger. Perhaps John had been right, had been on to something. It was *right* that she got what she wanted now. She had suffered too many wrongs. Andreas also got what *he* wanted. It was a win/win. But she held the power. And she liked that.

Careful, I mustn't abuse it. To be used in moderation only.

She told herself that she was only playing at it, trying control on for size. To her delight, she found it a perfect fit: as if it had been made especially handcrafted for her. It felt snug and warm, but she knew that it had to be nurtured correctly. In the correct way. It mustn't be used carelessly or with cruel intent. Together, her and her control would learn their boundaries. She hugged her new-found power to her like a newborn creation, wanting to caress it.

And she couldn't deny that having control over others made her feel powerful. She liked that. It opened up her world;

offered her new and exciting opportunities. But she'd be careful with it. Gently, gently. No nastiness permitted. No bullying.

Unless it was called for of course, and then all bets were off.

John had spoken *some* sense, she had to admit. And it was *he* who had given her back her control. But she wasn't about to thank him. Because having her control again was her God-given right. John was still culpable for the murder of Lucy, and it was Lucy's killing that she couldn't, *wouldn't* forgive. Not ever. That wrong had to be righted. And it was clear who the wrong was, in this particular story, and who would be punished.

Hermione.

It was *she* who gave birth to John, and John gave birth to carnage. He had obliterated her family and now was dead himself.

Because I killed him. And it felt great.

But for real revenge, to right an impossible wrong, to take control and make the world perhaps a better place, Becky had to go back to the source of the evil. The one who had created both life and death in one human child. Hermione must be punished for unleashing her son into the world, who had in turn, killed many, many people. Most importantly, John had killed Becky's child.

Badness bred badness. John's mother had bred, fed and ultimately led her son astray with her mothering. And for that she would pay with her life. Make no mistake about *that*.

I'm coming for you, Hermione.

I know where you live. It is the place where you will die.

I'm coming, Hermione, I'm coming.

I'm taking back control.

No one could blame her. For all bees had a sting. And Becky Bee was true to her namesake. *Mess with me, and you'll know all about it.*

John had awoken Becky's own drowsy bee and everyone knew, bees get more than a little annoyed when provoked.

THE END

ACKNOWLEDGEMENTS

A big thank you to all at Bloodhound Books: especially Betsy Reavley for accepting this, my second book, and to Tara Lyons, Editorial and Production Manager, who always makes the transition from my hysterical track changes into a beautiful book, a happy and seamless one.

Thanks to my editor, Morgen Bailey.

I am very grateful to Donna Wilbor, my wannabe-psychopath FB friend, who has always given me huge support and encouragement and who relishes very dark humour, so needless to say, we get on. She was one of my beta readers, who coped with my doubts, queries and general panic throughout the writing of this book. (And thanks for introducing me to the written word 'pfft.' Sometimes it just says it all.) Donna has the gift of true kindness – a trait which I value enormously.

I also must thank the amusing and extremely intelligent, Tina Howson, who was also always there – with her harsh but fair criticism, (which frankly I was too frightened to ignore). Her help has been invaluable. See you down the pub for a pint and a thrashing out of the 3rd book with your terrifying analysis and literary dissection. I look forward to it. Many thanks.

And as always, most of all, thank you to Francesca. For everything. What the hell would I do without you?

A NOTE FROM THE PUBLISHER

Thank you for reading this book. If you enjoyed it please do consider leaving a review on Amazon to help others find it too.

We hate typos. All of our books have been rigorously edited and proofread, but sometimes mistakes do slip through. If you have spotted a typo, please do let us know and we can get it amended within hours.

info@bloodhoundbooks.com